HUNGER MOON

HUNGER MOON

NEWEST PRESS

EDMONTON, AB 2019

Library and Archives Canada Cataloguing in Publication

Title: Hunger moon : stories / Traci Skuce.
Names: Skuce, Traci, 1970- author.
Series: Nunatak first fiction series ; no. 52.
Description: Series statement: Nunatak first fiction series ; 52
Identifiers: Canadiana (print) 20190167513 | Canadiana (ebook) 20190167521 |
ISBN 9781988732800 (softcover) | ISBN 9781988732817 (EPUB) |
ISBN 9781988732824 (Kindle)
Classification: LCC PS8637.K69 H86 2020 | DDC C813/.6—dc23

NeWest Press wishes to acknowledge that the land on which we operate is Treaty 6 territory and a traditional meeting ground and home for many Indigenous Peoples, including Cree, Saulteaux, Niitsitapi (Blackfoot), Métis, and Nakota Sioux.

Board Editor: Nicole Markotić
Cover design & typography: Kate Hargreaves
Cover photograph by Leopold Camp via Unsplash
Author photograph: Crystal Chowdhury

NeWest Press acknowledges the Canada Council for the Arts, the Alberta Foundation for the Arts, and the Edmonton Arts Council for support of our publishing program. This project is funded in part by the Government of Canada.

201, 8540 – 109 Street
Edmonton, AB T6G 1E6
780.432.9427
NEWEST PRESS www.newestpress.com

No bison were harmed in the making of this book.
PRINTED AND BOUND IN CANADA
1 2 3 4 5 22 21 20

For my mother, Carla,
champion of all things literary

CONTENTS

"Arise, fair sun, and kill the envious moon,
Who is already sick and pale with grief..."
— Shakespeare, *Romeo and Juliet*

KICK

WHO CAN SLEEP WHEN THE AIR WEIGHS A thousand pounds? Not Heidi, all pinned to the top bunk, baby-doll pajamas pushed up, sheets bunched down. Plus her breath is gaspy, catching under her wishbone. And her ribs so tender, even though school's out and she hasn't seen Tony B in four days. She hopes he'll move away this summer, to Timbuktu or anywhere. Hopes she'll never see his white crusty mouth, his snot-crystalled nose ever again. He always finds her though. Right when she forgets about it, when she's alone, coming out of the girls' bathroom, sipping water at the fountain while everyone's in class. Behind the portable when the recess bell rings. Even at the 7-Eleven, where she buys her mom's seltzers, herself lime-grape Lik-M-Aids.

And that time too, when she stayed late to finish the Fun Fair banner. Red tempera blobbed onto the margarine lid, Heidi dipping her brush like a real artist, painting a puffy balloon beside the "R." As she finished the ruffled lip, Miss Frayne click-clicked down to the staff room with her coffee mug. The halls so empty when Heidi started another balloon, thinking yellow next, mix it into the blob: make orange. She didn't hear Tony B until she stood up and he was charging her with steam engine cheeks, snot running in two creamy lines. Paint dripped onto her shoe, the floor, the sign. He snorted and his nostrils flared. Why didn't she jab him with the brush? Why didn't she stab his eye? But no, he did what he always did, even after she'd told twice, even after the principal's office and the detention and the half-day suspension, he still lifted his right foot, aimed and—*boof*—into her belly. And the boot, that plastic snow boot, salt stains and loose laces, winter and summer, hooked under her ribs, squished everything to her throat and, for a second, made her eyes water. Then he planted two feet on the ground, face smirky and glazed with snot. And she said, "Tony you ass. You snotbreathjerkface."

No, she didn't. Only now, at night, when she's supposed to be sleeping.

She hop-skip-jumps her fingers over the achy skin. What did she ever do to him? Except in Grade Three when he asked for glue and she said "No, absolutely not," even though it lay inside her desk under brown construction paper, and he knew it.

AFTER THE KICK TONY B QUICK-FLASH DISAPPEARED down the boys' stairwell and Miss Frayne came back laughing with the janitor, never seeing Tony B or traces of Tony B. Miss Frayne just pointed her chin at the sign. "Nice work, Heidi," she said, and didn't notice there was only one balloon, a not coloured-in balloon, a balloon with no black squiggle string. She didn't notice the lonely stroke of the second balloon either, floating like a frown without a face. Instead, she snatched all the brushes, rinsed them under the classroom tap, told Heidi to please wipe the floor. So Heidi did, then walked home under just-going-on streetlamps, legs like wobbly elastic bands, stretching and flinging her home to where her mother was just her mother, hands busy in the sink, busy in a bowl.

"How was your day, Love?" her mother asked, and Heidi didn't want to say, didn't want her mother's face to crumple as though *she'd* been kicked, didn't want her mother back on the phone with the principal, the principal saying *he's a troubled boy;* her mother later explaining how Tony B's father *this,* how Tony B's mother *that,* how Heidi should avoid him, just avoid him, stick with a friend. No clue how Tony B always lurked.

"There's raisin bread, or crackers with cheese," her mother said, massaging ground beef. But Heidi said no, no, she wasn't hungry. Wouldn't be hungry for hamburgers either, not with the chokey feeling in her throat. Then Laura clunked the steps out from under the kitchen stool, clacked them back in. And Laura went on and on about Sea-Monkeys and how they should send away for Sea-Monkeys.

HEIDI CLIMBS OFF HER BED, STANDS AT THE BOX FAN that's wedged into the window. During the day, she and Laura sing *Oh Little Liza, Little Liza Jane* into the blades, warbling their voices. But now Laura is sleeping and Heidi is alone, arms stained blue with the night, fan-wind helping her breathe again. Outside, the bottomest sky is a fingerpaint smear: white caught in it, smudged with yellow. But the real night hovers above, a darker dark with one, two, three stars flickering, trying to shine. It's hard for them in the city. Not at all like at Aunt Marg's cottage, the night sky so black the stars shimmer like a million billion tambourines.

The fan whirs and whirs, but Heidi still hears the front door unbolt. Feels the house expand and close in. She turns the fan to low, knows it's her father. Hasn't seen him at breakfast—blue suit, face splashed with Hai Karate, Tic Tac knocking against his teeth—for days. Not at dinner either. Only her mother's, "He's working late again," as she scoops potatoes onto an empty plate. And her sister's, "What kinda business is it, anyway?" as she chews with her mouth open.

Heidi touches her sore ribs, wishing her father had turned the car around after he dropped her off at school, wishing he'd seen Tony B chase her up a neighbour's driveway. Her father wouldn't say, *He's a troubled boy,* would he? He'd jump out of the car, grab Tony B by the scruff, and throw him against the brick wall, wouldn't he? Same as when the dog chomped Laura's arm, and their father punted it clean into the air, dog squelching, Laura bleeding in a teeth-mark circle.

Floorboards creak and the hall lights go on. The bathroom faucet. Heidi creeps up the ladder, back into the heavy air, sprawls across her bunk bed, face close to the guardrail. Her heart beats everywhere: neck, fingers, eyes. The creaking stops outside the door and her dad cracks it open. Heidi breathes deep and even, then moans, just a little, as if she's dreaming.

Her father doesn't come in. Only stands, or so she imagines, one eye peeking in, thinking how big his girls have grown, thinking how they must dream of Sea-Monkeys and Fun Fairs and tambourine stars; thinking he won't ever, not ever, let anyone hurt them.

But it was Laura who followed them up that driveway. Laura who screamed at Tony B as his boot lifted Heidi's ribs. Laura who thumped Tony B's back and made him roar and run away. Laura who knows he'll do it again, knows he'll keep doing it until somebody stops it.

When her dad tiptoes away, Heidi's eyes fling open to the blue-black ceiling. Something whooshes beneath her ribs. As though the floor has disappeared and the bed falls and falls. Not down, but up. Float falling. The way it would in outer space.

PROMONTORY

NOTHING MOVED MUCH. NOT THE WATER, THE air, or the people on the beach. The hippie with ropey dreadlocks lay spread-eagle without a towel. He looked like every other hippie to Drew—macramé necklace, Thai fisher pants—and Drew had even heard him bragging to Zoe, that he'd been here *so long, man, like I don't even remember when I arrived.*

Drew crouched in the shallows, tepid water weighting his swimming trunks, and the tide either ebbing or flowing. Difficult to tell.

Nearby lay an orderly row of Swedes. Plus four British girls doused in oil, backs glistening as though wrapped in plastic. The whole scene—crescent of white sand, jade waters, the green backdrop of trees—existed in an all-in-one blister-packaged paradise. Most travellers preferred the world this way, served up like a drink, all grenadine and maraschino cherry.

At the beach's east end was an outcrop of rock. Drew recalled the map posted over their table at the café, and the *you-are-here* arrow that angled toward a trail in the forested park. Then the scalloped skirt of a headland, wrapping from this bay to another, more secluded, beach.

Zoe lay on her belly, arms folded to prop herself up, hair hanging over a book. The guidebook, *Roaming Planet*, with its facts and practical travel tips. Since they'd met, she flipped through it frequently, underlining names of hostels and backpacker inns, caging costs and must-sees into inky circles. She studied maps in the middle of walking or conversation, even while brushing her teeth. Said she liked to know where she was in relation to other things—beach to hostel, hostel to mainland, mainland to equator, southern hemisphere to northern.

His gaze swept down the swale of her back to her orange bikini bottom. One heel dropped to her buttocks, thin foot angled skyward, then flexed, dropping back to the sand before the other foot lifted. She did this several times, flutter-kicking into the hot afternoon. Her body was both girl and woman, brimming hips and breasts, but with angular sprawling limbs. He wanted to slide that bikini off her ass, rub over her gritty, salty skin.

He jumped out of the water, jogged the labyrinth of sunbathers, through the hippie's cloud of patchouli and pot, the British girls' reek of coconut, until he settled on her, straddling her back, his knees pushing to the sand. He leaned into her neck where she smelled of apple shampoo, sea water, and hot skin.

Hey, she said, her elbows splayed, scrunching the book's pages beneath her chest. Hey! But she laughed and stretched out her neck.

He licked the ligament ridges, a blend of salt and sunscreen, and pressed against her.

Let's go, he whispered.

She laughed again, nudging her shoulder into his chest, hip into his belly, until she'd flipped onto her back, bearing his full weight. His sky-contoured face filled her sunglasses: broad chin, three-day scruff, dark hair drying in clumps. He tilted his chin at his own reflection, and deeper, past it, into her eyes.

Okay, she said.

ZOE RAN A HAND ALONG HIS SHOULDER BLADE, reached beyond it for his spine and followed the vertebral knobs down to his sacrum. She hugged him closer, her body melting under his. He smelled peppery, like cardamom and cast iron, and she knew she'd always be hungry for him. They could go anywhere together. Everywhere.

Already they'd travelled a month, the two of them, lived the past three days, going on four, in a thatched hut, the contents of their travel packs intermingling. It pleased Zoe to think of her journal stashed beneath Drew's paperback, the last entry dated March, though it was nearing May. And their toothbrushes leaning together on the small sink, one shared toothpaste tube squeezed tight in the middle. And their clothes heaped carelessly over the floor, except Drew's denim shirt, which hung over the wicker chair, and which Zoe sometimes wore after a shower, or on chilly nights.

Sweat stuck their bellies together. She felt him hard against her pelvis.

Let's do it, he said.

He broke her embrace, the sudden weightlessness of his body lengthened away from her: thin muscular thighs disappearing into his sun-faded shorts, abdomen rippling. He lifted his arm and pointed. She followed the contour of his bicep, down the long forearm to the index finger. Beyond that, she couldn't see.

Over there, he said. There's a beach on the other side.

Zoe sat up. Bedsheets lingered in her mind. The shelter of their thatched roof. The fan that whirled beneath it, and the air that'd move over their naked skin.

She shielded her eyes with her hand, and gradually the land took shape. It sprawled into jade water, edged with boulders and fringed with scraggly forest; it pleated in, extended farther, folded again.

There? she said. In the forest?

He shook his head.

Along the rocks. It'll be fun.

There seemed a huge distance to cross and leave behind their small claim on the beach, especially for scorching rock. She wanted to suggest the hut, or the shady mangrove. But he engraved a trench into the sand, his heel dragging over and over until he reached the darker layers. You can stay here, he said, in a matter-of-fact voice.

Her Birkenstocks were filled with sand, the sarong that served as a towel and skirt half-buried, and a column of mango pits and peels teetered under a mat of gnats. If she stayed, he'd dismiss her like he'd done with the hippie. She groped beneath the sand for her Swiss Army knife, wiped it on her tank top, clicked it closed and dropped it into her pack.

No, she said. I'm coming.

The British women were now face up, sunning their bellies. The Swedes jabbered in their Nordic tongue and Zoe tried to decipher the singsong syllables, though she only knew two words—*tack* for thanks, *krlek* for love. Over in the shallows a woman walked on her hands, legs floating in front of her, a mask and snorkel dangling around her neck.

Zoe smoothed the pages of her guidebook, but they stayed crumpled and misaligned. Giving up, she packed it, then rummaged for a granola bar or dried apricots to stabilize her blood sugars. Instead, she found a ticket stub for the bus from Brisbane with a small game of hangman scribbled in the corner: k a n g a r o o and only a head in the noose. Also, folded at the bottom, beneath the camera, an airmail envelope addressed to her, care of the General Post Office in Brisbane, from her sister Emily in Toronto. In tiny, concise script, her sister had recounted their mother's plan and execution to sell the family home and move to Nowhere, North Ontario, where she could deal in antique spinning wheels, pine-scrubbed tables, and rusting farm implements. Strange because neither Emily nor Zoe could remember growing up with anything but Ikea bookshelves, broken futon frames, second-hand crockery. Their rooms, Emily explained, had been cleared out and whitewashed. No more stickers on the doors, or graffiti hearts in the closet. Zoe's stash of *National Geographics* donated to Goodwill. All those issues she'd thumbed through, lying on the floor, clock radio playing low.

Emily assured her that other belongings had made it into boxes—clothes, yearbooks, *Nancy Drews*, old stuffed animals—and into the basement locker of their father's apartment building. Emily, too, would move in with their father and his new girlfriend until graduation next spring. Zoe folded the envelope into squares. Dismissed that empty room. *Her* empty room. Nothing she could do from this other side of the world.

She brought out the water bottle. Heat had softened the plastic and it crinkled in her grip.

Do you think it's enough? she said, and held it soldier-straight: three-quarters of a litre.

We're not going far, Drew said. He shook sand from a faded t-shirt and tucked it into his waistband. A pale sliver of skin shone, and a smattering of thin, dark hairs. Come on.

HE WATCHED HER SCOOP SAND OVER THE MANGO peels and loosen her buried sandals. Her arms as thick at the wrist as at the shoulder. Almost. *She's never carried anything,* he thought, and tried to imagine her in the bush, slogging up mountain ridges with survival kits, hammers and heavy rain gear, full sample bags at day's end. No way. Those arms made only for flower baskets and shawls. He squeezed his hands and flexed his biceps. He felt jumpy, ready to fling himself into the landscape, discover his own animal presence.

He tightened the Velcro of his sandals. Let's go, he said.

Zoe slid her tank top over her bikini, then gathered the sarong around her hips; when she stood, sand flaked off in sheets. She cinched the backpack closed and threaded her thin arms through the straps.

How long will we be? she asked. There's not really any food.

Who cares? he said. Not long.

He set out, walking past the Swedes. The hippie groaned

and his leathery skin grew darker. Something gasped in the shallows, a lone snorkel rising above the surface. Another exhalation issued, the swimmer turning in circles.

THE SUN HAD SLIPPED FROM ITS HIGH-NOON POST, and all cloud and moisture vanished into the atmosphere. These were dry tropics and weather made a fast exodus inland to saturate rain forests, or up along air currents toward the festival of monsoons. The sea stayed on, of course, swooning in its delicious love of the sun.

Zoe wished for her sun hat, the thing her mother had insisted on stuffing into the side pouch of her travel pack. *The Irish in you, darling,* her mother had said. Zoe wore it once in Fiji, her face still pasty with winter. Another time, she'd shielded herself from a disquieting stare on the Wellington ferry to Nelson, and the last time, in the Blue Mountains, because she'd heard the UV Index increased with elevation. Since she'd met up with Drew, the hat had stayed balled up tight. The wide brim gave her a virginal look, a pale innocence she'd tried to lose for years.

She followed him, his calves filling and emptying as he tramped through the sand, and composed postcards in her head. *My lover took me to a secluded beach . . . My lover and I will dive on the Reef . . . My lover will escort me to Indonesia . . .* Drew was her only lover on this trip. Ever, really. Back home she'd had a couple of boyfriends, but Drew fell into the lover category. He was older. Not much—twenty-five to her twenty—enough to assume experience. More than that, she thrilled remembering how he touched her, reviewing and savouring what she referred to, never aloud, as their *love-making*. She knew enough to feign casualness with him, suspecting he'd had dozens of flings. He told her he'd travel up the Coast with her, before he moved on to something else. She hoped *she'd* be that something else, their affair continuing, on and on, throughout her seven-stops-around-the-world trip (next stop: Bali) and eventually into Vancouver, a place she figured she'd settle, maybe even return to school.

She hummed the song they'd sung last night, sitting on the front steps of their hut. She'd assumed Drew was like all the guys from her dorm the previous year, the ones that strummed "Helpless" relentlessly. But under the Southern Cross, Drew had fast fingered a couple blues rifts, then played a song about mountain ridges and an unidentified *you*. As she'd sipped wine a longing loosened through her body, a sense that she wanted to expand and spread her arms and embrace the whole of the world.

I wrote that one, he'd said, tapping the song closed on the guitar.

A possum swung off the roof and opened its arms as though giving accolades. Zoe laughed and clapped, cuing Drew into a bow. The Swedes next door then popped their blond heads out and requested "Three Little Birds." That song so ubiquitous Drew shook his head, softened into Bruce Cockburn's "Wondering Where the Lions Are." She'd listened to it on her Walkman over thousands of miles. And when their voices met and blended, she realized she'd never sung the words out loud.

DREW HOOKED HIS FINGERS OVER THE GRANITE SHELF, dug them into a gritty crevice. He wedged a foot into a triangular crack and, with an orchestrated heave, climbed onto the surface. He stood, arms raised in victory and then noticed Zoe. Still on the sand, she palpated the rock as though checking for the lever to a secret cave. A mix of tenderness and irritation filled him as he crouched to offer a hand. She gripped his wrist and leaned back in counterweight. When she stepped up, she stumbled, one of her Birkenstocks, with its thinning sole, slipped into a gap.

These aren't the best shoes, she said.

He shrugged and wiggled it free. They'll be fine.

He faced the direction of the headland. They'd have to

walk with both arms and legs, leaning and calculating pathways over and around fissures that gaped and filled with water. Or up domed boulders, some the size of Volkswagen Beetles, others like giant tortoises. Sunlight gamboled over mica and feldspar. Seams of dulled quartz crisscrossed the granite. No doubt gold threaded through it, or deeper, in the bedrock. Not enough to make extraction worth it. Still, that gold vein reassured Drew, like money in a vault.

Around that first fold of land, the boulders flattened out and he quickened his pace to reach the next bend, where the human-strewn beach would vanish from sight. He wanted to imagine this place before Captain Cook's ship sailed past— undisturbed and unspoiled.

He did that on those long days when helicopters dropped him onto mountain tops or deserted icefields, with only his shotgun, his hammers and bags, a thermos of coffee. He'd wait for the silence and when it came, it filled him like wind, attuned every cell to the mineral voice of the land. *Ancient*, his father used to say. *The planet's oldest stories embedded in the rocks.* And his father had gone searching for them, discovering planetary climate shifts, or unearthing invertebrate fossils, those he called *ancestors*. Drew thought of the labradorite in a cloth sack, alongside his passport. His father had given it to him years before the apprenticeship, years before he died. He'd taken his research team to Labrador, and when he'd returned, he held the iridescent stone in his palm, pointing to the lamellae, blues and greens shifting like a hologram. *The closest thing to touching infinity,* his father had said. Then he'd tapped the stone three times, as though releasing a charm, and handed it to Drew. Now he wished he had it in his pocket, to finger and worry.

Zoe's voice strained over the distance: Wait up! She scurried like a child.

He leaned against a boulder and waited. The beach was barely visible except for the far crescent tip. A blue sailboat had anchored offshore, its main sail wrapped around the boom, but the jib stayed open and slack over the bow. Voices carried across the bay, then a series of splashes.

Mangrove trees bracketed the west end of the beach. Yesterday, he and Zoe had walked there, on a winding board-walk over networks of roots that plugged like wires into the sand. Afterwards they'd sipped pulpy shakes, pureed with mangoes that grew right there.

I could have one of these every day, Zoe had said.

Drew had wanted to tell her this island was a limbo-land, a holding place between his last thing—a cycling trip through New Zealand—and the next. When he'd met her in Byron Bay, he'd thought the restlessness had worn off for a while. Thought he could travel to the Reef, take the five-day diving course recommended by *Roaming Planet*. He wasn't sure anymore. It wasn't Zoe, exactly. Or diving. More the predictability. Small talk in close boat quarters. He didn't want to listen to the litany of places to see, countries to visit. He didn't want to hear about another madcap mishap on a Thai tuk-tuk, nor swap tales of dysentery, of nightmares brought on by malaria pills.

Drew stroked the boulder. This island had once been cov-ered in volcanic rock; the whole thing rising from the Earth's hot core only to harden and coarsen and wear away. *Permian. The Great Dying.* He closed his eyes as though to summon that Age; the underside of his eyelids swirled with red and fila-ments of gold.

Do you know why this island is called Magnetic?

Zoe eclipsed the sun and he opened his eyes. She stood holding the backpack straps like a parachute and panted a little.

No, he said, guarding against her affection for trivia: *The most easterly point of the continent . . . the aboriginal word for kangaroo . . . number of cattle ranches in the Outback.*

She bounced her pack, wiped her forehead. Strands of hair loosened from her bun. Her complexion had reddened.

Well, she said. Captain Cook sailed by and his compass went all wonky. He thought the island's bedrock must be full of magnets.

Impossible, Drew said. The crown of his head drew heat like metal. He snapped the t-shirt from his waistband, opened it and tied it into a headdress.

No one found any, she said. But do you think we'd feel it?

Feel what?

A magnetic pull.

He imagined the ions in his blood rushing toward the ground, fastening him there, making him a permanent fixture like the hippie on the beach. A person incapable of moving along.

No, he said. I don't.

ABOVE THEM, HOOP PINES AND STRING-BARKED eucalyptus popped in the heat. A bouquet of salt rose from the water. Every few metres, Zoe stopped to scrutinize the trees. She wanted to see a koala. All these weeks Down Under and she'd only glimpsed the tail of a kookaburra and countless possums. According to *Roaming Planet,* hundreds of koalas lived on the island, a veritable sanctuary. At the café she'd picked up a pamphlet that advertised tours with guaranteed sightings.

Guaranteed! Drew had said. What's the fun in that?

She'd wanted to tell him she'd gladly pay the extra ten bucks to have her picture taken with a cub. But he'd snatched the pamphlet and wagged it.

People want to devour the world like a goddamn hamburger, he'd said. They want McWildlife.

She knew what he meant.

So far the world hadn't proven as wild as she'd imagined. Back in stuffy lecture halls, she'd daydreamed herself dancing on clifftops. Wild coloured fabrics fluttering from her body, and the sky above, the vast waters below, all imbued with a pekoe light. That image kindled in her a sense of freedom and heart-soar. True life wasn't in the classroom or in the nine-to-five job that would follow, but out there, waiting for her, somewhere in the wider world. She'd tried to talk her friend Kirsten into accompanying her, but Kirsten waffled, opting for a boy-friend and home. So Zoe, chomping and restless, saved the money and booked her ticket anyway, knowing she couldn't wait for anyone else. Her mother called her brave and an inspiration; her father hoped she'd find herself and gave her a credit card for emergencies.

But once on her way, she realized the world was a well-mapped thoroughfare, the *Roaming Planet* so clear you couldn't get lost. *There and Away* sections provided exact co-ordinates and schedules for bus stations and landmarks. Listed names of taxi drivers and where to find the cheapest, best coffee, anywhere. *Roaming Planet* eschewed bus tours but encouraged bohemian walking tours and kayak guides. Freedom and adventure were catalogued and copyrighted, and Zoe admitted it was easier that way. The transience, though, demanded a fortitude she hadn't expected. Travelling alone meant picking up new companions every few days. And while New Zealand had a summer camp feel, backpackers on practically every corner, Australia seemed desolate, a party she'd arrived at too late. Sure she'd exchanged pleasantries with fellow travellers in hostel kitchens, the usual where-have-you-beens, and she'd dutifully walked from must-see to must-see—Botanical Gardens, Opera House, Blue Mountains—hoping for a local to befriend her, show her the untapped secrets of this country.

Finally, in Sydney, she took the advice of a Dutch couple and hopped onto a bus to Byron Bay. "It's brilliant," they'd said. But even those empty beaches seemed more lonely than beautiful and she spent hours writing in her journal, wishing Kirsten sat on the beach with her.

One morning, as per *Roaming Planet*, she rose before dawn and followed a scrubby trail toward a lighthouse, the continent's most easterly point. When she reached the bluffs, the sky brightened, and the last stars faded out. Drew was perched on the cliff's edge, facing the horizon. Weeks before, they'd met in New Zealand, spent several days trekking the Abel Tasman together, swimming in quiet bays, and once, kissing under a stone arch, never expecting to see each other again.

It's you, she'd said.

And he nodded, as though he'd expected her all along. The sun rose then, slipped from behind the ocean like a ripe and skinless peach.

A BREEZE MUMBLED OVER THE BLUE-GREEN WATER and sun reflected in trapezoids and diamonds. The air seemed to stop at Zoe, moving around her to continue up the slope, where it lazily shook the trees. She wished Drew would wait for her, grab her urgently, lower her onto the rock. She could add this to her tally of interesting places they'd *made love*, along with the tour boat in Brisbane, the mine shaft relic in Gympie, those sand dunes on Fraser Island. But he only moved faster, his sun-browned back churning as he loped over a series of boulders.

The climbing made it harder to breathe. She sipped warm water in small sips, swished it in her mouth, between her bottom teeth. When she swallowed, only a trickle went down. She closed her eyes, repeated the process a second, then a third, time.

The bottle down to half full. They must've walked an hour now. Or more. And she was still thirsty, would probably be thirsty the whole time. She took another quick sip, hoping Drew wouldn't ask for some too, but he was too far ahead. The sun burned hotter. Freckles spread down her forearms. Small sweaty pearls. She blinked one slow blink, the dizziness coming on, that feeling of the horizon swaying upward, then recoiling, then settling back down. Her blood sugars. All she needed was a handful of raisins. She squatted and rummaged through her bag. Six sunflower seeds. Nothing else.

THE TIDE ROSE, BUT ONLY ENOUGH TO SPILL INTO spaces where the lower boulders and rock shelves came together. Where the island rounded east, a big boulder domed and Drew climbed on top, studying the patterns of stone and rubble, scrub and trees which repeated, first cinching in, then jutting out to a distance twice what they'd walked so far. The sun dropped a fraction westward, its rays long and unimpeded, every shadow lengthening by inches.

Down below, rocks entered the water and he scrutinized them to see if he and Zoe could ease down for a dip. But beneath the jade surface lurked a jagged darkness. Reefs girdled the island and he couldn't gauge how close they came. If only he'd rented a mask and snorkel from the backpackers' earlier to scout it out.

He cleared sweat from his forehead and looked behind for Zoe. There, not too far back, she dropped to her knees, close to the edge, too close, giving him a moment of vertigo. She fumbled with the bottle, not drinking it, but shaking to see how much was left.

He cupped his hands around his mouth, called to her: You okay?

She screwed the lid, exchanged bottle for camera and smiled a strange, diluted smile then disappeared behind the camera. He swept a hand over his head, removed the ridiculous headdress, tossed it down and yanked through the salt clumps of his hair. Then he placed one hand on a hip, the other over his brow and gave his jokey catalogue pose. The shutter released. He stuck his chin forward and grinned. His sister called it photogenic botulism, the contrived smile that had filled their family albums.

Zoe clicked again. And again. He had the feeling she'd fire through an entire roll today alone. He'd never see these photos, doubted he'd ever see her again, once they separated. Though they'd done that before, first meeting in Nelson, on the south island of New Zealand and again, by fluke, in Byron Bay. This circuit guaranteed you'd cross paths with someone only to cross them again in another time zone, another latitude. Zoe said fate brought them, two Canadians, halfway around the world to meet not once, but twice. Still, it wouldn't happen again. Soon he'd get off the beaten track, back into the bush. Maybe find work in the Outback, prospecting for gold or copper. And the only people he'd meet there would be Aussie men with leather hats, men who shot kangaroos to roast and eat.

Where are we? Zoe climbed on the boulder alongside Drew, then sat with her legs dangling.

Drew nodded toward the far jut of land. The beach must be on the other side of that.

It's hot, she said. Let me have your shade.

He put his t-shirt back on and Zoe leaned against his legs, squeezing into his shadow's narrow girth. She took out her guidebook, the pages warped and stuck together in the top corner. She opened and ironed them out, then flipped back and forth. One page showed a road map of the main village, another the whole island: solid road lines running around the southern perimeter, a few broken trail lines wending through the park land.

We're not even on here, she said.

He tapped the spot he swore represented their very boulder. It's here, he said.

When she tugged the book away, the page ripped, a fissure through the island's centre. Zoe clucked her tongue and repositioned the map, pressed the tear so it held together.

Then what we're looking for is way over here, she said. Drew saw how once they rounded it they'd have to walk to another point. If it weren't for her, he'd be there by now.

It's not that far, he said. Your sense of scale is off. Another hour if we keep moving.

He reached into her bag and grabbed the water, tipped his head skyward and took three gulps, draining the bottle to a quarter. He passed it back, along with the lid.

That's all we have, she said, and sipped through pursed lips. Maybe we should turn back.

He tightened a fist, his biceps slow to flex. He released and the muscles relaxed.

We'll be fine, he said. An hour. Tops. We'll go back through the forest.

He slid off the boulder. Didn't she know if you stopped anything halfway, you ended up stuck?

But I . . . she said to Drew.

He glanced at her legs, the way they hung over the boulder, at her thin square shoulders that appeared to carry the sky.

You what? he asked.

She shook her head, then blew into the near-empty bottle. It sounded like a foghorn. She bounced her heels against the rock, said, The kangaroo is the only animal on the planet that can suspend gestation. In times of scarcity and drought, the kangaroo's fetus will stop growing and wait.

Is that right, Drew said. Then scampered up the next rise of rubble, bits of rock shifting under his feet.

Zoe held her index finger and thumb to the scale on her map, then lifted them. Through that small window she watched Drew move farther and farther away.

INSECTS CHIRRUPED, AS THOUGH ALL THIS TIME THEY'D been waiting under dried leaves and shredded bark for the right moment to stir. The eucalyptus above released a clutch of fresh oxygen. Its medicinal smell encouraged Zoe to move, continue along the arrangement of the headland. She hadn't said anything to Drew about her blood sugar, and good thing. Drew had survived much worse. He'd been drugged on a Philippine boat, chased by a grizzly in Northern BC, and caught once in an Indian street riot. She only felt lightheaded and trembly. If she wanted to travel with him, she'd have to be adventurous otherwise he'd hop on the next ferry off the island, leaving no note behind. Next time she'd make sure to bring granola bars, an extra bottle of water.

Just then, a kingfisher swooped off a spindly hoop-pine branch and over Zoe's head. Not too close, or with any particular sound, but a rare sight, its bearings confused, too far east of the mangrove marsh. Mere metres from Zoe, it hovered: feathers arching in a flash-pan of azure and copper, an alchemy of sky and metal.

Its black eyes steadied on Zoe, its white throat puffed as though to speak. Zoe fished out her camera, fixed the bird's bright body to the centre of the viewfinder. As she pressed the shutter release, the bird, without warning, without squawk or peep, directed its heavy beak toward the ocean and plummeted out of the frame.

She lowered the camera, stepped closer to the drop-off and peered down. The ocean moved as a mass, like a satiated belly, jiggling.

She turned toward the beach, saw the stern of a distant boat, then the trees and the enduring tangle of branches and needles. Then Drew scurrying over endless potato-coloured rocks. Finally, she faced the uncluttered sky and the sea again. The bird had dissolved. As if its fantastic wings had been made of nothing but sugar.

She found herself awash in an unaccountable sadness, an ache that leaked down her arms. She clutched her camera by the lens and spun it as though she might rewind the bird from the water. She pressed her lips together and shook her head, her brain knocking gently against its skull until her mother's face appeared. *It's just a little bird, darling*, she said. And Zoe squinted, praying the bird might rise from the water. *I know*, she said. *I know, I know.* But still, sadness spread, rolled over the winking, indifferent Pacific all the way out to the shores of strange islands and continents, where it poured into mouths, speaking every language, and roved through cities and mountains, deserts and savannahs. Had she been foolish to travel so far? She returned the camera to the bag, withdrew her sister's letter with its frail, piqued handwriting, and tossed it. Water bled into the paper, turning it dark, then darker blue. Zoe's empty childhood room swamped with a green sea, with angelfish and scuba divers, with starfish and the sugar-bird, water swelling up the walls and over the windows, right to the square light fixture: her whole room drowning.

THE END OF THE JUT RIGHT THERE. IT HAD TAKEN HIM, what? Twenty minutes? When they made it around the bend, the sun would tone down. He nodded the way he did when a project neared completion. They'd get to the beach, swim, fuck in the shallows. Head back through the trees. Drink cold beer and eat battered shrimp.

Something forced him to turn. Zoe lagged behind again, now back where the land pinched in and rubble tumbled from a steep pitch. Rocks, so much smaller there, stacked in a cleft and rose up into the forest. A gully, he thought, a riverbed where water would flow, if it ever did flow. Zoe sat on the shelf at the foot of the slide. He called and she lifted an arm, waved something white before letting it drop.

You can't stop now! he yelled. Come on! Hands motioning like a man directing planes or training an animal.

He started back toward her, heat lifting off the granite in thick layers. He called again, his voice skipping over the water, bouncing off the rocks. She didn't hear, and couldn't know, how much he sounded like his father, that same impatient inflection.

The white square flapped and landed near her feet. Another went up and landed in the water.

He climbed over rocks he'd just traversed, hating to walk the same tract twice, his thighs quaky. He dug his fingers into a long crack on a large boulder and this time decided to cross on a narrow ledge. He inched along the shelf, cursing Zoe. She'd botched the only excursion they'd taken without following *Roaming Planet* guidelines.

As he set his left foot down again, his right slipped into a crack between smaller boulders. He tugged, but the sandal only twisted, strap tearing away from the bridge of his foot, his toes sinking deeper. He cursed and reached down with his right hand, left still holding tight. He hooked his thumb under the heel strap, strained and yanked, but his foot wedged tighter. He returned his right hand to perch alongside the left. Leaned his forehead against the boulder. Okay, he thought. Okay.

He kept his fingers anchored and slowly revolved the right foot. Once, in the bush north of Terrace, he'd had to tap rock lightly with hammers, flake away outer layers of schist. He needed that patience as he narrowed his foot, pointing it downward, lifting millimetre by millimetre. The sandal sole flapped against his heel, and he felt some release before his foot sank even deeper.

Saltwater lapped at the granite far below him, grinding those micas and feldspars. Time would go on like this, stone turning to sand, sun beating his back. He needed to get the fuck out.

From the top of his femur, he rotated his leg outward. The foot moved. He paused and secured his fingers. Revolved his pelvis and his knee began twisting and the foot freed up a fraction. His knee twinged, but he had to keep twisting, keep bringing the whole leg around. He clenched his jaw, almost there, and with one fast turn of the hip, jerked his whole body.

Something popped, pain shooting down his shin into his ankle, even as it radiated up his thigh. The foot hung limp, streaked in blood, the sandal dangling off his heel.

He shimmied across the crevice, hopped the left foot over and when his right leg swung to the other side, he flung onto the flat ridge. His hip took the fall and he rolled onto his back, howling and swearing at the sky. His knee swelled, the skin growing fat and angry and red. He tried to bend it.

Fuck, he said. Fuck fuck fuck.

He placed his hands over the radiant joint. The beach had disappeared entirely from sight. The boat too. He called up into the forest, metres above him, but heard no human noise. He turned to find Zoe. Her legs draped over the far granite shelf, and she was throwing paper into the water. Had she not even seen him? He yelled, but her hands swatted the air above the water. She needed to get help. Maybe together they could hobble into the forest. Maybe she could help him up to the crest of the high ridge. He thought of her thin arms.

Fuck, he said again, and dragged his ass closer to where the land rose. He bent his good knee, jammed that heel into the rubble, pushed with his quads. Sand and hot gravel slipped under his waistband. He bent his knee again, pushed. Again, his shorts filled. The soil loosened and the next push brought him far enough away from the waterline, closer to the pine smell. He clawed the ground for purchase, but it gave and he slid from the forest edge to the lower ridge, bumping down and down, until his straight, swollen leg hit the sharp square of a boulder, filling his knee with barbs and electricity.

THE SUN ROARED LIKE A HOT MOUTH. IT MELTED THE solid lines on the map, liquefying them, so they seemed to slide off the page. The island itself might slip from beneath Zoe's feet, land ready to glide toward the horizon and disappear.

She could disappear. And who would find her? She remembered that boy, Eric. His face small with a nose that scrunched when he'd told her about tadpoles. And she'd followed him, through a thicket, branches rounded and forming tunnels, nylon windbreaker swishing, and Eric's jacket stuffed into a pocket pouch, fastened around his waist and wagging as they crawled away from frozen tag, from mothers unfolding wax paper and slicing apples. No one noticed them leave. And they'd crawled a long way to the fast skimming water, brown and reeking of frog skin. Eric stood and pointed to a fallen tree, Zoe a little behind. Before she reached him, the ground gave way under Eric's feet, a collapse of sand and mud and new shoots of grass, and as he slid into the creek, his face slapstick cartoon in surprise, Zoe laughed. She remembered how she'd laughed. How he hadn't shouted or called out, water fast and brown and never caring he was in it. She'd thought he'd come back. Fastened her hands to a branch and waited.

Now she ripped the map from the guidebook and held it,

compass arrow pointing skyward and the sky arching away. She released the page; it sliced through the air, then flattened with gravity, sailing side to side onto the water's surface. It took its place in line with the others, the page with all the places to eat and stay on the Gold Coast, the photo of surfers at Coolangatta, listings of jet ski adventure shops, and the brief history of Captain Cook's navigational confusion. The paper chain drifted out onto the water and she wanted to walk across it, dive in and come up, floating like another map, sea undulating all around her. She tossed the book in a perfect arc, a full gulp and swallow into the jade.

Once, before Eric swept away from her, her father had risen out of water this same colour, mask over his face, a snorkel, and hands full of starfish. Where? Mexico, maybe. Her father draping the starfish over a white wall. The orange one. The blue. All day Zoe had touched their rigid backs, watched their limbs move as slow as crooked clock hands. Her mother had told her they were living things, that the sun would dry them and did. Legs forever shaped like wilting petals. Now she lay over the hot rock. She'd become like them, those starfish, colours fading, and reeking of the sea.

BREATHE, BREATHE, BREATHE.

INSECTS EMITTED A HIGH-PITCH THAT RATTLED THE SKY like a pane of glass. A bellow resounded over the slack-tide. Zoe opened her eyes, the sun lower now. She must've dozed. She licked her lips, tasted salt and iron. She wanted to suck on an ice chip, but it seemed to her now she'd never known ice.

It sounded again—a shout—and she sat up, fixed her hand to her forehead and scanned the glaring water. Then her vision clarified to the pattern of the too-familiar, dun-coloured stone. She surveyed each one, from the tip of the jut inward, as though reading words. Halfway between her and the far point, a flag rippled. Drew against the incline. She nodded and waved, thinking it'd been so long since she'd seen him. And she wanted to see him again.

Come here, she yelled, her voice a whisper.

FINALLY, SHE WAVED BACK, AS HE POINTED AND pointed to his knee, now three times its regular size. I can't move, he hollered, over and over.

He thought of the way he'd circled his thumb and index finger around her upper arm, how he'd asked whether she'd ever chopped firewood or built a shelter. She'd given him a puzzled look, said she wasn't a Boy Scout, that the closest thing she'd come to wilderness camping was swinging in the hammock at her aunt's cottage, roughing it in the cabins at summer camp. Still, she had the knife. Maybe they could fashion a rope or harness out of bark. Something to hoist him up into the forest. From there, he could hop or hobble, hold each eucalyptus for support. He wished he'd broken his ankle or leg, something he could splint, but the only remedy for swelling was ice and ibuprofen. And if he'd torn the wrong ligament—he didn't want to think about it. If only she'd hurry the fuck up.

He watched her crawl over a boulder, turn toward the next one, pat its wide curve before mounting it. He flagged her again and she nodded and moved with the same caution. Hours could pass before she made it, he thought. Fuck. He hated that he needed her, hated her cautious nature, her constant checking for provisions. Hated that she didn't have any more water. His knee throbbed, but he tried to bend it again, wondered if he could spring-load it with enough adrenaline to push past the pain. He squeezed his eyes, tried to recapture the panic the grizzly mother induced that day in the high Chilcotins, the only time he'd ever been that scared. Nothing but wit, an empty shotgun and a can of bear spray. She'd growled from a higher ridge, beginning low in her gut, then fiercer, up into her teeth-baring mouth. He'd held the shotgun over his head, growled back like the experts tell you—appear bigger than you are—though he'd only wanted to run like hell. The standoff lasted five minutes, or fifty, he didn't know, before he started backing away. That's when she dropped to all fours, descended toward him, rank and gamy smelling. He tossed the gun and it thudded to the ground. She advanced and he, still facing her, fumbled with his belt. She was ten feet off, maybe less, when he released a thick cloud of spray. She bounded into it, roared, then became disoriented enough for Drew to sprint across the open range. His whole body pounded, feet barely touching the ground, he ran and ran until he reached the lip of glacial debris and radioed the helicopter.

But now there was only the hard rush of his heart and the Lord's Prayer he muttered like an obedient schoolboy, even though he didn't want God, but the labradorite, its smooth store of luck. And all his father's best moments. Whatever his father was now—ghost, spirit, stardust—Drew spoke to him, apologized for not speaking in all the days since his death.

He promised to call his mother first off, forget the Outback for now, and fly home to apply for those doctoral programs, get on with the rest of his life. No more languishing on beaches, no more forays with women along the travel-beat. He had gold to find, a small empire to build. He even had a company name picked out, honouring his father: Grant's Frontier Gold.

Groundwork first, Drew said. Like you always say.

He needed a little help was all. A reorganization of the day's events. Reduced swelling. And water. Definitely water. When he opened his eyes, he felt a little better, as though he'd placed an order and, without question, it would be filled.

PATTERNS BECAME PUZZLES. A JAGGED EDGE followed by a gap, then a smooth surface with no foothold. Sometimes cracks formed eyes, or dark ancient mouths. Here, a ladder Zoe had to descend, as though fetching something from a cellar. Only now she had to twist halfway and reach for the narrow waist of a neighbouring stone. She hoisted herself over, panting, then spread flat out. Inertia overtook her, and she closed her eyes, stayed as still as possible. She used to lie on her bedroom floor, not twitching a muscle. Barely breathing. She'd wanted her mother to find her, worry for a fraction of a second that she was dead. Wanted to know her mother's life would become another life without her. Less. But when Zoe had listened through the floorboards, she'd hear her mother talking on the phone, or listening to Bach cello suites, or kneading bread, never once wondering: where's Zoe? And now, again, on this hot afternoon, she wanted her mother to find her, to slide the horizon open, poke her head through, say: *Come on, darling. Stop playing silly games.*

Something hollow scratched beneath Zoe, a deep grinding rising through the granite. The globe in the living room, her mother's hand spinning the world on its metal axis, spinning and spinning, until the colours of the continents and oceans blurred. Zoe felt dizzy, nauseated. Stop, she said. Just stop. But no one stopped the momentum, no one peered in close.

She sat up, opened her eyes to the low hum of blue. She needed to keep going, even if every step filled her head with sparks. But she couldn't rest, not now. Drew kept calling, needing her, though she couldn't understand why. She wondered if he was speaking another language, German or Swedish. Another thing she didn't know about him and wanted to. Like the guitar and the song he'd written, but never played for her again.

AT LEAST ANOTHER HOUR BEFORE ZOE COLLAPSED beside Drew. As though she'd run a fucking marathon, as though she'd just crossed the finish line. His shoulders dropped, the pinch in his jaw was gone. He rolled his eyes and muttered thanks to his father.

Listen, Zoe said.

He cocked his ear and heard the cicadas, the rustling branches above, and the eternal lapping water below.

What?

She motioned toward an airplane, a silver needle way up in the ozone. Zoe waved.

It won't see us, he said.

The last of the day's sun glazed her cheek. He saw how red it was, saw her throat pulse like a tree frog. Then for a moment, his father's stern face. *How lucky you are . . . Next time you might not be . . .*

I can't move, Drew said. You need to get help.

She noticed his knee, naked and vulnerable, a thing freshly birthed. She wanted to cradle it, kiss it, rub it with salve. But he grabbed her pack and said something about her knife, something about breaking wood, something about the trails.

Orange streaked the horizon, then a pale blue. Zoe started up the slope, magnet legs plodding forward. And when, at last, she reached the trees, she slid back, fell to her knees. Drew yelled and yelled.

Never mind. She stood back up. She'd carry on.

HUNGER MOON

YOU FOLLOW FOSTER THROUGH THE SIDE DOOR. He chucks his jacket and gym bag onto a row of boots, taking down a pair of salt-stained lace-ups. You attempt to hang your jean jacket on one of the seven occupied hooks. First try fails, and your jacket skims into a gritty puddle. Second go 'round and Foster's laughing saying, "Just throw it anywhere, man." But you're persistent, and finally, with some rearranging, it stays put over a trench coat and rain poncho.

You kick off your high-tops, only a couple months old and already too small. You won't report this to your mother, not until your feet bleed or she's better, back at work. *Great.* There's your big toe. Jabbing right through the fresh hole in your sock. *Goddamn.* Somewhere between wearing shoes all day and removing them, it's happened: your feet have taken on another centimetre.

You are like the fucking universe, expanding.

Or like that kid with a messed-up gene. The one you read about, his DNA gone haywire, pumping out signals to never stop growing. At sixteen, the guy's legs are so long he had to remove the driver's seat of his Volkswagen Golf to work the pedals from the back bench. And still he had to bend his neck funny to peer out the windshield. He's probably eight feet by now or exploded right out of his skin. That could happen to you. *Is* happening. Every night you feel bone-splintering pain, as though tiny people are scaling beneath your shin bones with crampons and pickaxes.

Now your stomach groans. Foster's mom peeks around the partition wall, says, "Derek!" She folds her arms, flicks the filter of an unlit cigarette with her thumbnail. She's wearing a fuzzy teal sweater which gives her an out-of-focus look, especially with her smudgy green eyeliner.

Foster runs past her, does a sock slide across the kitchen floor, right to the fridge. "You hungry, man?" he says.

You're never *not* hungry.

When you step into the kitchen, Foster's mom tugs your sleeve, says, "Jesus, Derek. You join the basketball team yet?"

"It's not really my thing," you say. Every other person begrudges the fact you don't put your height to good use. They must picture you slam-dunking a million shots, and not how you trip down the court in gym class. Especially your dad who, when not in the Caribbean with his new girlfriend or closing another so-called deal in New York, hassles you to try out for volleyball or *B-ball* like he did. He's always recounting his glory years, captain of this and that, telling you about team trips he went on, cheerleaders he dated.

Foster's mom says, "What *is* your thing, Derek?" You shrug, mumble something about guitar, though you only play an A chord and a G. She places the unlit cigarette in her mouth and opens the oven. Lasagna smells waft out. "You staying?" she asks.

For the past two months, you've eaten mostly grilled cheese sandwiches, Doritos, cereal, and those bags of deli corned beef. Occasionally, your mom's friend Evelyn drops off a casserole or a pot of chili, something your mom cries over, thanks her for and doesn't touch. Supper you and your brother eat for two or three days in a row.

Your stomach groans again and you say yes to Foster's mom.

"Yes *please*," says Foster and crams a Kraft Single into his mouth.

"Hollow legs," his mom says, turning oven knobs. "The both of you." She lights her cigarette, coughs, shuffles out of the kitchen. "Four o'clock," she says. "*Oprah*." And she disappears toward the TV room, in slippers that look like mini sleeping bags.

Since she's pretty much bedridden, your mom watches *Oprah* on an old black-and-white TV. Last fall she was diagnosed with lupus, and now she's in the midst of a flare, every joint swollen and sore, her mouth full of cankers, hair falling out in clumps. According to her doctor, it's preying on her kidneys. She swallows pills which bloat her face and make her look like someone else's mother.

You hope that soon you'll wake up and she'll be chopping onions and carrots for stew or scraping paint off the tallboy in the middle of the dining room or rushing off to work in her white sneakers. You keep waiting for her to use that jokey voice, the one like a secret code between you. Instead she asks you to sit on the rocker beside her bed, the lights dim or off. She says, "Derek, this isn't how it should be for you. It isn't." Her voice thin, like an echo, like a sound lifting out of a deep and lonely hole.

There's hope though. A friend of a friend of a friend found Longwei, a Chinese doctor with a reputation for miracles. For the past two Tuesdays and Thursdays he's knocked on the door, told you that you're too tall, and handed you a paper sack stuffed with dusty herbs. First day he showed you how to simmer them low until the water transformed into a black potion. "To tonify kidneys," he said. Then there's the *qi*. Longwei says your mom's is stagnant. You have no idea what qi is, but you've watched him encourage it, waving burning sticks over her wrists, inserting needles and twisting them deep into her joints.

FOSTER'S GOING TRIPLE-DECKER WITH THE SANDWICHES.
"Toothpicks, toothpicks," he says, chomping on a piece of ham,
opening every drawer. "Like at Yitz's, you know? Olives and
fucking toothpicks." You jam your fingers into the olive jar,
fish around until Foster slaps your hand. You flick olive juice
at him, and he whips you with a tea towel. One giant step and
you're out of reach, twisting the egg timer by the stove to sixty.

You really should call your mom. She's always saying, "At
least do me that courtesy, Derek. Otherwise, I'm thinking
ditch." Probably she's with Longwei, or Oprah; probably she
isn't worried about you at only four in the afternoon.

"Mustard?" Foster says, clinking a knife against a jar.

You say sure, sure, then you're over in what Foster's family
calls The Nook. It's more of an eatery, where you've downed
glasses of freshly squeezed OJ and baskets of croissants,
where Foster's parents spend most Sundays smoking, drinking espresso and filling in *The Globe and Mail* crossword.
This house has other luxuries too: wide staircase, basement
mini-gym, outdoor pool, indoor solarium. None of your other
friends even know what a solarium *is*.

Frozen rain taps the sliding glass. Outside the sky isn't
really light or dark. More that indecisive blue-grey. And
the pool, covered in an undulating blue blanket and crusty
mounds of snow, is nothing like last summer at Foster's pool
party. That's when you made out with Jaime Harris under the
diving board. One hand gripping the ledge, other hand, roaming. You would've slipped it beneath the bra part of her bikini,
but Foster charged overhead, canonballed into the water.
Jaime sputtered, submerged and swam wide frog strokes along
the bottom. Now chickadees drop from bare branches, peck at
a smattering of seed, and no one's making out with anybody.

Meg appears, reflected in the glass, a smear of white and
powder blue. You turn around, and your heart plunges a little, though you wish it wouldn't. She's fourteen to your seventeen, wears turtlenecks and sweatpants, school mascot on the
bum. Not at all like Jaime. But there's *something*. The theatrical

fedora, brim casting blue over her face. The spin and moon-walk, half-Michael Jackson, half-*Flashdance*. You shove your hands into your pockets, concealing your boner. Plop into the nearest chair.

She tosses the hat, which lands over the cat dish, and laughs. Straightens her glasses, her spine, and salutes you. "Hello Derek. Howst art thou?"

"Stop it with the fucking Shakespeare," Foster says.

To Foster, she says, "Excusez-moi, oh brother mine." Hip checks him away from the fridge. To you, she says, "Do you know *Antony and Cleopatra*?" But you don't. She's playing one of Antony's daughters; she has one line.

"One word, more like it." Foster peels four slices of bacon from a pack, sticks them on a paper towel and into the microwave.

"One word. One line. Same same." She displays a container, does a plié. "Fruit bottomed yogurt anyone?"

The microwave whirs and Foster butchers a watery tomato. "Yeah, and we had to sit through five hours of *thou* and *art* and shit, and all she says is *Father!*" His voice rises in girlish pitch, tomato dripping from his fingers, and you know he'll never not go to his sister's plays.

Years ago, she lost her eye. Foster's fault: he lobbed a snow-ball, aimed at his buddy, packed around rock and ice. It caught Meg, ruptured the vitreous humours, inside liquid of the eye leaking out. He's told you the story a couple times, and once, when you were both high as shit, he brought you into her room, tiptoeing to the dresser, where he opened a plastic container and her backup eye ogled you. At first you both laughed your asses off. The weirdness of a disembodied eye. Then he dumped it onto your palm. You thought it'd be a sphere, but it spread across your palm like a fried egg. It felt strangely cool and you imagined Meg sliding it through the socket, position-ing it like a board behind a broken window.

You always forget which one is the fake.

And now she joins you in The Nook, straight hair staticky

from her hat. She's eating from the yogurt container, licking her spoon, asking if you've ever seen a lunar eclipse.

You pick the dried petals off a potted African violet, rub them until they crumble into dust. Tell her about the solar eclipse, the grade six art class where you cut cardboard, glued tinfoil, and designed special viewing devices. You tell her how your mom shut the curtains so your little brother wouldn't sear his retinas, and how you stood at the bathroom window, door locked, and pointed the device at the sky. The thing didn't work. Biggest celestial event of your life, and it didn't work.

"That's too bad," says Meg. "Tonight's the lunar. No special device required. Only clouds in the way." She lowers the right eye, obvious now it's the living one, and you study the left, the way it stays wide, doesn't move at all.

She's scooting a chair closer to you, warmish and girl fragrant, and you can't remember when you started to notice-*notice* her. Maybe by the auditorium doors at school, hanging out with the other drama kids. Or the cumulative days you've spent watching *Star Trek* with Foster, Meg curled on the saucer chair. It doesn't matter, because all you know is you want to place her whole and pure in your mouth. "Meg," you whisper, not really meaning to, but she's heard you and says your name with a big fat question mark. You clear your throat, shift over, knock your knee and ignore the pain. In that stupid Shakespeare voice you say, "Thine mother. She dost callst thou."

She laughs, shakes her head, and starts orbiting the yogurt container around the African violet, the salt shaker around the container and explains the Earth's shadows. Surreptitiously, you close your left eye. In your periphery, her wrist revolves the Earth, but beyond it's only a black border. When you open your eye again, her elbow and shoulder come back, wisps of hair. Sun and moon.

Foster delivers your sandwich on a plate, cut into triangles, olive on each section, speared with toothpicks. Three bites in, your tongue prickles with heat. Four and your head is on fire. "What the fuck—" you say.

Meg giggles, fetches you water. It helps for a moment, then doesn't. Foster shrugs, takes another bite.

"Foster?" Meg says. "Did you use the spicy mustard?"

"And the jalapeno!" He laughs like a maniacal cartoon bad guy, a class-A asshole. "Not to mention the banana peppers."

Meg slides the yogurt your way. "Try this," she says. "It'll cool you down way better than water."

ONCE THE HEAT TEMPERS, YOU'RE UPSTAIRS SPRAWLED over Foster's futon. It's on the floor, like yours. Yours used to be in a frame but you outgrew it and now sleep diagonally, feet hanging off the end. Your mom said it made your basement room *college-ready*, along with the too-low ceiling and milk crates for books. Never mind your grades have tanked. Never mind you won't be going to college or anywhere at all.

Foster starts up *Dark Side of the Moon*, volume low. The only album he plays these days. He hooks up the Nintendo console and turns the TV to its blue screen. Close to the bed are coins scattered across a fat dictionary. You pick up a fifty-cent piece, roll it from finger to finger, one of the few party tricks you're actually good at. Foster places a charred roach on the windowsill, opens the window so that cold air pushes in. He's on and on about dropping acid tomorrow night, tripping out at the Laser Floyd show. You steady the coin on your thumb toss it into the air, catch it and slap it on your hand. Tails. You think about the weight of Meg's hand on your shoulder as you slurped her yogurt. About how she daubed sweat off your forehead as though sponge painting. Her easy laugh. Her eye. You ask if Meg can come too.

Foster snatches the roach. "What the fuck, man? Laser fucking Floyd?"

The coin slips to the floor. If Foster actually knew you wanted to hold his sister—even just for a minute—and sniff her hair, if he knew you wanted to talk about eclipses and black holes, he'd pummel you. *Pummel.* So you back track, remind him there's a Meg in Calculus, the girl who always wears braids.

"You mean Marsha?" he says, leaning against the radiator, patting pockets for a lighter.

"Yeah, exactly," you say.

"Invite her if you want," he says, but he's using that skeptical tone and looks as though he might hurl the Zippo at your skull.

You reorganize the coins into a pyramid then a circle. Foster leans against the radiator, clicks open the lighter and sends you a sideways scowl. You feel like your own understudy, the fool who doesn't know all his lines. You shouldn't think about Meg as anyone but your friend's kid sister. Let alone ask to invite her along. But somewhere in the past months the real you's gone AWOL. Detached like a rocket booster and burning away in the stratosphere of your future. Meanwhile you're just an asshole fumbling through the present, dividing coins into copper and silver, hoping Foster will forget about it and light the fucking roach.

You move to the window where a few needles of freezing rain prick your back. Heat rises from the radiator, burning your ass. Foster drops the roach into a film canister, seals the lid and shakes. He squints and swivels his stout body, first away from you then toward, and his spine snap-crackles all the way up. And maybe as a diversion or because you haven't talked about it with anyone, not even your brother, you tell him about your mom. About Longwei and qi, all the needles, and a meridian called the Gushing Spring.

You knock your knuckles against your teeth, scanning the three posters on Foster's walls: Toronto Argos, Toronto Blue Jays, LA Kings. You say your mom's never been this sick. *Never.*

Claire Torry's voice wheels from the speakers and around the room in its exquisite torture, and when it peaks, Foster lights the roach, draws hard and deep. "Shit man," he says, his chest puffed, voice tight. "I had no idea." He exhales, passes the stubby remains over to you.

WHEN YOU SIT DOWN FOR DINNER IN THE NOOK, the rain, though less insistent, still patters against the sliding-glass doors. It's dark now. One light hangs over the table, spreading its yellow over the bubbling lasagna. Everything's mirrored in the dark glass. Foster's mom tongs salad onto her plate, encourages you to take multiple helpings. You start with two.

Meg forks away the top layer of pasta and slices it, then sets her cutlery across the plate. "Pass the parma," she says, and you slide over the shaker. She opens it and powders her food, and you watch how the eyelid over the prosthetic is broad, almost bulging, as she focuses on her task. You want to trace the eyelid, circle the iris, tap the black pupil and look behind it. She catches you staring and you flash an apologetic smile, shovel in another bite.

"Did Foster mention my telescope?" she says. "Views aren't great from the city. Too much light pollution." She tsks and shakes her head. "Next summer Foster's taking me north for meteor showers. Right Foster?"

Foster grunts and stabs at his croutons.

You're wondering if she's always aware of the emptiness behind her eye, the way you're always aware of hunger. Or if it's different, if it's like a blank wall she turns into and away from, all the time.

Her fork clatters and drops to the floor; she claps her hands together. "Do you hear that?" You stop chewing, and everyone hunches forward, straining to listen. The rain has stopped. Meg rushes the window and, framing her face, presses into it. Her breath fogs the glass and she reminds you of the Little Prince, stranded on her own tiny planet. Then her shoulders drop, and she draws an x in the condensation. She sits back down with a pout. "Still cloudy," she says.

"Maybe it'll clear," you say. And it might. But you wish you had a guarantee for her, that when the time comes, this close to midnight, she'll be able to see the moon disappear.

"Yeah," Meg says, picking up her fork. "Maybe."

HOURS LATER, YOU'RE WALKING AWAY FROM FOSTER'S listening to the ice-coated branches tinkle, someone's heat pump kicking on. You expect hunger to hollow you out, thighbones to toes, belly to throat, but there's only the pleasant gurgle of digesting. You slip-slide toward the corner, tramp over hardpacked snowbanks, briefly nostalgic for the tunnel networks you and your mom and brother used to dig. You pause under a cone of orange streetlight, cold rising through your canvas shoes, seizing the one big toe. A raccoon humps diagonally across the street, lifts onto hind legs at the stop sign, and casts its metallic gaze toward you.

It's then you realize you haven't called your mom, that you're half-high and a James Bond flick later than you planned. She's probably in and out of sleep, listening for you, and you wish you had some sort of phone in your pocket. But that's way off in the future. Along with the day you finally stop growing, reaching six foot eight. And before then, when your mom dies, not of lupus, but a cancer so fast and rare doctors hardly know a thing about it.

And the day, years after that, when you'll meet Meg in Vancouver, where you'll have lived for a decade. She'll play Viola in an underfunded production of *Twelfth Night* and it'll take you half the play to recognize her. But once you do, you'll send your date home while you go backstage. You'll attend the play twice more, hanging out in Meg's dressing room afterwards to drink wine and talk and laugh. Then, on that third night, an understudy will play Viola and no one can tell you where Meg went.

But now, as you move through the side streets, the houses return to normal size. Some curtains open, families watching TV, reading on couches and wingback chairs. You're cold and getting colder and you wish you had a teletransporter or a jet pack, things that won't exist in anybody's future.

You approach the Jewish cemetery and head west. Frozen rain falls again, needling into your ear and down the back of your neck. It gains speed. Heft. And you squint through the silver lines, your strides wider than sidewalk squares, completely forgetting that above all the clouds, the Earth continues rolling over, eclipsing the moon.

ELEPHANT SHOE

T HE NIGHT OF THE CAR CRASH, GABE LEFT FOR work in his usual way. He took a hit from the bong and offered one to Tess. She refused, asked him to please, *please*, blow the smoke out the back door. He did, said he always did, didn't he? The baby's sweet lungs were everything.

Tess held Willa as Gabe stuffed earbuds into his ears and licorice into his pockets, along with a lighter and a flattened pack of unfiltered Player's. When he leaned in, Beastie Boys thumping through the earbuds, Tess smelled the baby oil in his hair and turned so his kiss landed right below her ear. Then he dove in for Willa, brushing her cheek with his, and Willa swivelled her head, this way and that, as though trying to get away. Tess hated his insistence, kissing Willa, blowing on her neck, rubbing his wiry chin against her skin, saying, "Who loves her Daddy?" until Willa either smiled or cried. If she cried, he'd storm out. If she smiled, like now, he clapped, performed his pirouette, and said, "See you lovely ladies later."

From the other side of the door, he tapped the glass, squinted James Dean-style and mouthed *elephant shoe*. Then disappeared down the zigzag staircase, clomping all the way.

Outside the larger casement window, November pressed its purply-black sky against the glass. Gabe reappeared in the road and looked up, Tess's cue to wave the baby's hand. Tonight, though, she buried her face in Willa's neck, wishing he'd just go already.

When she finally lifted her head, Tess caught his fast-marching figure crossing the road, heading downtown toward his night janitor, twelve dollar-an-hour job at an upscale harbour hotel. Then he disappeared and only her own image was left, rippled and distorted in the glass, her already long limbs and neck elongated further, and waves cast over her regrettable haircut and the baby's bald head.

She dropped into one of two kitchen chairs and the apartment reconfigured the silence around her: rafters creaked under the upstairs neighbours' footsteps; a laugh track filtered from downstairs; the radiators ticked and water rushed through the plumbing. A half-eaten tray of nachos lay reeking on the table. The onions burned Tess's eyes, already stinging from a string of sleepless nights. Last night Willa had awakened every hour. Was it even possible to heap sleep deprivation on top of sleep deprivation? Plus, the doctor had told her her iron was low. For months, it felt as if she'd been breathing sand, as if sand had replaced the marrow in her bones.

She blinked away the nightly assembly of tears, hugged Willa, who rubbed her face back and forth over Tess's collarbones, hooked her toes into Tess's ribs. Tess rose, patted the baby's back, hushing and saying, "There now." She kissed Willa's downy head, swayed, and sang the first and only verse she knew of *Amazing Grace*. She did this for the baby, yes, though lately, with earlier and earlier nightfall, she imagined herself putting on a show for passers-by and people waiting for the bus. She'd never draped the windows, tall and reaching the height of the twelve-foot ceiling, and now rocked her baby in front of them, showing all those strangers how patient, how loving, how nurturing she was.

What they couldn't see, what they'd never know, was how foolish she felt. How she didn't mean to, or want to, end up here. She loved her baby, of course, *of course*, but if she could rewind time, take it all back, she most certainly would.

THE CONTRACT HAD FALLEN INTO HER LAP AND SHE'D almost turned it down: three weeks in July on the border of the Northwest Territories. Two hundred and fifty bucks a day. She'd already worked a six-week stint in northern BC, and part of her had wanted to return to Victoria, find a waitressing job, take a late summer course in political science. But she couldn't turn down that kind of cash, so she flew to northern Alberta, farther north than she'd ever been.

Gabe picked her up at the tiny airport in High Level. He'd printed her name in block letters on a piece of paper, waved it casually in front of the arrivals door. Lean and dark, his hair cut short then, his face clean shaven. He wore black Carhartt overalls, no shirt beneath, eagle tattoo visible beneath the strap. "You the cook?" He nodded at her, pilot goggles perched on his head.

They drove through the town, past motels and silos and abandoned rail cars, then out along the flat roads. She slipped off her shoes, pressed her bare feet to the dash, and the pick-up's shadow cruised along jack pines and balsam. Gabe lit a cigarette with the truck lighter, asked if she wanted a drag. Then he mentioned the last cook. "Total nervous breakdown. Over bread or some shit," he said, fixing the goggles to his eyes. "Hope you're not like that."

He was a vegetarian, he told her, a rare breed in these parts. Only him and another girl in camp. "But it doesn't much matter what you make—Greek, Indian—I put salsa on *every-thing*." He said the word loudly, enunciating each syllable.

"Even pancakes?" she said.

He smiled. "Sure. Even pancakes."

They turned onto a bumpy logging road and Gabe swerved

around the big ruts and told her about the movie he'd been filming. Blocking it out, really. In his notebook. The truck-in-the-mud scene. The moose snagged in barbed wire. End-of-contract party in spring, drunk planters walking through the bonfire. "Tree planting is non-stop," he said. "Perfect for film."

He parked the truck alongside a cut block, the camp there behind a thin screen of trees, a collapsible village of tents and generators among stumps and fireweed. Gabe toured Tess through the cook shack, orienting her to the dried goods and freezers, water systems and coolers. Then he reached behind a stack of mixing bowls, presented a two-litre bottle of Old El Paso salsa. "My secret stash," he whispered. "Take what you need."

For the rest of that week, he rode his quad back to camp while everyone worked. He delivered the seedlings, didn't plant them; he took long smoke breaks, and imitated the voices of Clint Eastwood or Robert De Niro while she kneaded bread, peeled potatoes, prepped salads and sauces. He asked if she'd seen this movie or that, and if she hadn't, he'd say she *had* to, it'd be his personal mission to show her *Taxi Driver* and all the Dirty Harrys.

Sometimes he mentioned his ex-girlfriend. "She just didn't *get* me," he'd say. "Stifled my creativity." And Tess mentally noted she'd never do that to him—stifle his creativity. Other times, he recounted backyard shinny antics from his boyhood, flooding the rink, scraping it clean, his mother's strict rule about snow pants. He even broke down a cardboard box once, flattened it into a flimsy yet serviceable ice rink, and reenacted an elaborate puck pass that goose-egged his forehead. That devolved into a breakdancing demo, the worm and back-spin he'd perfected in junior high. In more serious moments, he told her none of his family ever graduated with anything beyond a high-school diploma, and though he'd completed a year of community college, he really wanted to go to the Vancouver Film School. They'd already rejected him once but wouldn't again when he blew their minds with the tree-planting proposal.

Tess would listen, cook grilled cheese, dump salsa into a shared bowl, and chop a bunch of carrot sticks. These lunches were invariably interrupted by someone calling Gabe on the radio, and, sandwich in hand, he'd dash off. Alone again, she found herself wishing he'd return sooner than later.

Into the second week of the contract, thunder rolled over the camp and lightning forked in furious scrawls, rain poured in a thick wall. After she'd finished with the kitchen, Tess ran with Gabe down a muddy path, through puddles, shirts soaked and sticking, all the way to the treeline. He'd pitched his tent between the two tallest pines, stretched a tarp to create an overhang. The rain hammered it. Tess yelled over the din. "What if lightning hits these trees?" Her teeth chattered; her arms covered with goosebumps. Gabe unzipped the door and she followed him in. He arched his eyebrows and curved open his mouth, his front two teeth overlapped and hooked over his bottom lip, his whole face glistening in the bluish light. He wrapped her wet hair around his wrist, pulled her in to him.

All her life, people told her she reminded them of someone else. She attributed it to her plain brown hair, her pale, reddish skin. But in that moment, when Gabe stripped off her shirt and jeans, when he kissed her belly, her breasts, even before touching her mouth, her ordinariness slipped away. She didn't say, "Let's be careful." Or, "Hey, do you have a condom?" And though she'd thought about it, and though her mother had drilled safe sex into her since sixth grade, she didn't want him to stop. And he didn't. Not for the remaining two weeks of the contract. And, during that brief time, Tess felt as though she'd stepped off a cliff and discovered she could fly.

AS SHE RUBBED THE BABY'S GUMS, SHE THOUGHT HOW she hardly let Gabe near her now. Not without double protection. Condom, foam, pull out . . . even then, sex was the last thing she wanted, the absolute last.

Willa whimpered and fussed; two sharp ridges finally broken through her gums. She clamped Tess's finger, her eyes drowsing and angry. Tess whisked her into the dark bedroom, the window there blocked by a mounted Klimt poster: *Mother and Child*. The hall light reflected off it and made a silhouette of the laundry basket. She groped through the clothes, clean or dirty she didn't know, for Willa's sleeper, and sniffed. Everything faint with soured milk.

She lowered Willa onto the queen-sized bed, built a pillow barrier on one side, reclined on the other, latching the baby to her breast. Willa gulped and drained the first side, suckled slowly on the other, pausing longer and longer. When Tess tried to eek her nipple out, Willa picked up speed, as though she meant never to stop. Tess prayed this wouldn't be a repeat of last night's marathon nurse. When she'd been roused for what seemed like the fifth or sixth time, her nipples raw and the clock reading 2:07 a.m., she'd wanted to pound the walls and run outside. Instead, she'd gripped the baby's ankle, pulled her too-hard down the mattress, then in her meanest, growliest voice told her own sweet daughter to fuck off. Not her finest moment. And worse, the yelling felt momentarily satisfying. Until Willa flinched and shook, her face contorting seconds before she wailed. Wailed as though Tess had thrown her or broken her bones. It didn't take long for regret to swoop in, for Tess to gather her baby close, both of them sobbing, and Tess saying, over and over, "Sorry. I'm so sorry."

When Willa had finally nursed back to sleep, Tess shut herself in the bathroom and wept. Gabe found her there, fetal on the bathmat after his shift. Sitting beside her, he stroked her back until she could explain what happened. Then he filled the tub with steamy water, perfumed it with lavender oil. He brought her scotch, which she didn't want, then kneaded her shoulders, circling one knot then another with his thumbs.

"Maybe you should let her cry it out."

Said the world's deepest sleeper.

The week before she'd left a full bottle, twenty minutes worth of hand-pumping, and went downtown to deliver resumes. When she'd returned, Gabe was passed out on the couch, the bottle full and the baby in the playpen with soaked pajamas, red-faced and screaming. Even after Tess punched his arm, called him an irresponsible motherfucker, he'd hardly roused.

"She must've just woken up," he said, creases down his face and eyes puffed. Then he headed for the back porch, fired up the bong.

Tess had followed, Willa still nursing. "You can't do this if I go back to work," she said. "You can't fucking do this. Someone might call social services. Think we left her alone. Or worse. She might choke."

"Come on, Tess." He held the smoke tight in his lungs. "She won't choke." He exhaled away from her, but a slight breeze blew it back. She returned to the kitchen, livid, hearing him say, "These night shifts, Tess. They're murder on my sleep."

TESS SLIPPED STEALTHILY OFF THE BED. SHE LANDED ON hands and knees, peered over the mattress edge to watch the baby's arms fling up in surprise, her mouth searching for a nipple. Tess waited and waited until at last Willa settled.

Then she tiptoed backwards out of the bedroom, her sock snagging on the wood floor. Something jabbed her toe, sent her silently hopping and cursing. She leaned against the door jamb, plucked out a two-inch splinter. *Goddamn.* They'd have to sand these rough spots before the baby started crawling. Already Willa rocked on her hands and knees, gathering momentum. The last time Tess went to the Healthy Babies group, she'd witnessed a dozen mothers crisscrossing the room, frantically chasing their babies. "It's an exciting stage!" the group leader, a fifty-something nurse always said, with that annoying cheer of someone who didn't live it twenty-four-seven. Tess, barely twenty-two, hated how they divided child-rearing into tidy phases and stages. When—she wanted to ask the nurse—was the stage she got her life back?

MAYBE IT WAS OVER BEGINNING IN NINTH GRADE, when her breasts began to get tender. When she'd been seized by a foreign kind of tired. Then her first period coming on during a grammar lesson. Comma splices. She told that story to Gabe in the motel room, two days after the contract ended, somewhere west of Edmonton. A painting of a bridge above the headboard, and Tess smoothing the sateen bedspread, praying the test wouldn't be positive, that her body had just done something weird and irregular because of the electrical storms and the long northern daylight. Until now she'd always been a twenty-eight-day-to-the-minute girl.

The curtains stayed closed except for a narrow crack. Gabe rolled a joint on the dresser, hair and forehead caught in the one sunbeam.

Tess wanted to savour the final moments when a negative result was still possible. If she wasn't pregnant, she'd smoke that joint with Gabe, get rip-roaring drunk and toast her life with a sense of relief and narrow escape. If she wasn't pregnant, she'd forget the road trip they'd planned, beeline it back to Victoria, find that waitressing job and register for fall classes.

Gabe poured himself a finger of Jack Daniel's. "Feels like fucking Christmas or something," he said, then opened the bathroom door.

"Wait two more minutes," Tess said.

He didn't wait. He passed her the wand without looking at it. The blue line ran straight and clear across the plastic window. She handed it back.

Gabe's eyes went electric, his voice ecstatic. "Fucking-A," he said, kissed her hard, leapt up, did a James Brown spin. He giggled, circled his fingers around one eye, made turning motions with the other hand. "The perfect ending scene," he said, panning out. "And you, baby, you're the star."

Tess shook her head, felt nothing like a star. She curled her legs to her chest, sank her teeth into her knee tasting the motel lotion. What she felt was betrayal. By her body. By her own good sense. "I'm scared," she said.

"Don't you get it?" he said, dropping his hands. "This was *meant* to happen." He tapped her forehead with his. She smelled the whiskey, cigarettes. "We're *meant* to be together and I'm totally with you on this one. I'll move to Victoria. We'll get married if you want. Shotgun-style." He grabbed her hand, pinned it to his chest, his expression a hybrid of earnest and ready to laugh.

She could feel his rapid-fire heartbeat, her whole life shifting with the very fact of him. She loosened her hand, said yes, yes, he could move in with her, they'd see how it went. Marriage, though, was too much too soon.

"No problem," he said. "Elephant shoe."

"What?"

Then he mouthed it—*elephant shoe*—and it looked like he said *I love you.*

"I don't get it," she said.

"It's what we'll say until we're sure," he said. "We'll keep it at elephant shoe."

Then he lit the joint, closing his eyes with what seemed hallucinatory joy. He tossed out names: Grover, Marley, Madison, Art, Bob. "A blend of you and me?" he said. "It'll be the best little monkey ever."

Tess asked him to put out the joint or step outside, told him she had a headache. But what she had was not a headache. More a dull pulse nested in the back of her skull. Gabe exited, then stepped back in. Light fanning in behind him.

TESS IGNORED THE DIRTY DISHES, PILED TWO DAYS, going on three, and headed for the living room. The overhead light buzzed, also the two Y-shaped halogen lamps, their beams bouncing off the ceiling. She clicked off the one behind the scratchy plaid couch, noticed the baby bottle, half-filled with breast milk, on the table alongside the retro movie theatre schedule and Gabe's beloved bong.

Earlier that afternoon, he'd fed Willa while Tess dashed out to fetch baby Tylenol and liquid iron; the first time she'd left him alone with the baby since last week's debacle. When she returned, he'd been spinning records on his turntable, calling them up like a DJ—Isaac Hayes, Miles Davis, Frank Zappa—and dancing with Willa in his arms. "See the happy baby?" he'd said. "See how she loves her old man?" Spotting Tess, Willa had kicked her legs and whimpered, ready for a nap, and Gabe passed her over, snubbed.

The milk had probably curdled by now, and Tess, irritated, bent to pick up the bottle. Her sweater sleeve caught the bong which teetered, toppled, first onto the table then to the floor. The glass cracked and the fetid water spilled out. Tess retched, reached for a flannel receiving blanket and tossed it over the mess, the dark water leached into the yellow print of rattles and bowed babies.

A sob released from deep within her body. These days it happened frequently, unexpected and primal, and now she covered her face, took a few stuttery breaths.

The phone rang, that obnoxious bell on their old-school rotary. She lunged for it, gulped hello.

"Did I wake you, Tessie?" Her mother, whispering. "Sorry if I woke you…"

"No, Mom. I…"

"I'm sorry to disturb you, honey. I just had this—what do you call it?—a premonition about you and wondered if you were all right. That's all."

"The baby's teething," Tess said. Another swampy, putrid stench bloomed from the bong. She twisted away, into the corner of the couch, picked at the upholstery.

"And Gabe? Is he helping?"

"You called because of a premonition?" Tess said.

"No, honey," her mother said. "I just worry is all."

Tess squeezed her eyes, her face. She wished her mother lived in the same town, the same country, and not across the border, three states away. She wished her mother could take Willa for a night, maybe two. Just from time to time.

"Tess? Are you there?"

"We'll talk later, okay?" Tess's voice sounded compressed and small and far away. She cleared her throat. "I'm just so tired."

"Sure, honey. We'll talk later."

Tess set the receiver in the cradle, considered the disaster on the floor. In the halogen light the yellows were yellower, the soaked blanket almost sinister. She leaned forward, elbows on knees, head in hands. Back when she'd told her mother about the pregnancy, her mother, devoid of any excitement, asked, "Are you sure? You're so young. At least wait until you're both twenty-five." For whatever reason, Tess wanted to prove her mother wrong. People had babies all the time. Why not her? Now she realized she knew none of those people, had become an anomaly among her friends. Friends who'd offered to henna her pregnant belly, cast it in plaster, transform her baby shower into a goddess ritual. They'd snapped pictures holding the newborn, begged to be godparents. Then, they disappeared, back into the world of their own lives. Tess had no one, not even from the Healthy Babies group, those moms all older, more married, and definitely more moneyed.

She picked up a blackened piece of glass near her foot. It matched a corresponding hole at the base of the bong, still lying on its side. How long would it take for Gabe to figure it out? Two minutes after he walked in the door? Three? Maybe he'd find a new hobby, though what, she couldn't imagine. He'd smoked more and more pot since her pregnancy, said it boosted his creativity, helped him sketch kick-ass film ideas. A cure-all too for boredom at work, stress about money. He'd even encouraged her to toke when the contractions had started. "Better than an epidural," he'd said. She thought he'd tone it down after the birth, but it only got worse.

These days, after they paid rent, he withdrew the last of their funds, postponing hydro and phone payments, to buy dope by the ounce. Just the other day he said he planned to grow or deal it. Supplement their meagre income. He'd grown frustrated, scouring the classifieds for a higher paying job. Nothing but retail and service and minimum wage. "Not even construction," he complained. "At least in Edmonton I had construction." Marijuana, he assured her, was the only way around here to make any real money.

TESS FOUGHT OFF THE URGE TO SLEEP. HER BONES, her head, everything ached for it, but this was the only time of day she had to herself. So she abandoned the mess, wiped her hands on her jeans and slipped through the pocket door into the darkened parlour. The outside streetlight diffused through the darkness, and the traffic signal stained the south wall green.

In their search for an affordable apartment, the parlour with its window seat, the fir panelled walls and wainscoting sold them on this one. "Six-thirty a month," Gabe had said. "And with *character.*" Tess imagined this room had once housed an upright piano, a mantle clock, a silver tea service. Tiffany lamps, a butler, wingback chairs with footstools, and an easel with watercolours in various stages of completion. Now the room contained a salvaged futon in one corner, mildew stains and blotches of breast milk all concealed by heaps of newborn clothes already too small for Willa. Plus, that old computer, cord wrapped around the base, her last semester's essays immortalized on the hard drive.

There was an old coal stove, too, cast iron grill where fuel used to go. Quaint, except for the hearth overrun with garden gnomes. They looked creepy now, strange creatures lurking in the shadows like horror film tropes. When they first moved in, Gabe had abducted each and every one from flowerbeds throughout the city. "If people are stupid enough to buy them and leave them lying around," he said, "they deserve to have them stolen." This justified the car magnets he'd peeled off car doors too, advertising realtors or dog groomers, and stacked in their closet, or the garden flowers he snatched and gathered into bouquets, presenting them to Tess. She'd tried to convince him theft was theft no matter what, but he said who cared, everything belonged to anyone anyhow. So now they were stuck with stacks of car magnets and a dozen garden gnomes.

Tess perched on the built-in window seat, back pressed against the frame. The red traffic light tinted the wood, her fingers, the tops of her knees. During the days a steady stream of stop-and-go cars rolled down Quadra Street, these corner windows vibrating from subwoofers and busted exhausts. By late evening traffic became sporadic, the roads mostly running clear.

Not much to the view, only a hodgepodge of apartments and commercial buildings—a grocer, a tire repair, and down the way, an indoor public pool. She wished instead for a moor, a river, a boulevard of broad-leafed trees.

Wind chimes clinked on the front porch and a car squealed to a stop. Right now, Gabe lugged a contraption to polish marble floors. Soon he'd move on to the brass fixtures and posts. He hadn't complained in a while, but she knew he hated the job, wondered how much longer he'd stick it out. One day, when she'd been five months pregnant, he'd stayed in bed as though fevered. She'd gone to class, her job at the Student Union, a meeting at the feminist paper, then arrived home to find Gabe sitting in this same window, naked, drinking coffee and violating his promise to only smoke outside.

"Shouldn't you be at work?" she'd said. He'd worked at a coffee place as a barista.

"Yeah," he said. He looked skeletal. Not bony but haunted, his pallor yellowed, even the whites of his eyes. "They rejected me again. No to the tree-planting idea. That fucking awesome idea." He leaned back, his lips almost white with flaking skin. "I can't do this," he said. "I can't keep working shit jobs with no future. You're better off without me."

At that moment, something inside her collapsed, her bones and flesh flimsy, as if they were simply tent poles and canvas, ready for camp teardown. She couldn't raise a child by herself. She couldn't. If he wanted to pack it in, she did too. Keeping the baby had been his idea, really.

All his backspinning enthusiasm on the motel floor, and his *best blend of you and me*. His insistence on filming the birth for the final movie scene. Plus, his designs for a steampunk crib, the *Mother and Child* poster for her birthday. The baby fluttered in Tess's abdomen, reminding her that at five months abortion was no option. She wanted to drag Gabe from his despair, bring back his earlier, enthusiastic and animated self. The one who'd made her laugh and feel like a goddess, the one who called her *eye candy* and *destiny*. She knelt down, actually knelt, wove her fingers through his and squeezed. For a full minute, maybe two, she reeled through her brain, searching for words, some phrase of wisdom, that would lift them from this dread. She only came up with, "Everything will be all right."

But things weren't all right. His moods fluctuated, peaking when he smoked pot and landed on another great film idea, then plunging again. He blamed his despair on the constant rain. On this goddamn city with no opportunities. If they lived in Vancouver, he'd at least get work in the industry, production assistant, location scout, whatever. He felt useless as a barista, as a guy waiting for the baby's birth, as her partner. For weeks, she tiptoed around his bleakness, pretending to friends and professors, to her mother, that she'd built a solid relationship with Gabe, that the baby would only increase her sense of joy and commitment, that she could hardly wait another day to meet the little person she carried. Meanwhile, Gabe spent an inordinate number of hours sleeping or down at the retro theatre, while they lived off the scraps of Tess's tree-planting savings, her part-time cafeteria pay, her student loans and credit cards, until spring rolled around and with it the sun, and right before the baby was born, he found work again.

OUTSIDE THE STREET HAD EMPTIED OF CARS. A shopping cart rattled over sidewalk cracks and a homeless man appeared in Tess's line of sight. He trundled his belongings toward the public pool where she'd seen him sleeping over open grates. He stopped at a trash bin halfway down the block and recovered a couple of cans. Shook them, held one against his ear as though listening to the sea. Then he lifted a plastic cover off his cart, stuffed his treasure beneath. The November wind billowed the plastic awning around, and he had to capture its edges, stuff them down into the insides of the cart.

Past him was the jagged configuration of lights and buildings on the downtown borders. Then above that, the hazy city glow. Not a single star. She searched for the moon, its radiance behind a cloud, when she heard a metallic scraping along the pavement. An unmufflered engine growing louder, an old station wagon, one headlight flickering, the other burnt out. Tess rested her chin on her knees, noticed the car listing to one side, its tires low or flat. It crossed the double centre line, half its wheels in that lane. The engine revved and Tess's windows shook. She cringed, wished it would hop back into the right lane, then hurry away. An oncoming car honked and swerved and the station wagon, unimaginably, headed straight for Tess's building.

The crash came next. Crumpling metal. Showers of glass. Followed by silence, a tinny pitch in Tess's ear. The traffic light switched from green to yellow, and the darkness broke around her into electrons and amber motes. After a second or two, she hurried to the front porch, clanging the chimes as she hung out over the rail. Below: the car had rammed into the corner of the building, the hood crunched and pleated, the windshield webby and cracked with a hole in the centre. More a piece of installation art really, except for the stink—hot metal and gasoline. A dim light shone from the remaining headlamp, and the radiator, or maybe the engine, clacked and hissed. From where Tess stood, the car appeared impossibly vacant. She knew she should call 911, should feel compelled to help. But she didn't, and this quietly shocked her. Later, she'd tell Gabe she almost ran to the phone. But she only waited, the air in that moment charged with possibility. She waited, knowing everything in the aftermath would shatter.

Neighbours appeared in small numbers, some popping onto stoops across the street, others onto the sidewalk. The homeless man lumbered toward the car, his shopping cart abandoned, yelling for someone to call an ambulance.

Tess watched the headlamp fizzle and extinguish, heard the driver's door clunk and creak, inching open. Out stepped a boy, maybe sixteen or seventeen, gangly and tall and suited up in denim, baseball hat on backwards. He jerked his head around as if he'd dropped from the sky and attempted to get his bearings. People called to him, said, "It's okay! An ambulance is coming!" The kid froze, hunched, hands held wide as if waiting for a basketball pass. For two or three seconds no one moved.

Then a woman stepped onto the street and the boy bolted, rounded the corner at Empress, so fast his shoes squeaked. The downstairs neighbour, a middle-aged bachelor with a beer gut, chased him. The ambulance arrived, two cop cars and a fire truck. Lights swirled over the faces of witnesses as they pointed and recounted and shook their heads. The beer-gut man returned winded, empty-handed. Tess bit her lip. Her body contracted, and she hoped, though didn't know why, the boy would get away.

IN THE MORNING, SHE'D TELL GABE ABOUT THE CAR, THE strange randomness of the accident. He'd ask questions, sorry he missed out. Even forgive the broken bong. For all that day and the week after, they'd live on the rush and mystery of the crash. They'd spend an hour picking up tail-light shards and stucco chunks, they'd scrape away kitty litter to examine the gas stain, they'd deposit bits of windshield into a ceramic bowl and stow them with the car magnets. They'd piece together whatever they could, chatting with the downstairs neighbours, asking about the kid. Gabe would buy the local paper, a thing he never did, come across a tiny column devoted to the wreck: car stolen, the driver, the thief, unknown.

A MONTH LATER, CLOSE TO CHRISTMAS, GABE READIED to leave in his usual way. He kissed Tess and the baby and said, "I love you." Tess shifted Willa from one hip to the other. Knew she couldn't, wouldn't, say it back. Couldn't even mouth "elephant shoe."

So Gabe hightailed it back to Alberta, leaving behind his garden gnomes and film sketches and the last of his dope, while Tess sat in the welfare office, rent receipt folded in her pocket, along with her latest bank statement, telling the case worker the baby's father had left the picture. She cried. Snot and tears, not because of Gabe, but because she was too exhausted to support herself, her baby. The case worker patted her hand, exclaimed over Willa's fat healthy cheeks and said Gabe wasn't the first daddy to skip town. Then she said: "We're here to help you navigate these bumpy roads. To set you back on course."

WHEN TESS THOUGHT BACK TO THAT NIGHT AFTER THE crash, she remembered how awake she felt, how alive. That beside her Gabe's breath grew whistly, dovetailing into a snore and the baby squirmed, ready any minute to nurse. Tess's mind crackled with thoughts of the kid thief out there, crouched beneath someone's back porch or deep inside a laurel hedge. Adrenaline buzz wearing thin. Neck hurting, head too. Cold seeping through his denim, his knees gone totally numb. She wanted to step out of bed and into that night. Run down the streets, feet bare and breasts leaking. Every part of her wanted to find him. Pull him from his hiding. Stroke his cold, cold cheek and follow him home.

TO THE RAVINE

VERY NIGHT BETH LIGHTS THREE CANDLES AND
places Toby Forbes into a pink bubble. A technique she's
learned from the reddish blue mystical book she found
while babysitting on New Year's, full of exercises to help man-
ifest your dreams. She tore the Pink Bubble pages from Mrs.
Wilson's copy and stashed them in a box under her own bed.
They're still there, tattered and dog-eared, because although
she's memorized the instructions, she skims and reaffirms
them before and after every meditation.

She's supposed to relax her body—toes, feet, legs, all the
way up. Hardest to quiet are her eyes, which flicker and buzz
in the sockets. She presses her palms against them, focuses on
her breath and builds a slow image of Toby.

She starts with the back of his head because she's studied
it a thousand times in English 11. He sits in front of her and
sometimes, when Miss Finch lectures them on AB rhyming
schemes or the central motifs of *Romeo and Juliet*, Beth studies Toby's brown-blond shag, how it curls and crisscrosses at
the ends, how it hides his jean-jacket collar when he tips his
head back. Below his hair, a Led Zeppelin logo arches between

his shoulder blades; *Zoso* is written in bleedy blue ballpoint halfway down his back, a word she says silently, over and over.

At this point the visualization usually stalls. She wants the imagined-him to turn around the way the real-him does in class, but he won't. And so she waits, drifts into a half-dream where she's dancing. Stumbling really, her legs heavy and clumsy and clueless, her ballet teacher yelling and yelling. Usually some noise—her dad backing into the drive, her mom creaking downstairs to have words—pulls her back. Then she squeezes her eyes tight, relaxes them, squeezes and relaxes, until Toby's face appears—fuzzier than real life because she can never quite recreate it. Angle of jawbone, silver scar above left eyebrow, things she collects from him every day, never appear in the right way or order. She hopes her mental sketch is enough for the universe to go on, that she won't end up with an inferior Toby, some cheap knock-off she has to endure, like those faux-Topsiders she wore in eighth grade.

If she's lucky, her vision morphs, and his mouth opens. He tells her she's beautiful, tells her he loves her, wants only her. And then there's a mirror ball and they're slow-dancing— *Stairway to Heaven*—and he leans in to kiss her.

At this point she casts a thin pink substance over the scene. Wraps it up and inflates it like a balloon, releasing it up up up past her ceiling and into the universe, where it's supposed to unleash vibrations that will attract other, similar vibrations. These assemble somewhere in space then zoom back to Earth in real time, uniting causes and conditions so that Beth's dreams, her *visualizations,* become physical and true. Mathematically it makes sense, in an x+y sort of way, but the trick is: you have to emerge from your meditation feeling like you already have the thing you want. Manifestation depends on it. But Beth's heart *always* strains. Strains and strains to feel what it doesn't feel—elation, jubilation, Juliet when she first kisses Romeo. And after minutes of effort, she blows out the candles and doubt hatches in the centre of her brain. Toby will never love her. Even though the book promises he will.

Promises that when you put your order in with the universe you shouldn't question *if* it will happen, only *when*.

TOBY HAS A GIRLFRIEND. CHRISTINE MEYER. WHO, FOUR days before Spring Break, hugs all her friends in the north parking lot after school, saying she'll miss them but she'll totally send postcards. She asks Beth and Sally to scribble their addresses into a Hello Kitty autograph book with a Hello Kitty pencil. It's an unmistakable form of charity but Beth writes her address anyway and tells Christine to have a really great time—so much fun!—in Jamaica. Jojo, who flies off to Disney World on Saturday, unworthy of Christine's pity or postcards, says, "Bring back rum! And ganja!"

Christine says, "Yah *mon!*" And it sounds as though she's coughing up a pearl.

Christine reminds Beth of weddings, her curly blond hair, more white than yellow, like a frieze of baby's breath. She's tall too, wears a prim white ski jacket and loose white jeans. Once, during a snowfall, Beth saw her standing on a snowbank, and she looked like a bride, veil of snowflakes over her face. So when Beth fantasizes about Christine's death—car accident, leukemia, drowning in a lagoon—there's often a tragic white gown involved.

Raw wind tunnels into Beth's ear, giving it a sharp, swift ache. She winces, wonders if the universe will punish her thoughts. You aren't supposed to wish ill on anyone. Only trust that the outcome of what you want will benefit all involved. From her corner of the parking lot, she watches Christine thread her arms into Toby's, nuzzle his neck, kiss his throat, and she revamps the death scenario, praying Christine will fall in love with a Jamaican boy on her vacation, never to return.

"She won't bring back rum," Sally says. "Or ganja."

"Who can bring back ganja?" Beth says. Then she entertains Christine's arrest at customs, her prosecution and punishment for the pound of weed sewn into her suitcase or underwear. Neither Sally nor Jojo know about Toby or the pink bubbles. They think his going out with Christine cured her crush months ago. And before she found Mrs. Wilson's book, she tried not to like him. Spent six weekends in a row watching *The Breakfast Club* so she could swoon over Judd Nelson. Plus she upped her commitment to dance, three times a week instead of two. None of that matters, because there are still moments when tiny electrical pulses leap from Toby's fingertips to hers. Passing notes in English, pretending to everyone else, even to each other, nothing exists between them.

On the opposite side of the lot, Toby climbs into Christine's Pontiac, and Christine waves to them—Jojo, Sally and Beth—smiling her wedding cake smile. Jojo says, "Do you think she'll deliver? This afternoon before she flies away?" Ever since Jojo came *this* close to losing her virginity last summer, she likes to talk about who delivers and who doesn't.

"I heard they did it like a month ago," Sally says.

And Beth's heart dispatches a battalion of envy. She's never had the chance to deliver. And she curses the universe for failing her.

A squall snaps across the parking lot, a whip of old dirty snow. Beth digs around her pockets for one woolen mitten. Where the other one ended up, she has no idea, so she slips both hands in and blows warm air between her thumbs.

Sally pulls a scarf over her face, tugs at the too-short bangs she bleached last week.

Jojo tosses a chunk of watermelon Bubblicious into her mouth and slides a heel across a grimy patch of snow. "Anyway, Christine won't send you postcards," she says. "I'll send you fucking postcards."

True. Beth still has the Mickey Mouse card from last year, the one that says, *Jealous of my new boyfriend?!* And *Kidding! I'm with Pinocchio!*

THAT NIGHT BETH'S MOM SUGGESTS THEY DO something as a family over the break. She's always saying that these days—*as a family*. She slops potatoes onto Beth's brother's plate, a sliver of roasted pork, and Beth votes for a week in Myrtle Beach, a two-day drive each way, but at least it's warm, if not exactly Jamaica. But her mom says they can't afford it because of the dollar, plus it's too much time away from work. Then, as if she's just thought of it: How about a couple days at Niagara Falls? Beth's little brother sputters milk through his missing front teeth, widens his eyes and tells them that a guy once tightroped across the Falls, right across, and *didn't* plummet to his death. Her dad pours gravy in a perfect ring on his plate and says there are some definite daredevils in this world. Then he raises his wine glass and winks at Beth's mom saying Niagara Falls is a fabulous idea and he'll arrange everything— motel, Maid of the Mist tour, reservation at some swanky restaurant he's heard serves lobster and the most unbelievable mousse. A real treat.

Beth cuts meat away from fat and shoves the fat to her plate rim. She remembers Niagara from a long time ago. Summer sky and cool spray on her cheeks. A blue windbreaker that billowed with wind. And how she clutched the rail against a churning, frothy roar. Didn't she drop something? Her plastic barrette? Sent it hurtling down the rock face, losing sight of it long before it hit water.

The water's probably frozen now. Even the Falls. And how long can you stand around admiring a glacial curtain? No, she'd rather stick around here. Besides, it occurs to her that with Christine gone, Toby might invite her to his family's place in Collingwood. Or, more likely, he'll say they're all going to the Bloor Street Diner on Tuesday and does she want to come? She divides her potatoes into islands and asks if she can stay home while the rest of the family goes. She won't have a party or anything, just hang out with Sally, drink coffee, and watch *The Breakfast Club* a few more times.

Her mom frowns, the corners of her eyes harden. "As a *family*, Beth," she says. "Aren't you part of this family?"

Her dad says, "Come on, sweetie. We'll make it fun."

She hates that he says that. Because she can almost guarantee that the day before they leave, he'll bail. Apologize, feign disappointment and declare a very important meeting, one he just can't miss. He did this in August before they headed to Montréal to visit family friends. And last Thanksgiving, before going to see her aunt, *his* sister, he'd received an "urgent" call from his boss and had to fly to New York to bid on a crucial account.

So she knows she'll end up on the trip with her mom and her brother, no dad. That they'll drive in silence, and when they arrive at the Falls, her mother will ask strangers to snap pictures of them, and force everyone to smile.

Her mother points to the heap of fat on Beth's plate and says, "Still good meat on that."

Beth's appetite shrinks to nothing. She excuses herself, tells them she has homework. She has to read the last act of *Romeo and Juliet*. "You must remember it," she says, scraping fat onto the edge of her father's plate. "The one with the double suicide."

THE NEXT DAY TOBY DRAWS A COMIC OF MISS FINCH and passes it back to Beth. Wings, beak and a bubble over her head that says, *Oh happy dagger!* In real life, Miss Finch stands in a tweed skirt and rust-coloured turtleneck in front of the blackboard. She's stout, mouth cast in a sly, literary smile, and her nose is unbirdlike and wide. Today, they're finishing up the crypt scene, Juliet awakening, dead Romeo beside her, her own tragic stabbing. Miss Finch currently reads the Friar's long speech, wrapping her mouth purposefully around each vowel.

Beth adores this play though she doesn't always get it. Like that Mercutio part, where he argues that dreams come from

Queen Mab. She loves when Miss Finch reads aloud, language leaping and arabesquing about the room. Then there's the story. The love! The tragedy! She wants to ask Toby if he'd die for Christine, for *anyone*. Instead, below his comic-drawn Finch, she writes "Kill the envious moon," because that quote—act two, balcony scene—has spent days looping through her head.

When she drops the note over Toby's shoulder, Miss Finch glances at her. Beth freezes, feels the paper release from her fingers, the heat of Toby's body. Miss Finch tightens, shuts her text and recites the last lines from memory. Beth slides lower in her seat, bows deep into her binder. Miss Finch knocks the board with a piece of chalk, says she'd like them to write a full page, no less than five paragraphs, about the stark example of dramatic irony in this final scene.

Toby returns the note. Beneath his drawing, beneath Beth's envious moon quote, is a sharp-handled question mark. Nothing else.

Heat pricks her throat, spreads into her cheeks. His inky question mark looks like a sickle. Something that can peel open her psyche so he can peer in. Maybe Toby doesn't get the reference, has only skimmed the play. Only half-listened to Miss Finch, relying, really, on his *Coles Notes*. It doesn't matter; she's positive he can see her floundering crush on him. And she crosses her fingers tight under her desk, hoping, hoping, he can't.

She writes "Arise fair sun" above the question mark but doesn't pass it forward. The quote in its entirety might worsen things. He might think she thinks he thinks she's his fair sun. Which she doesn't.

But she does. Only she can't let him know. Her face grows hotter and hotter and she flips through the play searching for dramatic irony. Words swim and hop around the longing and tragedy, and she thinks of all the pink bubbles she's released into the universe. Every single one floating above her head, ready to pop.

THE QUESTION MARK ACCUSES HER ALL DAY. HOW could *she*—not a fair sun at all, more like puny little Pluto—kill the envious moon? Especially compared to Christine Meyer, who really, hands down, would be cast as Juliet. Beth would play the nurse, or worse, Mrs. Capulet.

She leaves school through the front doors, avoiding the north parking lot and its cliquey minefield, even dodges Jojo and Sally. She hops on a bus, then the subway, ends up at Bloor forty-five minutes early and decides to walk to the Danforth. But as soon as she exits the turnstile, she regrets it: the outside air is icy, full of pelting rain.

A car rushes by and slushy water sloshes over her cheek, soaks her coat sleeve. She cringes, freezes as though playing statues. Slush runs down her neck, beneath her sweater and between her breasts, full of cold city grime. Fuck fuck *fuck*. Her little black flats have soaked right through, each toe completely numb. Christine Meyer's on a beach. In a climate exactly opposite to this. Beth fishes out her single mitten, wipes her face with it, her coat, picturing Christine in a lacy white bikini, sipping drinks from hollowed-out pineapples. Everything's so easy for Christine. Luring Toby in, right after dumping Eric Tattersall. Meanwhile Beth has had precisely zero boyfriends, unless you count Greg Abbott from sixth grade, but they only ever bought slushees together and played kick-the-can and held hands twice.

When Beth finally reaches the other side of the bridge, smells of rosemary and roasted lamb, olive oil and mint, drift from a dozen Greek restaurants and assail her. She's starving, having spent her lunch hour doodling Toby's name in the library, cross-hatching over it, feeling stupid, caught out, disgraced. She'll feel sick if she eats then dances, regurgitating spanokopita or baklava whenever she lands her assemblés, so she hurries up three flights of stairs and lets those deep fryer smells pang her stomach.

Inside, her toes tingle. She hears Ms. Belle finishing up with the littler girls. A few mothers wait in the entrance hall, but she's the only one in the change room. She shucks off her street clothes, dampens a paper towel and wipes mascara smears off her cheeks, slush stains off her throat. Then she dresses in tights, leotard, slippers. Slicks her hair into a bun. Her spine immediately straightens and takes on an inch. "Do not slouch girls!" Ms. Belle has told them six or eleven times a lesson. "You are not apes!"

In the studio, Beth takes hold of the barre, the first sure thing she's felt all day. She hoists a foot onto it, bends to the side, feels the tweak and pull down her hamstrings. In the mirror she watches stragglers from the earlier class leave. Then focuses on the curves of her ankle, her calf, the inside of her thigh. She straightens up, searching for redemption. Not in her too-long neck or slight under-bite. Not her wide blank forehead. She brings her right foot down, changes sides. Scans the mirror and makes sure she's totally alone. She touches a breast. Jiggles it. The way she might pick up a snow globe, shake and return it. Yes, her breasts. Their newness and shape. They could definitely deliver.

A few girls enter the room and head for the barre. Beth raises her arms into a hasty fifth. The girls titter, talking about the upcoming recital, an abridged *Swan Lake*. Beth brings her arms down, her leg. No matter what ballet they do, she's always, *always*, chorus.

Ms. Belle appears in a graceful flounce, slips a cassette into the stereo. The first piano notes sound dim and melancholic. "*Cou-de-pied* front," Ms. Belle says. "*Cou-de-pied* back . . ." The music sweetens, saddens. Soon enough Beth's slippers sweep in unison across the floor with a dozen other girls. Her body becomes a suite of muscle and movement, blood flow and intelligence. And, for now, all her rambling thoughts about Toby and his punishing question mark, about Christine and her undeserved vacation, ease and . . . *jete* . . . *pirouette* . . . *jete* . . .

THAT NIGHT, AFTER BALLET, AFTER DINNER, BETH DOES not do the Pink Bubble Technique. Decides that the universe has rejected her pleas, that her pink bubbles have shrunk and withered in the dusty corners of the cosmos. She writes a clunky conclusion to her dramatic irony essay and watches David Letterman. At midnight, she turns off the TV and tip-toes into the dark kitchen. She opens cupboards, closes them, hungry but not. She fishes the emergency flashlight from the junk drawer and waves light over the fridge handle then down the hall where it lands on her dad's rubbery overshoes.

She listens for upstairs sounds. Nothing but the humidifier in her brother's room. She assumes a furtive walk, quieter than quiet, heads to the hall closet and all the pockets there.

Her mom's wool coat procures two lozenge wrappers and a grocery list, with only four of ten items crossed off. Her dad's spring and fall jacket: a folded racetrack programme, subway tokens, a crumpled two-dollar bill. She moves onto his winter coat, finds waxy chapstick and a spent Tic Tac container, three pennies. Hardly incriminating.

She's never sure what she wants to find. Or she is. Ever since the summer after grade six. Since that humid night when they sat on the back porch and she asked about the Ten Commandments. They never went to church, but she knew Moses carried those stone tablets off the mountain, knew something about not killing or stealing. "But what else can't you do?" she asked.

Her dad said, "Do you still have that Bible from Grandma?" He left his wine and they went upstairs, giddy, an almost-adventure. She flipped through the onion-thin pages, found the Commandments in Exodus or Deuteronomy.

She read about idolatry. "No posters or statues of other Gods," her dad explained. "Like Buddha. Or that elephant from India."

"India?" she said.

He rolled his hand in the air so she'd keep reading. *Honour thine parents.* "Any problem with your old man?" He swayed and pointed at his chest. She giggled but carried on. "You must not murder," she read.

"Duh," her dad said, and they both laughed.

When she read the next one, she stumbled over the word adultery. Barely sure of its meaning, she pressed her finger into the text, about to ask. But her dad leaned against her desk. "Well . . ." he said and winked.

Something squirmed in her belly and she knew. Her father a bit drunk, tipsy, had let something slip. He'd hardly noticed what he was admitting. But in that moment, everything shifted.

Off and on since then, she's searched for hard evidence. The nights he doesn't come home. Trips he forsakes. She can never prove he's not doing what he says. So she doesn't expect to find much of anything. Then she spots his unguarded briefcase leaning against the couch.

It's easy enough to open. The number combinations: her birthday on the left, her brother's on the right. Inside, his daytimer. She flips through it, interrogating each page with the flashlight. Penciled-in meetings, the word Niagara across next Monday and Tuesday, the letter M triple underlined below that. In fact, as Beth turns the pages back—February, January, November, October—she discovers at least ten other M's. Someone's name. *Her.*

She feels queasy, closes the day-timer. Should close the briefcase but doesn't. She investigates the accordion pouch, extracts a single file folder with a single black-and-white photo in it.

Her dad, dressed in a suit, his arm loose and casual around a dark-haired woman. Young. More buxom than Beth's flat-chested mother. Neither look at the camera but off to the side, toward something Beth cannot see. What she does see: a bright and obvious elation.

The pulse in her throat swirls and swirls. This photo is more than evidence. It's a grenade. If her mom sees it, their whole family will detonate. She slides the picture back, closes and locks the briefcase. She snaps off the flashlight. Immediately turns it back on. She holds it between her teeth, beam facing out, retwirls the briefcase combo, and retrieves the photo. She tears it down the middle, between the two heads. Then again across the shoulders, decapitating them. She returns the empty folder to the briefcase and leans it innocently back against the couch. Tiptoes into the kitchen and throws all four quarters of the photo into the garbage under the sink.

ENGLISH THE NEXT DAY AND SHE'S SO TIRED. This morning, when her dad asked if she wanted a ride, she'd thought *liarliarliar*, said no thanks, Sally wanted to meet at her place. And he said fine, fine, but he'd pick her up from ballet at six-fifteen.

Now, at her desk, Toby's empty chair in front of her, she folds her arms, rests her head down. Then his voice, close and conspiratorial in her ear, says, "You can only kill the moon with mega gamma rays." A full moon shatters like a clay pigeon under her eyelids. She lifts up and Toby's plopped in his seat, twisted toward her, his sweet, slouchy smile. "But what would happen to the tides?" she says. Meaning what? To start a silly banter—no moon! no tides! haha! But it comes out sad, full of aimless waters, lost oceans, woe for a disappearing moon. His smile shifts, fades, and a steady naked current passes between them.

So thank God Miss Finch comes in, bustle of bags, and a pimply guy behind her, pushing an AV cart. "Treat today!" Miss Finch announces, pulling a thick album box from her bag. A recording of *Romeo and Juliet*. Toby leans toward Beth. She smells his morning cigarette, his buttered toast. Feels the thunder of her heart. He points to Miss Finch and rolls his eyes. Turns and peels a mandarin.

A citrus tang overlays the crackles and pops of the record. Beth's heart settles down. She opens her text and listens. Enters fair Verona.

Halfway through the first act, there's a skip so Benvolio

stutters. The class collectively groans, and Miss Finch lifts the needle, blows off the dust, places it back down. But the skip persists, and Miss Finch removes the album, inspects for scratches. It's then that Toby tosses the mandarin peel over his shoulder. Like he's casting a spell or playing a challenging version of hopscotch. The peel splats across Beth's desk and she notices a jaggedy scrawl etched into the pith. *Ravine after school?*

She doesn't ask why or tell him she has ballet at five. Doesn't want to jinx it. Or refuse the universe if this is the answer to all her pink bubbles. So she rips off a corner out of her textbook, writes in all caps: YES.

For the rest of the day, she furtively pulls the peel from her pocket, reads and rereads it. She can't risk telling Jojo or Sally. Besides, it might be nothing. Maybe she and Toby'll just smoke a joint. Discuss wild, impossible ways to annihilate the moon.

AFTER SCHOOL, THEY HANG OUT IN THE NORTH PARKING lot, as per usual, socializing in separate clusters. Toby's in a hacky-sack circle with Damian Cowan and a couple of the drama kids. The sun shines and everyone's upbeat, high-fiving and hopping around, ready for the break. Beth stands with Jojo and Sally, but her gaze follows the beanbag rolling down Toby's arm, bouncing off his poised knee.

"My plane leaves in seventeen hours," Jojo says. "Thirty-six and I'll be making out with Pinocchio behind It's a Small World."

Sally giggles. Later she'll probably call Beth and say, "Can you believe her?" But for now, she says, "Do you think you'll deliver with Pinocchio?"

And Jojo says, "Sure, you've seen that nose." Both Jojo and Sally laugh. Beth only wraps her hand around the peel. She hopes Toby will give her a signal. But he keeps on with the hacky-sack and she feels her heart shrink and ball up like a hedgehog.

"I'm going to drink eight cups of coffee every day over the break," Sally says. "Do you want to come over Beth, and drink eight cups of coffee?"

"I have to go to Niagara," she says.

"Falls?" Jojo says.

"Of course the Falls," Sally says.

"There's also the lake," Jojo says.

"Right," Sally says. "The lake."

"Family trip," Beth says. "A hundred bucks, my dad won't come."

"Why?" Sally says.

She hasn't thought of it since before English, before the mandarin, but now she pictures her black and white dad, his shining, exuberant eyes. "I found a photo. Remember how I thought he had another woman? I found the other woman." Now that she's saying it, it sounds like fiction. A thing she's dreamed up. The ripped photo in the garbage can. No big deal.

Jojo's gum cracks. "Were they like . . . you know? *Delivering?*"

"Jojo!" Sally tugs her bangs. "They weren't, were they Beth?"

"Then how do you know she's the other woman?" Jojo says.

"I just know," Beth says.

A car circles around the lot and breaks them apart for a few seconds. Beth notices the hacky-sack has fallen into a puddle. Toby picks it up, shakes it off and sticks it into his pack. He tips his head toward her, then the side street. She nods, gathers her things. "Gotta go," she says.

And Sally says, "I thought you had ballet."

"Yeah," Beth says. "But my brother. I have to babysit him." She leaves and knows they'll debate about her dad and the other woman, but she doesn't care. Because now they won't notice her following Toby past the flagpole and front lawn.

IN FRONT OF THE SCHOOL, BETH WATCHES HIS ARMS swing, the Zeppelin logo rippling, his jeans hanging around his skinny ass. Toby Forbes! Toby Forbes! Every cell trills. He disappears down a set of stairs into the south parking lot. Two beats later and she's down the stairs too. He pulls her arm, ducking into a doorway and kisses her. There's the sudden presence of tongue in her mouth, a hand shoved against her breast. But she gets into it, kisses back, and as soon as she does, he pulls away. "Come on," he says.

The afternoon sun glares off crusted snow. Trickles of snow-melt spider over the asphalt and the air feels like winter's finally swapping out for spring.

Toby's a long stride step ahead and Beth hurries behind him, down the ramp into the junior schoolyard. Far away, kids shout and a dog barks. Up close, their feet crunch. For once Beth wishes she'd worn boots, snow granules already sneaking into her flats.

A zillion conversations eddy through her, each one sense-less and irrelevant, so she keeps quiet, doesn't want to ruin whatever they're doing. They cross the whole field and Beth wishes Toby would say how he really likes her, has always, always liked her. But he seems solemn, concentrating on climbing the hill.

In the shade that skirts the ravine, it's cooler. Even more so once they step on the path that runs through a stand of trees. In junior high Beth avoided this ravine, the rocker kids lurking, smoking cigarettes and dope. Back then she always dashed past the entrance as if a troll would leap from the shad-ows, snatch and eat her up. Now it's quiet, only the white noise of traffic from Yonge St. and a couple crows calling from invis-ible perches.

Toby leads her down a steep slope where the trees thin out and become thick brush. More snow slips into her shoes, chilling her feet. No matter. Toby's in front of her, holding up a branch, ushering her to an exposed semicircle of thawed ground. Then he widens his arms as though he's presenting her with the heart of a palace. But there's only a sludgy, half-frozen stream and relics from a bonfire. Charred logs, crushed and burnt beer cans, a shredded windbreaker hanging in the shrubs. Beth hugs herself, shivers, and stomps her feet. She's missed her bus and Miss Belle will note the rupture in her perfect attendance.

The sun shines only on the high tree tops, leaving Beth and Toby in a trough of blue, shadowy light. The stream emits a rankness that reminds Beth of fish scales and swamps. Toby's shoulders hunch in his jean jacket, hair hanging in his eyes. She steps closer, hoping he'll kiss her again. She even adjusts the angle of her face like she's seen in a thousand movies.

But he doesn't kiss her.

And she doesn't know how she goes from standing to kneeling. From waiting for that kiss to sucking him off. He's not forcing, she knows that. She wants to, even with his hands on her head, pushing her. She gags once, twice. Clasps his wrists, moves his hands. Then finds a rhythm. Back and forth, back and forth, her jaw unhinged and, after a few minutes, aching. She counts in her head—one two three, one two three—and soon there's a groan and a warm salty gush.

He slides from her mouth and she's still on her knees holding the mucusy liquid like a raw oyster on her tongue. She pretends to cough, spits it into her hand, a white gooey snot. She smears it on the ground, her coat, as he tucks himself away.

He helps her up and they face the poor excuse for a stream. Beth wants to ask if she did it right. Because did she? She's only read about it in *Cosmo*. Like eating a popsicle, the article said, which it really *really* isn't.

Toby lights a cigarette and offers her a drag. And though she doesn't smoke, she takes one. Wants the taste gone from her mouth.

WINTER CLASPS ITS HARD SILVER BUCKLE BACK ACROSS the sky. Out in the open again and cold burrows into Beth's bones, clings to her throat. She can't, though she wants to, speak. It's as if she's already said all the words and what's left is a framework of simple, soundless nouns: tree, snow, school, boy. She wishes Toby would open the conversation floodgate. Tell her he's already written a letter to Christine, breaking it off. And then she could explain the magic of the pink bubbles, and how it brought them, finally, together. But for two whole minutes there's only an exchange of breath. Dense, jagged clouds: his then hers; his again.

His lips hang slightly apart and twist to the left; his gaze darts above her as though tracking sparrows. He swallows hard, Adam's apple up and down. "I forgot my math book," he says. "In my locker."

All Beth says is, "Oh." A tinny squeak of sound that reverberates beneath her skull.

Toby turns away and sprints across the field.

Oh. Oh. Oh.

SHE STANDS THERE LONG ENOUGH FOR THE MUD stains on her knees to congeal. For a crust of cold to form down the shins of her jeans. She keeps hoping Toby'll come back, math text under his arm, all insistent and Romeo. But he keeps staying away.

The sky dims, dusks, and the first glimmer of Venus flicks on.

He's gone. Except for the metallic oyster taste on her tongue. The cigarette.

A chatter of three women amplifies and comes closer. Beth turns toward them. Joggers, one suggesting to the others they should run the ravine. Beth steps forward. Wants to tell them she's left something down by the creek. Something small but essential. If they could take her down there. Help her find it. One of the women pauses, jogs on the spot and says, "You okay?" Beth worries the mandarin peel in her pocket. Brittle now, cold. She feels the women's eyes lock on her knees. "Just waiting," Beth says. "For a friend." They nod and, with furrowed brows, disappear into the dark ravine.

Then Beth rushes away, as if the troll might spring from the trees. She follows the walkway that encircles her old junior school, breaks a crumb off the mandarin peel and drops it. Another and another. A whole orange trail down to the northeast corner of Avenue Rd. and Glengrove where all she needs to do is cross the street and hop on the 61 Southbound. She's too late for ballet, for her dad, who already waits for her at the studio. But she can still make it home before her mother. Pull the photo pieces from the garbage. Shake them free of coffee grounds and banana peels, hide them in that box under her bed.

Instead she lets the 61 sail through the intersection and buttons her coat to her throat.

The temperature drops again. Zero, minus two, minus five. Then a wind chill.

Beth pulls out her one lone mitten and stuffs both hands inside. For hours she'll walk like this. Meandering the side streets with hands pressed together. Sending out one plea, and then another, to the wide empty ear of the universe.

AT THE EDGE OF
EVERYTHING

FOR THE PAST HOUR, ALLI HAD BEEN SITTING against the small oak, her eighteen-month-old son latched to her breast. His molars had finally—finally, finally, *finally*—broken through, and now he suckled, cheeks sticky, eyes lolling. Alli hoped another mom would show up. She hadn't had an adult conversation since Jeannie had taken off to visit her parents in Vancouver. And Clay? Well, he was just plain off. And now she wanted someone, *anyone,* to gab with about the impossibility of lost sleep, errant husbands, and teething. But there were only the crows, waddling around the rim of a garbage can, diving in for pizza crusts and flying across the playground over to the giant cedar.

Alli's daughter, Tavia, checked out the birds from under her floppy sunhat, and then dumped a handful of sand onto the accumulating pile beside Alli. Alli mimed eating, mumbled *yum-yum* for the umpteenth time. "Do you like it Mommy?" Without waiting for an answer, Tavia ran back to the production centre beneath the slide.

Jack continued suckling. He'd drained both breasts; Alli had become a giant pacifier. His eyelids fluttered and his blond feathery hair stuck to his forehead, ear crusted with milk and peanut butter. She picked at it and he swatted her, still sucking hard. *Enjoy them while they're young,* people said, but she couldn't wait to toss these days onto a slag heap.

A forty-something woman walked past, leading a sturdy four-year-old boy by the hand. She released him at the edge of the playground then sat on a bench. She wore a creamy blouse, puffs at each shoulder, and a beige skirt exposing powdery legs. She turned toward Alli, zinc-white streaks across her bony face, and Alli nodded, about to say hello. But the woman dug around her purse and covered up with dark, owl-like sunglasses.

People circulated this small town like so many white blood cells—from the busking tuba girl to the old timers on coal-cart benches—but Alli had never seen this woman before.

If Jeannie were here, they'd speculate: staunchly married, conservative investment portfolio, subscriptions to *Canadian Living, Martha Stewart,* and *O.* Penchant for butterscotch candies, sweet liqueurs, and casseroles topped with crushed-up Carr's Water Biscuits. They'd name her too, the way they'd christened the buff mom Chin-Up, because that's what she did on the monkey bars while her kids ran amok. Or that blond grandma—The Fuming Miss Clairol, for her consolidation of bottled platinum and mentholated cigarettes.

This woman was obscenely beige. Like rice cakes. Or pablum. Cream of Wheat.

Wheatie.

Just then Wheatie's son stomped up the tube slide, all force and yell, probably a sugar tantrum. Tavia winced below, scrawny shoulders lifting against the noise. The boy shot down backwards, then charged his mother, who wiped his face and hands with a readied Wet One. He growled, turned around and launched belly first onto the swings, dragging sand with his feet. Wheatie folded the soiled wipe in quarters, brushed her son's residue off her skirt, and adjusted her sunglasses.

What nickname would Wheatie give Alli? Mother Without A Cause? The Stench Wench? After all, Alli hadn't showered in days; her hair fell in disobedient strands, which she tucked behind her ears, gritty and sticky like everything else. And she probably gave off an offensive odour she could no longer detect. Soured milk, diapers, ripened armpits. Wheatie had probably caught a whiff. Or marvelled at Alli's stained and too-small *Righteous Babe* t-shirt. Not that Alli was actually *wearing* it—Jack had yanked the collar around her right breast, lifted the shirt to fondle the left.

Alli tugged the nipple from Jack's mouth and his eyes sprang open. "All done," she said. He squirmed and head-butted her breastbone. She plopped him on the grass and rummaged through the diaper bag for Cheerios. He screamed until Tavia returned with raspberry sand and said, "You can have this one, Jack." He extended a hand and she filled it before running blissfully away. Jack showed it to Alli as she repositioned her bra and adjusted her shirt. Then he threw it in her face.

She fell onto her hip, tightened her eyes. Opened them a slit, felt the sting, the burn, and closed them tight again. Jack climbed onto her thigh, forced her shirt collar wide. "Damn it, Jack." She clamped his wrist, blinked the playground into a staccato smear.

When he screamed and hit her chest, she clasped that arm too, squeezing it harder than she should. She wanted to shake him, abandon every parenting book she'd ever read. *Give them words for their feelings! Give them gentle redirection!* A not-so-gentle scream built in her throat and she almost, *almost* released it. Then she became hyper-aware of Wheatie's steel-wool gaze, so she lightened the pressure, spat sand off her lips, converted her voice into sugar, anger turning, as it often did, to a deep and shameful heat.

"Don't throw sand," she said, trying to think of the positive phrasing—not don't, but *what*?

Her vision returned, briny and blurred, though something still scraped her cornea. She drained Tavia's sippy cup into her eyes, blinked them clear, then shook a few remaining drops over Jack's head. "Nonononono . . ." The only thing he ever said.

"Let's try the swings," she said, clutched his overall straps like a suitcase handle and carried him past the monkey bars, past Wheatie's bench. Alli heard her titter.

She stuffed Jack into the toddler swing and stepped back. Even without him in her arms, her body felt like a thing she hefted around. Baby weight massed around her arms, and her thighs chafed. Even after Tavia, her thighs hadn't chafed.

"Richard!" Wheatie called her son. "We need to go. Now!" He whined and scampered onto the climbing-gym suspension bridge. "One!" she yelled. He grinned, bounded on the bridge, producing waves. "Two!" Alli wanted Wheatie to climb, cinch the boy around the waist, and sail down the slide in her beige skirt, but she just kept counting.

Alli pushed against Jack's back. The metal chains creaked as the swing went forward, as it returned. Two and a half hours until dinner. Since Clay had left all they'd dined on were marbled cheese cubes and cucumbers, noodles and butter, cereal (*sans* milk) and fishsticks.

God. She was a *fishstick* mother now.

Jack held the chains, bucked his head forward and back, a complaint that Alli hadn't sent him into orbit the way his dad used to. Swings made her motion-sick, so she kept it at lullaby speed. A shrill "Ten!" came from the slides. The boy now wedged in a plastic tube, Wheatie alternately thumping her hands against it, and yelling into the opening.

"Hey Alli!"

Mounting the slope beyond the soccer pitch Dr. X held two ice cream cones, posing as though he'd been photoshopped. A little girl, who might be mistaken for his daughter, trailed behind. People admired him, called him by his first name, but since he'd walked out on Jeannie for an OR nurse Dr. X suited him better. An ears, nose and throat specialist. His face a polished bronze; teeth sending off sparks. Alli hadn't seen him for months.

Now he arrived, leaning against the swing set, tongue working the melting vanilla. He'd just come back from five days paddling Desolation Sound, had she ever been?

Beyond him Wheatie threaded her arms through the bridge ropes, shackling her son's ankles and pressing down with all her beige might. "Stop!" the woman said. "I *will* leave you."

Alli pushed Jack again, and Dr. X went on. Something about a mountain just south. A doable hike with kids. Oh, the view! Gulf Islands sparkling in the Salish Sea. The Coastals. She really ought to check it out. Clay too. He lowered his eyebrows, cocked his head and pointed with the cone. "Where's he at these days anyways?" he asked.

Did he really not know? Dr. X had started this damn contagion with the nurse, and now Clay was off with the Skinny Skank, making money, taking whimsical excursions on days off.

Wheatie started yelling. "Excuse me! Excuse me!" She pointed at the oak. Alli turned: a crow was having a heyday with Jack's Cheerios. It hopped on and off the stroller seat, pecking away. Another dropped from the tree, clamped its beak onto the diaper bag, opened it. Yet another swooped from the garbage can and sauntered right into the bag, snatched a dirty diaper. "Fuck!" Alli shouted.

Dr. X did nothing but laugh.

THE NEXT DAY WAS FRIDAY. JEANNIE WAS FINALLY back and Alli hung out on her back porch while the kids played inside. Jeannie watered bean sprouts in Styrofoam cups and four tomato starts in terracotta pots. Alli eased into one of the rockers Jeannie had refinished last summer, post-divorce, every night after she'd tucked in her girls. Small bugs were entombed in the shellac, and Alli picked at a gnat and told Jeannie about the crows, how they'd prized open the Cheerios, pecked the dirty diaper and took off with the last of her Medjool dates.

Jeannie stood, lithe and muscled, her skin shone with a vitamin radiance. Even her laugh was rich in carotene and omegas.

"Dr. X showed up," Alli said, knowing his name would momentarily eclipse Jeannie's glow.

Sure enough, Jeannie's mouth flatlined. She snapped two pairs of chopsticks apart, stabbed one into each bean sprout cup, spilling dirt onto the porch.

"The nurse? And the girl?"

"Just the girl."

Jeannie tied the stalks to steady them, then wrapped her hair around the extra stick, swirled it into a French twist.

"Do you know how many crows make a murder?" Jeannie said. She set two Mason jars onto an old TV tray beside an oversized pickle jar filled with amber liquid and shredded herbs.

"Three?" Alli offered.

She couldn't tell if Jeannie's hands shook as she nestled strainers into the small jars, but she muttered, the way Alli did sometimes, casting under-the-breath vitriolic spells. When Jeannie turned, her face settled. Alli wished she'd rage over Dr. X., tear him apart like she used to, and they could launch into catty commiseration. Instead she handed Alli a glass and clinked it. "Sun-steeped tea. Mint, chamomile and clover. For nerves."

Jeannie had tonics for everything. Tinctures of skullcap, reishi mushroom, valerian, nettles and god-knows-what-all. She pushed them on Alli: one for low energy, another for headaches, this one great for digestion, that for lactation. Alli liked the idea. Dandelion to cleanse the liver. Nettles to rebuild her blood. Though when she hit the afternoon slump, these days moving closer and closer to morning, she didn't reach for nettles but sugar and coffee.

Inside, Tavia's voice rose: "I'm the princess!" Alli leaned forward, awaited dissent, or, at the very least, a meltdown, but nothing followed. She crossed her fingers, hoping for another hour, the closest thing she'd had to a break since the night she'd pulled out a DVD and watched an uninterrupted episode of *Six Feet Under*.

She rocked back too hard and sloshed tea down her shirt.

Jeannie snatched a dishcloth off the rail and tossed it. Alli stilled the chair, wiped the spill, said, "I don't think I own one fucking shirt without a stain."

"You're still wearing your ring." Jeannie motioned toward Alli's left hand, sunlight streaking over it, catching the thin band.

Releasing the cloth, Alli twisted the ring to show Jeannie it wouldn't budge. Heat had swollen her fingers, not to mention the twenty pounds.

"You try soaping it?"

Alli nodded, though she hadn't.

Last winter, after Dr. X had left, Jeannie turned his departure into ceremony. *For closure,* she'd called it, sounding like *fore*closure, which, in a way, it was. Alli had hiked with Jeannie through a cold drizzle to the gushing forest spring while the kids stayed home with Clay. And she accompanied Jeannie as Jeannie wrapped prayer flags around a cedar, lit candles that hissed in the rain, and read poetry. Alli had tried to *feel* something, reverence or compassion, but she only felt the anemic grit behind her eyes, the overwhelming desire for a nap. Besides, ceremony—whether wedding or unwedding—always felt like contrived pomp, *death till you part* pronouncements while mothers and aunties wept in the crowd. Still, Jeannie cried and laughed and sacrificed a wedding photo to the sputtering flames. She'd recited an incantation too, downloaded from the internet, and vowed never to marry again. Then she laid her three-karat ring to rest, carved *RIP* in the dirt. Alli saw the appeal, the stamp and seal of it allowing Jeannie to move on. But surely bouncing back required more than a candle and buried ring.

"I did stuff my wedding dress into a garbage bag," Alli said. "Ready for the Sally Ann."

"Not the same," said Jeannie.

Alli sipped the remaining tea. In the yard, an empty bird feeder sat on a fence post, its roof streaked with sun-faded purples and oranges. Below, garden beds had been turned and worked, soil dark as chocolate cake; popsicle sticks and seed packets marked the rows where baby lettuce and beets sprouted. There was the consolation-prize trampoline Dr. X had bought after he'd left, now overturned. Dandelions growing between springs, small serving plates and teacups arranged in its centre.

Jeannie called Clay Mr. Y. "If you can't call him ex," she said, "then consider why." *Why did Alli still love him? Why didn't she deserve better? Why did she think he might come back?*

Before he left, he'd said, "You used to laugh, Alli. A lot. Now you only complain about how tired you are." Admittedly, Alli's entertainment value *had* gone down, all those interrupted hours of REM sleep. Things could really do nothing but get better, she'd said, but he just couldn't wait around. So he took a job up in Haida Gwaii, two twelve-hour ferry rides up the coast, to the edge of everything, where you only got cell service on some guy's front steps and internet from dial-up at the library. "Just for a few months," he'd said, packing his planting bags, his best rain gear. "Clear my head. See if I've made the best decision." That was six weeks ago, and he'd still failed to mention the pierced tree-planter girl—her eyebrow, navel, and nose.

A wren pecked around the feeder then disappeared behind the fence. Alli twisted her ring to the knuckle, where it pinched; she pushed it back down. "Sometimes," she said, "I want to stab the crap out of him. Actually plunge the knife in. Her too. Skinny Skank."

"I used to dream of fires," Jeannie said. "The whole new family up in flames. Even the kid." She stretched a fist forward and traced a zigzag scar through the knuckles. Alli remembered when it'd been bandaged, though Jeannie hadn't offered many details. "That's from punching a mirror," she said. "If he hadn't ducked, it would have been the good doctor's face."

THE NEXT MORNING CAME TOO EARLY. JACK'S FEET jabbed Alli's hip. He'd awakened twice in the night, the second time pattering across the house and into her bed. Tavia had weaned herself at fourteen months—why not Jack? Jeannie once mentioned a woman who'd nursed four kids, five years each. A goddamn career. Anyway, Jack showed no signs of slowing and Alli wanted to cut him off, but feared he'd seek ways to fill the void she'd created—sugar first, then street drugs and porn.

Without opening her eyes, Alli lifted her shirt, stalling morning as long as she could. Jack latched on and suckled, and Alli drifted off.

She imagined Clay returning, surprising her at the front door with flowers and a plane ticket to anywhere, or maybe with a stunned look, as if he'd just come out of a coma or long hibernation.

In truth, he'd gone back to the same wilderness they'd visited after their first season tree-planting together. A freak winter-type storm hit the Hecate Strait late that summer and it took Alli two days to recover from seasickness. Then they wandered wide empty beaches with windy silences and nothing on the horizon. And those forests: crazy-big trees shag-carpeted with moss, russet rivers winding through them. Clay talked about someday building a log cabin there, living off the grid. And now he'd sort of done it, probably taken up a whole new identity. She bet he'd grown a bushy beard, caught salmon with his bare hands, designed driftwood shelters on the beach. In no time, he'd father a fresh batch of skinny kids too.

Jack pulled away and rolled around the mattress, singing in gibberish. Then Tavia flung open the door and bounded onto the bed. Her book nicked Alli's elbow and Alli groaned, stuffing her head under a pillow. "Ten more minutes. Please."

Tavia flipped through the pages, exclaiming over every 't' in her book. "Another one! And there!" Then, "Don't touch it!" and the slap of skin on skin. "Mommy!" Jack mounted Alli's ribs as though she were a rocking horse and bounced.

BY ELEVEN, THEY'D EXHAUSTED FOUR EPISODES OF *Bob the Builder,* two rounds of breakfast, a game of buy-something-at-the-store, Bulldozer-Boy, and fairies with glitter glue.

"Out," Alli finally cried. "All of you!"

They both froze. Then Tavia reached for Jack's hand, pulled him close, and Jack dropped to the floor and whimpered. Why did they always need her? At least with Clay around there existed the promise of a break. Hadn't her own mother shoved her out the door? Left her to play in the yard. In the street. Only allowed back in at dinner.

And look how that turned out.

"Fine," Alli said. "Fine." She scooped Jack up, told Tavia to put on her shoes. They'd go to the farmers' market. Somehow they'd find redemption in snap peas and fiddle players. And cookies, of course. She fastened them into their car seats and drove the fifteen minutes out of town in her old Subaru, down the highway connector, across the bridge and the estuary and around the corn field, to the mall with the drive-thru ATM.

Despite the *Idle Free Zone* sign, a pickup idled in front of them. Exhaust seeped through the vents and Alli shut her engine.

"It stinks," said Tavia.

Alli dumped the contents of her wallet onto the passenger seat to fish out the bank card. Clay promised he'd deposit money once he got paid. Surely he'd *been* paid. He hadn't called for three weeks, never said anything about a remote banking site. Yesterday the mortgage payment went through their shared account, but she'd stopped checking the balance, not wanting the reminder of how they hovered, always, around the maximum overdraft. Things would change soon, she'd find work. That was okay. People worked. *She* used to work. Only eight seasons as a tree-planter, true. And that one year ringing up booze at the liquor store. Then all those years playing house-wife. That would really dress up a resume: *Makes dinner and breastfeeds on demand. Can sing "Wheels on the Bus" inexhaustibly and rise hourly for new teeth, fevers, and vomit.*

Tavia kicked the back of the seat. "Mommy? Can we get mermaid cookies? I want a mermaid cookie."

The diesel pulled away. Alli's car clunked when the engine turned over then lurched forward. She slid the card into the machine, punched in the PIN and requested an even one hundred bucks. The machine gurgled.

"With green Smarties and pink icing!"

The ATM beeped, flashed *Insufficient Funds*. The card slid out and she pushed it back. She punched in sixty. Forty. Twenty. Then the machine threatened to eat her card.

Alli balled the receipts and tossed them. No money. Nothing. Maybe no money from Clay ever again. What if he was really gone? Totally disappeared. Okay. *Okay*. She could do this. People did this. The house. A little two-bedroom bungalow with dings in the walls. Hardly any kitchen counters. But she could paint, put in a new bathroom floor. Make it worth *something*. Then what? Sell only to rent a one-bedroom basement suite with two tiny closets, a stand-up shower, and black mould? Maybe Jeannie would take them in. Share that big house.

"I'm hot!" Tavia kicked again. Alli cranked the fan. It whirred and blew dust.

Two short bleats from the car behind, and Alli crept into the parking lot. An elderly man, hunched over a cane, hobbled by. She thought of things she could do immediately. *Phone sex.* Was that even still a thing? And how did you apply? A yard sale seemed more straightforward. She could throw up a couple of posters this afternoon. Put ads in the Buy and Sell. Sell Clay's CD collection, his tools, his bike, his vintage hockey cards.

She gripped the steering wheel.

"Cookies! Cookies!"

Fucking Clay.

"I'll always take care of you guys," he'd said. "You're still my family." She hated that she'd believed him, and hated, even more, that she still wanted to believe.

She headed back onto the connector toward home.

"Go back!" Tavia's voice keened. "What about cookies?"

"No money, sweetheart," Alli said. "No cookies today."

Tavia screamed. *Mean! Unfair! Hatehatehate.* Then her words dissolved into beastly sobs.

Alli picked up speed. Something clunked, or rattled, hard to tell with Jack joining in on the wailing. Alli glanced in the rear-view, Jack's teeth clamped on his stuffed tiger, Tavia yanking it away. Let them kill each other. Maybe then they'd fall into serious naps and she could drink black coffee, take inventory for the yard sale.

A light blinked on the dash, needle hanging over the E on the gas gauge. Usually that gave her forty kilometres. Or was it twenty? Enough to get home in any case. The kids grew louder.

When she and Jeannie worked as tree-planters they'd once waited five hours on a muddy logging road, their truck with a busted starter. Ravenous and cold, they'd played Worst Thing. Dexterous bear opens door and mauls. Axe-murderer smashes windshield. Moose charges truck into swamp. But they'd never imagined this: two children melting down, no gas, midday sun.

The accelerator didn't respond. Cars honked and she swerved to the shoulder, leaning forward as if to help the propulsion. Tavia got quiet; Jack too. Outside the scenery slowed until trees stood still. Something clicked under the hood.

"Mommy?" Tavia said.

Her cell phone had hardly any juice. She tried Jeannie, leaving a message on the home phone, a text on her cell, before the battery died. In the distance, she could make out the overpass. About a kilometre away. The gas station, another three.

She rotated the key, hoping to squeeze the remaining distance from the tank.

Come on.

It clacked, followed by a grinding sputter. A second time and the same result.

Tavia asked, "Why don't you just drive?" And Alli told her to please, *please* just shut up.

EVERYTHING GASPED AND HISSED UNDER THE HOOD. She studied grease spattered tubes, tarnished coils and radiator cap. Like visiting a back alley in a foreign country where they used another alphabet and all Alli could say was *excuse me, hello,* and *dipstick.* So she pulled the dipstick from its place, wiped it with a scrap of paper towel she'd found in the car. Nothing. Not a drop or evidence of a drop. And a fissure on the engine blocks, a thin crack with fresh metal gleam. It could have been there before, right? Like nicks on the windshield and rust on the wheel wells. She shoved the stick in again, pushed and twisted. But no. When had she last put oil in?

It came to her that the engine had seized. One of those vague automobile diagnoses she'd heard. Maybe she'd asked Clay what would happen if. More likely, it came from one of Clay's condescending lectures, his wide-eyed, arms-crossed, slowed-speech instructions on caring for things. The way he'd yakked on about the cast iron pan, insisting she should never, as she'd done for years, leave it to soak.

She dropped the hood, let it slam, wiped her hands on her shorts.

Cars passed by in batches of twos and threes, then long stretches of nothing. A turkey vulture perched on a road sign, feathers cloaked around its neck, sinister and expectant. A *turkey* vulture? *Seriously?*

BY THE TIME THEY REACHED THEIR STREET CORNER, Jack's arms and neck were bright pink. Tavia performed the limp rag over and over so that Alli had to carry a kid on each hip. Her right shoulder blade ached, sending pain up her neck to her skull, where it gnawed her brain. By the time they reached the front door, she discovered she'd left her ID and bank cards spread over the passenger seat along with her keys. She force-fed herself through the bathroom window, popped two expired ibuprofens and fetched her overheated children from beneath the apple tree. Jack was catatonic, drool spindled off his lip, and he refused the breast even when Alli shoved it to his mouth. Something irreversible must have happened. She shook him lightly, tickled his chin, his cheeks, but he pulled away, preferring the sippy cup and television. Tavia ate dry cereal and ice cubes, asked, "Where's Daddy anyway?" and "When will he come home?"

Alli felt her own forehead. *Kids are resilient*, Jeannie might say. But were they? Kids never remembered the thousands of mundane hours you invested in their lives. Only the irascible few. She thought of her own mother, swatting her away from a pregnant belly. Did it matter she hadn't paid attention to Alli's shock of rejection? And why couldn't Alli remember the hours before?

Alli knew no amount of positive wording could undo certain damages. Her kids would never forget a day like this. Never forget their father's leaving. Her misery. At least Tavia wouldn't. As for Jack, the confusion had seeped into his tissues, absorbed by his small, impressionable body.

No one would tow the car without a credit card. And a new engine? The quotes she scribbled on the back of an unpaid hydro bill all came to two thousand, minimum. That, for a used engine.

The voice mail kicked in immediately on Jeannie's home phone. Her cell too. Alli had forgotten about *me-time*. When Dr. X had the girls, Jeannie heeded the advice of mothering gurus and unplugged for twenty-four hours, committing one-hundred percent to her uninterrupted baths with lavender salts, and then her projects: knitting, tincture brewing, gardening, refurbishing old chairs. "So restorative," she'd said. "So necessary." And Alli wished she'd married for money instead of love, that she could divorce someone for a sizable alimony and every other weekend off.

She texted Clay, even though he probably wouldn't check it until his contract ended mid-July. She passed along news of her brain aneurysm, Jack's catatonia, Tavia's fresh abandonment issues, and the stranded Subaru.

BY EVENING THE SKY HAD MELLOWED, THE LIGHT MEALY and saturated with a boozy, nostalgic scent of barbeque grills and briquettes. Shouts and splashes broke over backyard fences, a couple of boys slapped barefoot on the sidewalk. Alli biked by, pedalling at a steady cruise pace. She meant to turn left, zip over to the connector, collect her keys, her ID off the front seat as she'd told Kate, the twelve-year-old babysitter she'd convinced to work on credit. Instead she veered right, avoiding the gravel shoulder where she sometimes skidded.

It calmed her, mountains solid and dark against the sky, that geological genius of time housed there, packing away the ruckus of another day. *This* day. She took the hill up the hypotenuse side of the Peace Park meridian, feeling lighter as she went, her skin like a ship's hull scraped free of barnacles.

The old railbed edged along the swamp, where—back in the day—they'd shunted coal. Now dust kicked up beneath her wheels and cottonwoods released their last perfume. She walked the bike across a gap-toothed footbridge. Water trickled in spidery threads down the culvert and Alli noticed a plastic fire truck half-submerged where the swamp pooled deep. Kids from the nearby townhouses. She'd seen them throw whole tricycles in.

She hid her bike in the brush and entered the trail they called *Mama Bear's*. The light dropped an octave, giving a bluish tinge to lichen-splotched trees. The trail was lined with wide-girth cedars and firs. Hemlocks stood on higher ground, amidst sword ferns and salal. These were only ribbons of forest. Ecosystems shredded and divided, aswirl in industrial cuts. But in here, Alli felt the air sweeten, the world still intact.

The path branched and she followed it, creaky-kneed, down through straight-postured firs. The ground loose from the dry weather. She passed the spot where chanterelles grew. She'd missed them last fall, caps beheaded by some other treasure seeker, but now she'd have to make extra efforts to forage food: huckleberries, blackberries, mushrooms. If things got really bad, maybe she'd even take up bow hunting.

The swamp released a damp taste into the air. Microbes going berserk in a rotting stump, breaking everything down, and the boggy spores of skunk cabbage. The trail levelled, then climbed. Here, the spring choked and drooled a wet lacquer over the chunky black rock. In a couple of weeks, it would dry completely. Alli found footing on the rock face, climbed to the cedar where Jeannie's prayer flags hung limp and battered down the trunk.

Then she stood, twisting her ring to the knuckle. Slicked it with spit and tugged at it until it slid off. She held it skyward, squinted through its centre. A chaste blue light hung above the tree crowns. Perhaps this was all she needed, like unhitching a belt after overeating. She tucked the ring into her back pocket, scraping it over her flip phone, then crouched low.

Dark collected at the forest floor, shattered needles and bits of leaf. Roots and the pair of rocks where Jeannie had burned two candles that day, where she'd placed a small Buddha, and called it an altar. Wax drippings scabbed the carapace, but the statue no longer sat lotus on the damp earth. Where exactly had Jeannie dug the hole? Alli felt the ground, hoping to read its braille *RIP*. Nothing. At the altar base, she peeled back a mat of needles, wishing she had a photographic memory, could hone in on the exact spot. She chipped randomly at the ground with a firm stick.

Once she'd read of a place, some high mountain village in Tibet or India, where the ground was too hard or frozen to dig, where the dead were left unburied, exposed to the elements, left for scavengers to feast. Maybe it was all like that. Maybe in the end we were just picked clean. Husbands from wives. Rings from fingers. Trees from land. All part of some mysterious cycle.

She twirled the stick around, widening the ground into a shallow hole. She'd never tell Jeannie. How could she? Besides, selling the ring would only buy her a little time. One month, maybe two.

The phone sent a sudden vibration, then rang. Digital *Ode*

to Joy. Alli leapt up, stood with the stick pledged across her heart. For a nano-flash she thought it might be Jeannie, out of her bath and ready to help. But Alli's own home number paraded across the screen and she felt a cocktail mix of relief and dread.

Kate.

Voice aquiver. An innocent: *I was just playing on my DS when . . .* Alli knew Jack's separation anxiety had kicked in, freaked Kate out. And then Jack's full gusto lungs in the background. Alli's breasts swelled and prickled.

"Are you almost done? I mean—"

Shit. She hadn't even recouped the ID yet. Didn't want too. Maybe someone else could grab it, do a better job of being her.

Jack yowled, the gagging cry that often ended in a puke. Pressure built in her breasts, each duct brimming, leaking into her bra cups, soaking layers of cotton and streaming down her belly. An overflow that hadn't happened in months. She suppressed it with her forearm but still felt that copper wire tingle, like a short-circuited transmission.

She held the cell glow above the hole, hoping for a diamond sparkle. Only stringy roots and the edge of a deeper rock. Kate's voice dumped into the ground, a stammer, maybe a gulping. Alli sighed, replaced the phone to her ear.

"I'll be home soon," she said.

She clicked the phone, crouched back. She'd return. Whatever else happened, she'd always return.

In the distance, a mourning dove hooted, sounding like an owl. Or an owl hooted, sounding like itself. The forest filled with dark shapes and the darkening spaces around them. Alli bowed her head, stabbed at a fresh piece of ground and broke it open.

INTRUDER

NEITHER SHE NOR MAX HEARD HIM COME IN. STEPH was upstairs in what for years they'd called the baby's room. Now it was empty. She'd moved the dresser and standing lamp into the hallway, along with the bookshelf and gliding rocker. She'd packed clothes from the closet—hand-me-down onesies and tiny pairs of second-hand socks—into a bag for the Canadian Diabetic Guys. Maybe she'd donate the furniture too, after she finished repainting. One red cushion should do it. Or a hammock, slung corner to corner, where she could spend her hours facing the muted walls, or the crows that roosted on the wires outside the window.

Of course, Max would never go for it. He'd say, *Let's get you a desk! A new career! A hobby! A little dog!* She'd nod, agreeing to get out more, knowing she wouldn't.

Steph peeled strips of green tape from around the window frame, rolled them into a sticky ball. With an X-acto knife, she teased out the stubborn bits. Halfway along the edge, her hand jerked and sliced the wall, opening the grey to the colour beneath.

They'd painted it a pale blue when they'd first moved in,

after she'd finished her master's in architecture, secured a job in a small firm, and finally went off the pill. Back then she'd imagined giving birth to an inquisitive and lanky girl, with Max's amber eyes and strong constitution. And when those first few periods came, she'd feigned casualness, telling Max, and herself, she was committed to the child but not the timing. After all, her body needed to readjust to its natural cycles, so she spent two years eating diligent portions of broccoli and kale, drinking gallons of raspberry leaf tea. Meanwhile, Max bought the rocker and unearthed a practically crumbling copy of *Goodnight Moon*. "My mother read it to me," he'd said, setting it alongside Steph's old Judy Blumes on the bookcase.

SHE HEARD WATER RUNNING IN THE PIPES. LATER, she'd tell police she thought it was Max hosing off his bike, or watering the delphiniums and daisies, although she didn't think that. The noise registered and melded with neighbour-hood sprinklers and power washers, followed by a siren and a chorus of baying dogs. Steph dabbed the last drops of Cumulus Grey into the gash and rollered over it. The work pleased her, even the splattered overalls and kerchief pleased her, though she felt a mild terror that the project was almost complete. She didn't want to reintegrate into a normal rhythm: barbecues at Fern's house, Pilates classes, once-a-week sushi with her mother. Nor did she want to bear the brunt of Max's enthusiasm on the trip he'd planned. Where he'd befriend every B&B owner, thrill-seek the steepest mountain bike trails and snap pictures of every single vineyard.

The neighbour's Bichon Frise yipped in clusters of four, and Steph resumed peeling tape, this time from the Thunderhead Black baseboards.

SHE'D TRIED CLOMID TO HYPERSTIMULATE HER OVARIES, became weepy and sensitive to noise, developed a deep aversion toward Max. She endured the love they'd made, wishing he'd finish things off and leave her alone. Finally, Fern, Max's sister, recommended the top fertility place in Vancouver and Max booked an appointment. The doctors harvested Steph's eggs, fertilized them with Max's washed sperm, then re-inserted two at a time, warning of twins. At last, in January, after their fourth and final round, a heartbeat.

Sixteen weeks in, she and Max went for the ultrasound. The technician looped the wand around Steph's navel, said, "Your baby is the size of a peach." Max filmed it: alien-shaped head, scramble of limbs, black-and-white staticky pulse. Steph had watched it over and over, Max's breath heavy in the foreground, his joyful, tearful joke: "Looks like she's trying to escape!"

A SCREEN DOOR SLAMMED, FOLLOWED BY A KERFUFFLE of cans. Max shouted. A panicked grunt. Steph immediately thought heart-attack. She dropped the X-acto, the tape, and listened. This time Max's clearer "Hey!" and the emergency she'd imagined slid down the scale: mild burn, sliced finger, small kitchen fire. Enough of a jolt for her to run downstairs into a miasma of melted plastic and cooked egg.

"Max?"

He spun around, his marathon-lean body crossing the kitchen. He bumped into the handle of the stainless fry pan, set directly on the laminate counter, then brushed by Steph, and cut through the living room to the front door. He opened the screen. Looked right and left and right again. Stepped back in.

Veins in his neck filled and bulged. "A fucking guy," he said, each syllable huffy and contained. "In the kitchen."

Steph surveyed their open-concept house for things turned over or out of place. The couch still orderly beneath the wide window, the four recent issues of *Outside* fanned across the coffee table. Even the gerberas in the vase hadn't lost a petal. What had he taken? What had he done? This intruder. Her chest tightened; her breath went gaspy. She grabbed the inhaler from her pocket, took two strong puffs and waited for her lungs to settle. "Did he have a weapon?" she asked. Max, incredulous, shook his head.

She stepped over a narrow puddle of water, headed to the Paris jar by the front door. It had its usual heft. She went to the oak chest in the dining space, opened the swollen drawer, so heavy she had to support it with one hand as she rummaged through birth and marriage certificates, bank statements, mortgage stuff, warranties, until she found what she didn't know she was looking for: passports.

"Planning a trip?" Max said.

"No," she said, nesting hers inside his. "I just thought . . ."

It sounded stupid to say identity theft. Most of that happened online, didn't it? Hackers who could decode bank numbers, run away with your money and half your life without setting foot inside your house. Still, she pressed her passport with its bleached-out photo to her chest.

Sunlight filled the room and she had to shield her eyes. "It's just," she said. "What did he want?"

Max shrugged and took the passports from her, shoving them back into the bursting drawer. Steph hurried to the kitchen and opened the top cupboards. She took a quick inventory of all her Mason jars, dried chickpeas and lentils, pasta and rice, her raspberry tea. The couscous they never ate. It didn't make sense, this impulse to check on dried goods, less sense than rummaging for passports, but she shook each jar and allowed the contents to crash against the glass. Then she walked out the front door to examine the daisies. Some white with saffron centres, the others vivid pink. They lined the path directing visitors toward the front door. Or arrowing them away again. Depending on the position of the sun.

Maybe now would be a good time to organize that oak drawer: file old bank statements, make an appointment for their upcoming mortgage renewal, buy a safety-deposit box for their passports and marriage certificate. Maybe she'd put her engagement ring in there too. An over-the-top diamond thing she hadn't worn in months, not since she'd dropped fifteen pounds drinking kale smoothies, not even after she'd put it back on with the hormones. She wore the wedding ring again, simple, unobtrusive, but cached her engagement ring in the bathroom of a makeshift dollhouse, stored on the shelf in the closet of the baby's room.

MAX CALLED FROM THE BATHROOM. CONDENSATION covered the mirror except for six lines, drawn like an I Ching ideogram with a vertical line down the centre. A message. Some hopeful offering. Or maybe an apology. On the counter, a years-old disposable razor clogged with hair and dry skin. Also, a used Q-tip, its middle bent, ends coated in pollen yellow.

"God!" Max said, pointing.

Guest towels, unused for months (years?) lay bunched under the towel rack beside a pile of soiled clothes. Max hooked a belt loop with his thumb and lifted a pair of dingy grey-brown jeans, releasing a sudden stench of ammonia and nicotine. Steph stepped back. Max dropped the pants, turned on the hot water tap full blast and lathered his hands with four pumps of soap.

"He took a fucking shower," he said, flicking his hands to dry.

The cops arrived then. An Officer Billings and another, Shand. Neither removed his boots, stepping inside with their imposing blue vests and holstered guns. Max escorted them to the kitchen peninsula, speaking quickly, his desultory nature in high gear as he explained the bike tinkering in the base-ment, then veered into a tangent about the thickness of walls, soundproofing he'd done when they'd considered adding a tenant suite. He circled his hand as though reeling himself in, and then pointed to the frying pan.

Two eggs: sunny side up. One with a broken yolk, fanning to the rim. The other, intact.

"Free range," Steph said. Billings clicked his tongue and asked what happened.

Max had done some improv when Steph first met him, and now he mimed stuffing his mouth with imaginary eggs, dropping the fork, wide-eyed, then charging the back door and disappearing long enough for the screen to bang. He reentered, glancing sidelong for approval or applause, but Shand only folded his arms as though waiting for the punchline, while Billings jotted down details. Steph imagined how the sketch would evolve at future social minglings, Max adding pinches of salt, sprigs of parsley, twists of black pepper.

"Was the front door locked?" Shand said, and stepped around Steph, over to the front screen where he jiggled the handle, opened it. Above his collar, his neck blazed red, except for a pale outline beneath recently shorn hair. He was young, not yet thirty. Good natured too, a cop out of a children's book.

"No," said Max. "Not locked." She knew he blamed her. Not that he'd say it, but thinking: *If she hadn't been painting the goddamn room . . .*

Never mind that she didn't know the screen *had* a lock. They'd never used it.

"He take anything?" Billings asked. "Jewellery? Wallets? Collectables?"

"No," Steph said.

Shand faced them again. "You're saying, perpetrator comes in. Unforced. Goes to the kitchen, helps himself to eggs. Cooks said eggs. Until you," he pointed to Max, "catch him. Then, he runs."

Billings tapped the pen against his teeth.

"Um," Max said, "actually there's more."

Billings followed him to the bathroom, Steph and Shand behind. Billings stomped onto the plush shower mat, shedding bits of grass and dirt. He pulled the shower curtain and the metal rings clattered down the rod. The four of them peered over the tub as though expecting to find a man wedged in the drain. Instead, a bar of artisan soap lay gummy and ruined beneath the faucet. Plus hundreds of wiry black hairs and thick patches of grit. Billings clicked again. Shand snapped on a pair of latex gloves, bent over, and picked through the clothes.

"He left the house naked? No towel? Or a jacket?" he said.

"Completely buck," Max said.

Steph hadn't thought about it, not even after eyeing the clothes heap. "Naked?" she said. She imagined the man streaking down the alley, though way more boyish in her mind than he probably was, stark white and hairless, scrambling past garbage and recycling bins, swiping laundry from someone's line.

Billings chuckled, squinting, and Steph knew the story would grow lewd at the station.

Shand dug into the jean pockets, removed a tarnished loonie, a cigarette butt, and a piece of twine frayed at both ends. He picked up the plaid button-up and shook it. The socks, drenched with sweat, stayed in tight balls. Each garment added another odour to the fug. The officers' exuded whiffs of cologne and fabric softener, and Steph's sinuses swelled, her eyes watered. She switched on the exhaust fan and a wonky rattle filled the room. Billings closed the curtain.

"Either of you hear anything?" His voice boomed over the fan. "Water running? Something like that?"

Max reached over Steph, turned off the fan; then, as it wound down, he leaned against the wall. He'd heard noises, sure. Running water. Footsteps across the kitchen. Thought it was Steph, even though she'd spent every moment after work upstairs painting. He'd assumed she'd come down to start dinner, but didn't check because they'd had, well, a disagreement—a *small* argument—the night before. Here Max flashed a smile at Shand who nodded and shoved the clothes into a bag, at Billings who tossed his chin forward and bit his lower lip, and at Steph, who closed her eyes and sucked on her inhaler.

MAX HAD OFFERED TO HELP WITH THE CEILING. He hadn't been wearing painting clothes, rather a new t-shirt embossed with his microbrewery logo. Didn't matter, she'd started without him, and had already finished the ceiling. Besides, she knew he didn't want to help, the whole project sidelined his positive thinking approach. On the other hand, Fern approved, thought it great that Steph wasn't *moving on*, but *moving over*. "Like me," Fern said. "It wasn't until I was ready to go on that volunteer vacation that Bailey came whooshing into the world." Never mind Steph had officially given up trying, her heart crumpled, tossed into the smallest corner of her chest.

"Why *this* colour Steph?" Max had asked. He'd brought her a cold beer, a sample of his latest IPA, set it on the stepladder, and she let it go warm and flat as she cut-in around the trim.

Last month, he'd erased the video. She'd searched both computers, old email attachments, his phone, hers, but nothing.

"You shouldn't dwell," he'd said.

So she started watching YouTube: ultrasounds at fifteen and sixteen weeks. She learned to decipher outlines of hands, feet, bums, noses. Even placentas and umbilical cords. Last week a new clip showed up. Twins, lying one atop the other, as in a bunkbed. The heavy breathing of the father. Then, *Tell us you find a heartbeat. Just one. Tell us.* The swoosh-woosh of the wand and the man's panic. *Both of them? Both of them?* The mother's blood circulated, but the babies didn't move. Steph watched the post in the middle of drafting, or over lunch. She thought often of the mother's belly, exposed and cold with gel.

When Max returned, his eyes bloodshot from the sun or the beer, he asked again, "How come this colour? I mean, it looks like a Vancouver sky, October to June."

She wiped the brush against the plastic container, her knuckles like small driftwood burls.

"You're right," she'd said, layering on more paint.

BACK IN THE LIVING ROOM WITH MAX AND THE TWO cops, Steph slid both panels of the front window wide open, breathed the warm air. In front of their house was an island of city green space. Ornamental cherry trees stood, evenly spaced, at the declivitous end. Steph noticed two boys scaling into the branches, bark loosening underfoot. A woman sat on the bench, facing the children, calling out, "Be careful, be careful." Behind her, a forty-foot cedar. Hundreds like it would have populated the street a century back, this park obviously some city-planner's concession to the forest.

Officer Billings probed Max for descriptors. "Caucasian. Mid-to-late twenties. Patchy beard. Five-nine or eleven. Hard to tell."

"Markings? Tattoos?"

"His hair . . ." Max said and wrapped his fingers around a hank of his own. Strands slipped as though freshly waxed and he seized a new batch then tugged. Next to the bulk of Billings, Max diminished. He'd always been shorter than Steph, but now his fingers appeared delicate above his scalp, even the hairy patches above his knuckles. He tugged again, standing on his toes, as though lifting himself off the floor. She thought if he pulled hard enough, he'd hang suspended from his own hand. She snorted—a giggle snort, a guffaw—so unlike her that her eardrums itched.

Billings furrowed his brow. She mouthed "Sorry," hitched her overall straps, and tittered a little more. Max glowered, stroked his hair back into its proper Max place. "It was matted," he said. "Sparkling with soap."

"Sparkling?" Billings wrote the word down, then flipped a page forward. "And you, Mrs. Edgar? Have you noticed anyone strange around the house? The neighbourhood?"

Her brain tingled. Every morning she left the house, bolted the secure, heavy lock. Then fleets of bicycles whizzed by her, their street part of the bike route. There was the neighbour who walked his Bichon Frise, cone of shame around its neck. The nanny who strolled the infant twins, one or the other always crying. She passed dozens of faces. Hundreds. Interchangeable and unremarkable. Bus drivers. More nannies. School kids with backpacks. Women and men rushing to work, ears or eyes glued to cell phones. Even the cops seemed the same cop.

The truth was, she could have seen the man who'd used her shower, who ate her eggs. She could have gazed upon his grubby clothes, his matted hair, then forgotten him seconds later. He could have stretched out on the bench across the street or tucked beneath the cedar tree. Sometimes she'd seen evidence of people living beneath it, flattened cardboard poking out, and once, a waterlogged sleeping bag. And maybe it had been his cardboard she'd seen. His sleeping bag. If she'd passed him, she hadn't noticed, the way she always absorbed herself in sidewalk cracks, or her own shoes.

"He could have been in the park across the street," she said.

"You saw him there? The man your husband described?"

"I might have," she said.

"You *might* have." Billings clicked his tongue, his pen, and then scratched something out.

THE OFFICERS LEFT. MAX OPENED HIS LAPTOP, POSTED something on Facebook. Then he went off to buy heavy duty cleaning products. "Like bleach," he said, though they'd phased out harsh cleaners years ago.

Steph locked the door behind him.

Crystal glasses on the hutch reflected the last of the sunlight, then the sun slipped away and the sky relaxed. Steph perched on the couch arm, turned toward the deserted meridian park. A squirrel dashed in figure-eights around the cherry trees, stopping to nosh a piece of trash, looped round again until something, the neighbour's dog or a cat, startled it, then it raced to the cedar, disappeared, shaking the limbs.

Billings thought drugs. People always thought drugs. And maybe the intruder had been high, incoherent and languishing under the tree as Steph passed by. Or possibly he'd studied them from under there, scrutinized their comings and goings: Max's daily return with a six-pack or growler strapped to his bike, and Steph's slow, mindless sorting of mail on the top step. Maybe he'd heard her drop her purse inside the door. Add a handful of change to the Paris jar, keys into the raku bowl. The door left open in invitation.

Or maybe early this morning a boy had walked by that tree, dressed in a pressed button-up shirt, smelling of Ivory or Irish Spring. And the man, asleep, caught a whiff above his own stench, and it stirred a claw-foot tub from some childhood memory. Songs his grandmother sang—"Darlin' Clementine" and "Lavender's Blue"—as she scrubbed his nails like baby potatoes, rubbed him briskly afterwards with line-dried towels. What if he'd smelled his fingers, all grit and nicotine, and wanted, not the cold communal rinse at the shelter, but hot restorative water? Fingers clean enough to break open an egg.

NOW PAST NINE, AND STEPH FELT FAINTLY HUNGRY; she hadn't eaten since noon.

The breadbox was open, plastic bags crammed inside, most containing just one heel. She reached into the middle for the walnut bread. Still half a loaf. She sliced a piece, dropped it into the toaster, wished the intruder had had time to spread on some apricot jam.

She noticed the eggs, the one bite missing, so unlike the forkfuls in Max's earlier reenactment. Broken eggshells scattered on the counter. She tossed and scraped everything into the compost. *The great egg heist.* Only not so great, the pan all crusty, the one they never used, especially not for eggs, so he must've clanged around getting to it. How strange neither of them heard. The walls not soundproof at all. She squirted liquid soap onto a scrubby, and thought, *Next time butter the pan, okay?* Wondered if there'd be a next time. *The serial egg thief.* Her painting muscles ached. She let hot water run as she picked half-consciously at the grey between her knuckles.

Then she remembered, cold water for eggs.

Max's cell rang from the table. Odd for him to forget it. Her toast popped and the phone went a second time, then beeped with a message. After that, the land line trilled and Steph dried her hands to answer.

"What happened?" The high-speed voice of her sister-in-law. "Guy broke in? Max Facebooked it."

When did Fern *not* revel in their struggles?

"Not exactly broke. Unlawful entry, it's called. The guy fried a couple of eggs." Steph cradled the phone, buttered her toast.

"Eggs?" Fern's voice became muffled, her hand no doubt over the receiver, passing the info to her husband. Then, "Did he take anything? Have you called the police?"

Steph didn't mention the unlocked door or the shower or Officers Billings and Shand. She bit into her toast, chewed for one thoughtful moment before Max knocked. Without saying anything, she set the phone down, heard Fern's voice call out as she walked to the door.

Max stood, weighted with Clorox and Mr. Clean, an extra bag of takeout sushi hanging from his wrist. She relieved him of it, abandoned her toast, and retreated upstairs with a California roll, tempura yam, and a pinch of pickled ginger.

THE CUMULUS WALLS GAVE OFF A PLEASANT GLOOM, especially with the dusky light outside. A sort of sensory deprivation tank. Noises, though, still rose through the floor: Max scrubbing the bathtub, Max turning on and off the water, Max exclaiming with Fern. Steph had often envied their closeness, the way he confided in her, the way they laughed as though no one else were in the room. Steph had grown up half an orphan. She'd had a mother, yes, who'd left Steph to live with Aunt Corrine, while she dug up relics in the Middle East. "Your asthma, dear," she'd tell Steph when Steph begged to go with her. Her father existed as a first name, coupled with her mother's brief description. "Serious, like you. Brown eyes." So for years, Aunt Corrine watched nature documentaries, crocheted dishcloths for craft fairs, and obligingly housed Steph, fed her cold food—carrot sticks, crackers and peanut butter, coleslaw—on little plates, never calling her to dinner, mostly leaving her alone to read and design her shoebox houses.

The houses Steph configured always had a centred front door, two long windows on either side, none in the back. Four rooms divided with walls cut from the cardboard lid. She even furnished them, placing a double-matchbox bed in the room she considered her mother's. On one visit, she toured her mother through the boxes, and her mother admired the ingenuity of a tinfoil chandelier, a cotton-ball hassock. "You'll be an architect," she'd said, and pride flickered briefly in Steph's chest. Her mother had seen her as *something*. But when she left again, this time for Peru, that something fizzled away.

MAX SLAMMED THE WASHER AND STEPH HEARD WATER percolate inside the walls. Had the intruder known they'd be oblivious to his noise? As though their house walls had been replaced with Plexiglas, like an ant farm, and he'd studied their scurrying, their long silences, their preoccupations with colour swatches and YouTube videos, Facebook and heartbreak.

Steph cleared the floor of drop cloths and newspapers and swept. As the hollow sound echoed, nostalgia wobbled through her. Once, all those years ago, with the renos finished and every box unpacked, they'd been on the brink. Of babies. Family ski trips. Birthday parties with sickly sweet icing. But no, the days just went on. Back in March, she'd celebrated ten years at the firm. Kathleen had handed her a fountain pen, the company insignia engraved on the shaft. The rest of the office staff tapped mugs, demanding a speech. None of her colleagues had known about the pregnancy and she'd been giddy, announcing it right then to a roar of congratulations.

The next day, though, as she rolled blueprints into a cardboard canister, her abdomen tightened. Then nothing. Except, not nothing. Sharp squeegee shrieks outside her window. A window washer's chair knocking into the pane. Steph stood still. Counting beats.

All the way home, she walked with slow tight steps, willing the tiny heart inside her to keep beating. Heel-toe, heel-toe, the whole offensive city rushing past. Night came. Rain too. Then Max opened their door, wrapped her in blankets, fixed her tea. She shivered and said nothing. For six days, she told herself she'd imagined things. Then the cramps knotted and knotted, and blood gushed. And the doctor with her hands, her cold instruments, said, "You'll feel a little pinch."

Steph wanted to hold it. Just that. Place it in a teacup and wrap her hands around it. *Size of a peach*. Keep it warm. One minute. Just one.

It's only tissue, the nurse had said. Clumps of tissue, which they'd sent to the basement for incineration.

MAX APPEARED IN THE DOORWAY, BACKLIT BY THE HALL light, face blue from his phone. He scrolled his finger along the screen, eyes cast down, then up, then down again.

"They caught him," he said.

She stopped her sweeping. "Who?" she said.

"The guy, Steph! The intruder!"

She reached the broom into the far corner, swept along the baseboards.

"In a dumpster," he said. "Just past King Edward." He flipped the light switch, bare bulb glaring from the ceiling.

"He made it that far?" she said. "Naked? In a dumpster?" She thought of razory can lids, broken glass, and the man's genitals mashed into rotting food.

"Serves him right."

"For what?"

"For breaking into our house, in case you've forgotten."

"He didn't break or steal anything, Max. He didn't even take change from the jar."

"Not to overstate the obvious Steph, but just where would he put it?"

Max's phone chirped with a text. "Anyway," he said, "they'll call me to identify him. In a lineup."

THE NEXT MORNING, MAX REMINDED STEPH TO LOCK all the windows, upstairs and down, before he rushed on. She wanted to call in, tell Kathleen she had to help identify the guy at the station, and then just finish the room, move things back, or place them in the alley with a "free" sign, but her dogged work ethic won out, so she dressed in linen capris and a shimmery grey blouse, combed her hair and tied it back.

Just inside the door, she gathered keys from the raku bowl, dipped her hand into the Paris jar against her own rules, then bent down for her shoes. She noticed a pair of black suede oxfords with thick creases across the bridge, toes worn, scuffed to powdery grey. Twine zigzagged through the lace holes, mended with knots. The shoes sat side by side, squeezed between Max's runners and the winter boots she'd never put away. He must've taken them off after he slipped through the door. Had he called out first? The way you do, entering someone else's house? *Anybody home?* If she'd heard him, would she have invited him in? Said, "There's plenty of hot water." Said, "I'll fix you something to eat." No, she wouldn't have said those things. She felt a pang in her chest. She'd have exclaimed, called for Max, asked him to leave.

She hooked her fingers into the back tabs, lifted the shoes and let them dangle. The sour reek from the insoles barely bothered her, the soles full of cracks and holes, both heels scraped down to nothing.

THE NEIGHBOUR'S DOG YIPPED BEHIND A BABY GATE
on the porch. The neighbour already out, pruning his cylinder
shrub. Steph crossed the street to avoid interrogations about
last night's visiting squad car. She stepped onto the meridian
park curb, over to the cherry trees. A grubby Canucks hat lay
on the ground. One of the tree-climbers must have dropped it.
She picked it up, hung it on the end of the bench. She expected
the currents of routine to draw her into the day, but the carved
graffiti on the bench stopped her, six horizontal lines, one vertical. She turned toward the cedar tree, as though she'd forgotten to lock the door or turn off a burner. She opened her purse
and jangled it. Nothing missing or forgotten.

The sun covered the cedar with fresh light. Its impressive
boughs broadened and drooped to the ground. Steph walked
to it, pinched new growth from the boughs, released the sharp
oils. A massage therapist once told her that cedar essence
cleared blocked energy. Like acupuncture or plumbing snakes.
But mostly it reminded her of saunas. Of split firewood.

She lowered herself down, nubby cones and dirt pressing
into her knees. She swept aside the low branches. No one was
there. No sleeping body, or cardboard mat. Only a sun-faded
Kit Kat wrapper, a lighter without spark wheels and several
spent cap gun cartridges. She bent farther, crawled through
the boughs until she fit all the way under.

The ceiling pressed low, flossy webs slung between spindly
brown branches, the trunk rising into a dead, cheerless centre.
Dust scratched her throat. She lay on her side, hip on the hardpacked dirt, between the lowest branches and the ground. The
frayed grass was visible, the curb, the daisies, their front steps
and the one ceramic pot with the whirligig Max bought and
stuck there.

She felt protected. Like when she'd built the platform in
her aunt's backyard chestnut. Three walls and no roof. She'd
wanted to live there, beyond Aunt Corrine's vague rules and
her own single bed, so she'd hauled up a sleeping bag and a
flashlight. All night, stars streaked across the sky. Wish after

wish. *Live with my mom. A puppy. A baby sister.* In the morning, her aunt had explained it was a meteor shower, that no wishes come true from meteors.

Now she listened to the neighbour whistle tunelessly, water from his hose spraying the walk. Then a herd of soft-soled pattering, the breathless conversation and collective laughter of women.

Steph had never had friends like that. A little in Kathleen. Lunch time strolls along the seawall. And in Fern, but only by the default of marriage. Then Max, of course, the optimist. When they'd decided to marry, she warned him, "I don't have your luck." *Or any luck at all.* At twenty-five, he'd won twenty-thousand dollars from a scratch 'n win. At thirty-one, he'd landed his dream job as brewmaster for a microbrewery. As he'd said, he had enough luck for both of them. Never mind his dad's heart attack at their wedding as they knifed the cake, or the carpenter ants that perforated the back deck after they'd finished the reno. Because even those things brought charm. His father transformed his life and health, and the infestation delivered the exterminator, an old high-school friend, to the door. "Can you believe it, Steph? Freddie Page!" Every disappointment generally followed by something better. Okay, so they didn't have *this* baby. *He* could move on. Why couldn't she?

They could adopt. Max had said that, people always said that. So many unwanted children in the world. As she had been. And likely the intruder.

The shade retreated beneath the tree, and sunlight blanched the grass at its edges. She saw the letter carrier's hurried feet, heard the brassy bang of her mailbox. Idly Steph broke a twiggy branch off the trunk, snapped it into even pieces, set the sprigs in a log-cabin square. Another four on top of that. Uneven corners, a bare, dirt floor, and still she wanted to shrink, fit her body into the small space, into all the small spaces. Instead she shredded the candy wrapper, crimped the strips to form a cushion. Placed it into the square. Then she sourced out more branches and tore them from the tree. Dust showered down. Her breath grew thin. Despite it all, she kept on. Building the walls higher, and higher still.

NEEDS

WE EMERGE FROM UNDER A STONE ARCH. Hungry and needing to pee, we've stopped in the Old City for relief and lunch. Three tour buses line the street. Two hundred nuns. *Les bonnes soeurs.* I dart through them like a minnow, but you are encumbered by that too-small stroller, your tall frame curved over it like a question mark. A litany of chattering sisters want to pinch the flesh of our baby. *Beau bébé!* They exclaim. They didn't see you last night, drunk with your bobbing erection saying: Forget the crying. You don't know how horny.

You may as well have said: A man has needs. And I could have cinched an apron around my waist, popped back the Valium, opened my legs. You may as well have said that, but you didn't; you disappeared into the bathroom, leaving me with weeping breasts to reach for the baby.

THE BOOKS TALK ABOUT SLEEP DEPRIVATION. SOME SAY a woman's libido might go underground. Some even say the man has needs. Not like that, of course, not like they used to, but like a warning, a red flag on the horizon. They don't say anything about the porn that will turn up on the computer or how a mother's body becomes utilitarian, something to drag around, satisfying everyone else's basic needs.

The pregnancy was bound in love and amazement. You rubbing my belly like Aladdin's lamp, whispering wishes into my womb. And then, the baby, born half-bruised from the pushing, blood vessels in his fresh eyes, broken. The pitch of his cry tilted some balance.

WE TRUDGE THROUGH CROWDS, TOURISTS ARMED with camera phones and shopping bags. This is a two-hour stop for us—between the Gaspé and your mother's house in the Townships. It's hot. This eastern summer swells my fingers, my brain, every one of my nerves. Our coastal home nudges up against temperate rain forest. We know mist and rain, and a summer heat. And, though I long for the hushed winter snows they have here, I cannot abide this humidity. It hangs like a thick net. All of us caught like lobsters. Crustacean claws climbing over each other, shells beginning to redden.

Where do we go? I ask. You point to a sign that says: *Vieille Ville*.

Follow the cobbled brick road, you say.

We cascade in a massive tourist flow. Down cobbled steps where the antiquated architecture is filled with Roots and ice cream and *fleurs-de-lis* and maple sugar. I reach into the diaper bag, slung over my shoulder. A sippy cup of water for the baby. He can't hold it himself, so I make you stop. People jostle past us speaking a dozen different languages. A Korean couple gestures a phone at us then points to the baby.

He's got to stay hydrated, I say.

I know, I know. And you click your tongue, nodding at the Koreans. They snatch a portrait or two and then wave their hands. *Merci*. Thank you. *Merci*.

Magané. Hungover. Literal translation: mangled. A new

word for me and I imagine twisted metal. Chrome. We have gone to your friends in the Gaspé, up the long thumb of this province, to show off the baby. Last night, you left me in the kitchen with the girlfriends and wives while you drank beer and scotch on the front porch. I used up all the words I knew with those women, and our conversation evaporated into a repetitive stream of c'est ça and bon and oui oui.

THERE'S A PATISSERIE WITH TABLES OUTSIDE. WE ORDER croissants—ham and cheese, spinach and cheese, cheese and cheese—and eat them in humid silence around a wobbly table. The baby nurses at my breast.

A woman walks by. Tight skirt and heels that click into the worn grooves of the brick. She holds a phone in front of her face, watching the screen. You smile at her and she catches you in her frame—she must because she smiles.

Slow spread of poison.

IT'S NOT LIKE WE HAVEN'T HAD SEX. EVERY ONCE IN A while, I relent. Give in because I've read articles that say: sex keeps the spark in a relationship. And if I don't, you'll go somewhere else. I didn't used to withdraw from sex. Ever. I didn't used to hold back. No, I pounced and clawed, always ready. None of that remains. My breasts touched a hundred times a day, always pumping out nourishment, sustenance, a means to pacify.

Six weeks after the baby. That's how long they say to wait. Until the woman's body heals from the birth. You timed it to the day, the hour, and reached for my breasts, marvelled by their fullness. These are ripe, you said, jiggling the right one before leaning down to lick the left.

I pushed your head back and started crying. It's the last thing.

You stood straight, kissed my hair. Okay. Maybe tomorrow. And I keep wishing the books would say it takes one year.

THE BABY'S HEAD LOLLS OFF MY BREAST, NIPPLE hanging just above his mouth, face glazed with milk and sweat. My shoulders ache from his weight in my arms. I lean into the cast iron chair back. You've gone in for iced tea, so you don't see her. The woman in the skirt passes by again, this time her phone tucked into her purse. She turns toward me and flips a screen of dark hair from her face. It shines like onyx.

She has you on her phone. Our whole family beneath this colourful awning. You with your sunglasses, your prize-winning smile. Me, with a halo of humid frizz, the haggard look of someone who never sleeps. I wonder if she'll download that photo to her laptop, enlarge you and wonder what you are doing with someone like me.

Why did you leave *your* culture? *Your* language? *Your* people? Why did you stop on the Trans-Canada that day? Why did you call and say: should we move in together? And why, before I could even think, did my heart leap out of my mouth screaming Yes! Yes!?

YEARS AGO, I LEARNED YOUR LANGUAGE IN STILTED, halting phrases. *Comment ça va? Ça va bien, merci!* Your mother says English is good for instruction manuals. But French is for love. Maybe I'm too much A into B and not enough blood on the page. I would never die for love. People ask that sometimes. They expect it. Once, after a fight, you even asked if I'd die for you. Because you claimed you'd die for me. I kept imagining you pitching your body in front of a bus. I might do that for the baby. Okay, if it came to it, I would die for him.

WE COULD GO ON A WALKING TOUR, YOU SAY, HALF-grinning. See the fort.

We've gone on walking tours of your old haunts, pushed the stroller all over your hometown. You've pointed to houses and mentioned parties, lists of lovers, details that make up the old parts of you. We ran into that woman with two-year-old twins outside the *dépanneur*. When she left in her minivan, you said, I went down on her in the shower once. Long before kids, and she had no breasts. Nothing. No softness there. Only a washboard of ribs.

You stated this as an interesting fact, something to ponder like the shape of someone's jaw or the colour of their eyes.

He's asleep. I nod my head toward the baby. Let's let him sleep for a little while.

You stay here then. I'm going to walk around.

You won't wait?

I'll come back. You flick your wrist. Ten minutes. I just need to move around.

Why can't you wait?

You lean over to kiss my forehead, to kiss the baby. Ten minutes. Then you disappear down the street where the woman with the onyx hair passed through.

Your mother said after you were born, she left you at the nursery for a week because your father suggested it. He thought it would be good for me, she said. To get my energy back. She shook her head. *Mon dieu*, can you believe that? I agreed to it.

All that week she spent her days at the nursery, breasts bound with tape. Nurses fed you and changed your diaper. At five o'clock they sent her home to make supper for your father. When finally he went to sleep, she cried.

All I wanted to do was hold my baby, she told me. All I wanted was to bring him home.

FIFTEEN MINUTES GO BY. THEN TWENTY. THE BABY'S HEAD presses into my arm. People pour in and out of doors. Buying things. Exclaiming. I wonder if you've navigated through the crowds, hard as a compass needle. I wonder if you're fucking her against the ramparts of an old fort.

I want everyone to disappear. For seasons to shift. The desolation of winter. Bitter cold.

I want to be alone on these streets, two hundred, four hundred years ago. For a door to open, a wise woman to pull me through. I want her to offer me elixirs for my blood, for my heart. Then a well-worn map, or a key, something, anything, to guide me along these perilous ridges without pushing you away.

I draw an ice cube out of your glass, hold it against my cheek. Drops of water splash onto the baby's arm. He stirs. And nuzzles closer in.

DESTINATION
SCAVENGERS

MAN, LEON HATED RILEY RIGHT NOW. FOR THREE weeks in a row Riley had ditched him. Flat out ignored phone calls and messages. And now, finally back on track, ready to roll, he'd invited his girlfriend to join in on their road trip. So here they were, practically midnight and up at her place near Dunbar, completely off track. She lived in one of those student rentals like the one he'd shared with Riley years ago, but instead of beer bottles and crusty dishes, squashed paint tubes and reams of paper, bits of shell and bark, driftwood and moss crowded this kitchen. Plus two clothesline cords strung between walls, paper pegged to them, kindergarten-style. Then this girlfriend on the floor, oblivious to Leon and even to Riley, bent over some old wooden cable spool, masked and gloved like a surgeon, doing arts and fucking crafts.

Her name dissolved before it reached Leon's brain. Disintegrated as Riley said it. Solvent fumes went straight for him though: instant headache behind his left eye.

A metal band girdled the spool and contained a pool of varnish. The girlfriend plucked an iridescent shell from a nearby pile and poked it into the pool. It submerged reluctantly, like a creature swallowed by quicksand. Leon's headache sharpened. The heaps of stones and shells beside her seemed infinite. They'd never get out of there.

Riley crossed over to her, rocked back and forth on his heels, nodded down at her masterpiece like some great appraiser and appreciator of art. "I saw the Mona Lisa in grade twelve," he said. "And the Sistine Chapel." The girlfriend grabbed another shell. "Anyway," Riley said. "You got a pack or a suitcase? We should go."

She mumbled something behind her mask and Riley spun around, disappeared down an unlit hallway.

Leon didn't attempt small talk. Instead buried his face in his collar, breathed in the cotton and his own ripe musk. His headache wouldn't simmer down, so he paced the clothesline gallery, watery landscapes and whorlly abstracts a smear in his periphery. Maybe he should bail. Slip out the door and walk back home across the freaking city. Forget about Riley. The girlfriend. The road.

"You can open a window," the girlfriend said. Leon dropped his face cover, ducked under the clothesline.

She slid the mask onto her head and smiled. Really, she looked nothing like he'd imagined. A couple months ago when Riley started bragging about this art student who gave him blow jobs every five minutes, Leon had visualized the milk-ad model, an unforgettable crush he'd had years back: a blond with a spritely face and a full suckable mouth. But this girl struck Leon as squirrelly, her slight, angular face and dark, receding eyes. And her hair. Brown at the top then switched over at eye-level to black.

She winked at him, repositioned her mask and examined her work.

Leon saw it more clearly now. A purple starfish in the centre, shells and stones spiralling outward, like a pinwheel, from each arm. She sighed and poked in a stone. "It's supposed to be a galaxy," she said, her voice raspy and dreamy. "But I don't know. Maybe it's more tidal pool." Leon said he could see it, sure. Very cosmic. Tidal cosmic. She laughed and said, "My mom made a table like this once. With coins. The Money Table."

She circled finger and thumb around one eye. "My favourite was the Chinese coin with the square hole in the middle." She looked at him a minute more, and he felt his shabbiness surface, his frayed sweatshirt cuffs, the rip along his collar. The two days he hadn't shaved, showered even, that stupid archipelago of acne above his eyebrow. And he worried she could see deeper beneath, to a more enduring flaw. He stepped back, stumbled into one of the clotheslines, loosened a clothespin, which sproinged and soared upward, dropped into a sink full of water.

"Nice shot," she said. And his headache throbbed full force.

Just then Riley reappeared, hooked his fingers over the door jamb, released his knees. He hung so his smiley-face boxers showed, and the bottom of his paunch. He'd been a skinny teenaged kid. Same as Leon. But at twenty-five, their high-speed metabolisms were failing them. Too much beer and road food. Leon had vowed to switch-up fruit for chips. A promise he'd already broken. He'd also started and stopped a regime of push-ups, sit-ups, jogging on the spot, at least a dozen times.

Riley let go of the door frame. "Don't you have a bag packed?" he asked again.

The girlfriend sank one more stone. Stood and peeled off her gloves, her mask. "Remind me where we're going?"

Riley rolled his eyes upward and Leon followed his gaze to a water stain near the light fixture. He studied the russet blotch, wondering what Riley would say and why the hell Riley had invited her in the first place. The only time a girlfriend had tagged along on one of their trips, a couple years ago, she'd fallen asleep before they left Vancouver and woke up way north, farther than she'd ever been or expected. She'd thrown a total conniption, demanding Riley find the nearest airport, some strip in a field, and fly her home. Instead he'd dropped her at a bus station north of Quesnel and gave her fifty crumpled bucks, a half-eaten bag of Doritos, and a promise that he'd call in a couple of days. Neither of them mentioned her again.

"Banff," Riley said. "Check out the Rockies. You know. The buffalo."

"Cool," the girlfriend said, opening the fridge, removing a thermos. "I'll grab my camera." She handed the thermos to Leon and ambled, unhurried, down the hall.

"Bastard," Leon said. "You said she'd be ready."

Riley snickered and Leon shoved the thermos into his chest. Riley grabbed it and yelled for his girlfriend to pack a pillow. A blanket too. By the time they got anywhere, it would be morning.

LEON RODE SHOTGUN. HE ALWAYS RODE SHOTGUN, the seat custom-fitted to his ass. So he didn't offer it to the girlfriend and neither did Riley. She sat in the back like a hitchhiker and leaned forward, wedging her shoulders between the two front seats. "I brought some CDs," she said. "The new Bjork. Some Cranberries."

"Let's leave the radio on for now," Riley said, turning it low. "Could be a road closure we should know about. An accident."

Riley had never cared about road closures. Even now, in the middle of November, the potential for rockslides or freak storms on the upswing, Riley didn't care. No, he just needed those late-night radio voices because they were part of it. Like the pre-rolled joints in the soapbox under Leon's seat. The extra stash in the trunk. Like the warm beer, the sleepless nights, the random destinations. Protocols they'd established years back. Leon pulled his seat belt into place, appreciated the sure sound of the click. Riley wasn't going to change things too much for this girl. Bad enough that because of her Leon had spent the past three weekends on his couch drinking cheap booze, playing rounds of solitaire with a worn-out deck, listening to the upstairs neighbours alternately fight and fuck.

Now, well after midnight, the streets were dark and quiet, except for the rattly growl of Riley's Pontiac Sunbird. He'd had the muffler fixed after their trip up the Hurly over a month ago, a switchbacky logging road that almost annihilated the undercarriage. Still the car quirked with noise. A buzz here, a clunk there. The odometer had exhausted itself after two times around and no longer tracked the mileage. Riley had inherited the car from his city-driving mom, had since replaced the brakes, the spark plugs, the battery a couple of times, but ignored the loose steering, saying it added character, and the upholstery shredded to shit.

"Well," the girlfriend said, "Banff'll be cool."

"Yeah," Riley said, glancing into the rear-view. Eyes darting from road to mirror and back again.

"My cousin worked at that big hotel in Banff," the girlfriend said. "I wonder if she still does. I'll look her up. Maybe we can stay tomorrow night."

Leon wanted to mention that they probably wouldn't get there. Or, if they did, they'd fuel up, grab a coffee, and maybe, *maybe,* stop at a diner. Some greasy spoon away from the tourists, from people really, where Riley could order his two eggs over-easy and Leon could choose between the western omelet and the waffles with bacon. Only after breakfast, depending on Riley's exact chemistry, would they circle a few main attractions, including the buffalo.

That's how they'd done it for the past two years. Riley picking Leon up on a Friday, asking, "Where to?" The farther, the better. Only the moving mattered, landscapes slipping past their windows like film strips. They played a destination scavenger hunt, ticking towns off a list they kept in the glove box: Likely, Oosoyos, Kaslo, Drumheller, Edmonton, Terrace, Smithers. Once they'd nosed up against the Alaskan panhandle, twice to the Yukon border. On their last trip, they'd followed the Fraser Canyon on a quest for the river's head-waters. Riley's idea. But because of a forty kilometre bush-whack, they never reached it, though they agreed they'd watched it fountain from the ground and flow out.

They agreed on other things too. Like how their lives stuck it to convention. How they'd never end up all nine-to-five, mortgages, and corporate ambition. Even if, with a little plead-ing, maybe a lot, Leon could return to law school. And Riley, whose dad offered him an entry level job at his plastics firm, whose parents built him a suite over their garage, who lived off an allowance, had been talking alternatives. Easy money. An indoor grow-show with premium bud. Riley had connections and promised to cash his bonds, his stocks, and fund the oper-ation. They'd rent a bungalow near Clark, foil the windows, fill the basement with lights and super skunky plants.

Leon heard a lid unscrew. Caught a whiff of boozy grape. The girlfriend swigged then extended the thermos forward. "Purple Jesus?" she said. Riley said no thanks, he'd rather a beer. Leon fished one out, handed it over, and then twisted toward the girlfriend for the thermos.

"Crap!" she said. "Why can't I remember the name?"

"Remember what?" Riley said.

"That hotel."

Leon gulped the Purple Jesus. It rushed sweet over his tongue, burned his throat. God, the fake grape tasted terrible.

THEY LEFT VANCOUVER AND ROLLED THROUGH Burnaby and eventually onto the highway. Riley accelerated and the Sunbird vibrated violently until it reached its sweet spot, the speed Riley called the cruising altitude. None of them spoke but Leon felt an energy in the car. Ions, electrons, pin-balling through the air, pinging him in the back of his head, his neck. It was the girlfriend. Her expectation that they'd reach Banff by dawn. See her cousin, the hotel, the buffalo. He hadn't said anything about not getting there, wouldn't say. He pulled up his hoodie, tugged the ties and focused on the news. A report about a suicide bombing. About a safe injection site.

Residual pain lingered behind his eye. He pressed his forehead to the cool glass to soothe it. Instead images flared and flickered: the junkie on his street corner, the change he put into her hand. His dad's bluing face, slow-mo and on repeat, all these past months. Those useless punches Leon had thrown at his father's chest. Other things too. His shit apartment, black mould in the shower, around the windows, along the baseboards, behind his bed. The miserable want-ads he coloured in with a ballpoint. And his mom's messages into his machine, "I know you're busy . . ." and the fact he wasn't busy, hadn't been busy all year, squandering away his student loans, his small inheritance, on anything but the law his mom believed he studied.

When they reached Chilliwack, static cut in and Riley searched out the same station on another bandwidth.

"Hey man," he said, "spark one up."

And the girlfriend chimed in: "Yeah. Spark one."

THE ROAD WENT STRAIGHT THROUGH THE VALLEY, past farmland and strip malls, then it curved at the foothills, eastbound lanes cleaved from the west by a scrubby meridian. There must've been a moon, gibbous or half, because the blackish-grey clouds towered and peaked, and the mountains appeared darker against them. Soft rain flecked the glass and the car shook and hummed as Riley lost and recovered their cruising altitude. Leon eased into the frayed upholstery and forgave Riley everything. They'd smoked that joint, and now it was no big deal about the girlfriend, no big deal about the weeks of silence, the procrastination on their grow-show plan.

They approached the sign for Bridal Falls and Leon searched the darkness for the narrow chute. He couldn't see it but had passed it a million times, knew it bubbled there, like champagne against the sheer black rock.

"Let's play Truth or Dare," the girlfriend said, raspy and sudden from the back.

The puzzling line in her hair flashed through Leon's mind. Brown turned to black. And then the starfish embedded in the cable spool. Entombed. "What?" he said.

"Didn't you play as a kid?" She leaned forward again and he could smell her, varnish and vodka, and something stringent, salty, beneath.

"What kind of dares can you do in a car?" Riley said.

"Truth then," the girlfriend said.

Riley turned off the radio, and hissed through his teeth, an unsettling half-laugh that Leon always considered part snake. "Truth?" he said. "Okay. Okay. Got one. But it's about Leon."

For a moment, half a beat maybe, Leon thought he might learn something new about himself. Then Riley chucked him on the shoulder and a familiar irritation rose up. "My buddy Leon here," Riley said. "Was born with an excessive number of fingers."

An old party trick, one Riley had marched out over and over back in the day.

The girlfriend giggled. "No way," she said. "How many?"

And Riley blinked out twelve in the dashboard glow.

"Twelve?" the girlfriend said. "Let's see."

Riley elbowed Leon and the car jerked. "Show her man," he said. Act two: the part where Riley tapped out a quasi drumroll and Leon released his hands and wiggled all ten of his unspectacular digits. The girlfriend reached for Leon's left wrist and tugged, twisting his arms so he had to turn. Then she lightened her grip, traced the contour of his fingers, palpating until she found the nubby scar tissue below his pinkie.

"There?" she said. "What happened?"

Leon recounted the story the way his dad used to tell it, and it spooked him a little, hearing his dad's voice in his own as he started describing the cigar-filled waiting room, the echoy walk into delivery where the nurse presented a blue bundled baby. "And what do you do with new babies?" his dad would ask, and Leon asked now.

"Count fingers and toes," the girlfriend whispered.

Leon's dad had always coddled an imaginary infant at this point, counting one, two, three . . . twelve! Leon skipped it, instead held up two fingers like a pair of scissors. "An extra on each hand," he said.

"And then?" the girlfriend said.

"My dad sliced them with a straight-blade."

The girlfriend let go of him. Riley sputtered out a full-blown laugh and slapped the dash. "Good one!" he said. As though he hadn't heard it a hundred effing times. Leon turned toward the girlfriend. She blended into the dark and he spoke toward her, searching for her face, wishing she'd move forward again, wishing he could remember her name. "I'm kidding," he said. "They removed them. Surgically."

"But why?"

He'd asked that same question when he was little. Why? And where were they now? And were they lonely?

"Are you kidding?" Riley said. "Do you know *anyone* with twelve fingers?"

Riley had always revelled in Leon's oddity, saying it was total freak show material, total Ripley's Believe It or Not. He didn't know that Leon had felt the scars throb on and off for years. Or that he'd traced his hands on construction paper or cardboard—how many times? Reaching the pinkie, shifting it, tracing it again. And the stories he'd built up, starring himself as Twelve-Fingered Man, his fingers not gone but retractable, and if he clenched his fists tight enough, said the right word, they'd sprout from his scars. The powers varied: antennae twitches to locate bad guy lairs, high-powered strength to sock it to said bad guys. Other times an extend-ability to pluck cats from trees, babies from water, shit like that.

The girlfriend scooted forward again. She placed his hand over top hers, stretched her baby finger from his scar and wriggled it. "I'd like to cast your hands," she said. "With those extra fingers."

Riley crunched his beer can, tossed it into the back. "Can I have that Purple Jesus now?" he said.

She didn't move and Leon felt the heat of her hand, its small size and intelligence. "Maybe metal," she said. "There's a forge at school." And Leon imagined his hands dipped in gold or bronze, hers working around them, moulding, restructuring, resurrecting.

"Hey? That drink?" Riley said.

And her hand fell away.

THEY STOPPED AT A GAS STATION IN HOPE. WHILE RILEY topped the tank, the girlfriend hurried to the washroom and Leon, munchies coming on, perused the store. He had a scrunched-up ten in his jeans, a bit of change, and nothing else. Riley would spot him whatever he needed, he always did, but Leon already owed him over a couple hundred bucks.

The dry-roasted peanuts and cashews were out of the clerk's sightline, so Leon fumbled, faked a drop, and slipped a couple packets into his pocket. He stopped at the pyramid of oil and mimed out a show of 10-40? Or 10-30? Then continued on to the beverage coolers, grabbed a Coke, returned it.

The girlfriend reappeared, the black half of her hair hanging forward like quotation marks alongside her cheeks. She winked at him, grabbed a bag of Miss Vickie's then stood by a postcard carousel and spun it. Swamped in over-sized jeans and plaid shirt, she couldn't have weighed more than a hundred pounds. Leon wanted to lift her up just to prove it.

"Always the same thing," she said. "Grizzlies. Wildflower meadows. Freakin' mountain goats." She waved a postcard in his direction. "Hey Leon! You ever, in all your Beautiful B.C. Living, see a mountain goat?"

Both she and the clerk stared at Leon and Leon felt the weight of the packets in his pocket. He picked up a Coffee Crisp and paid for it. The girlfriend joined him at the till with her chips and the mountain goat postcard. She nudged him. "Have you?" And he wished he could say he had, at least once. Hiking in the high alpine or from a distance. But no.

"WHO'S THAT FOR?" RILEY SAID.

The girlfriend scribbled on the postcard, using the front console and the weak gas station light. "I collect them," she said. Leon strained to decipher her writing, hoping she'd sign her name, but she clutched tight around the pen, her scratch marks furious and fast.

Riley cranked the key. "Coquihalla or Crowsnest?" he said.

"What?" She looked up, fanned herself with the postcard.

"Let's go Crow," Leon said. Not that it mattered, but he preferred the low road.

"What're you guys talking about?"

"The way," Riley said.

"Can I check out a map?" The postcard disappeared and she opened a bag of chips releasing a salt and vinegar bloom.

"No maps," Riley said. He pointed to a sign out by the road, with a crow's silhouette. "I don't even need the signs. It's all imprinted on my psyche. Like a homing instinct."

To call it instinct seemed a stretch. Riley had a photographic memory. Remembered side roads and alternate routes, even logging roads Leon had long forgotten about. His parents considered him a Mensa genius for all the A's he'd received in school. Mostly he'd used his talents to recite movie monologues and, lately, to elaborate on conspiracy theories, especially regarding reptilian shapeshifters and alien invasions. Now he told the girlfriend how the topography carved into his brain. How canyons, mountains, rivers, called to him in distinct voices.

"Voices?" the girlfriend said. She thrust the chips forward and Riley shoved a hand in, then nodded into the rear-view, excited. "More like a magnetic force," he said. "Like spawning salmon."

The girlfriend laughed, choked a little. Then slouched back into the dark and Riley turned onto Highway 3. "Salmon?" she said. "Salmon?!"

Leon dumped a pile of cashews into his palm, moved them like puzzle pieces. At Riley's mention of voices, his stomach hollowed out, his throat too. If it was just the two of them, he wouldn't have thought of it, just chalked it up to regular Riley logic. But now that Riley'd told the girlfriend, Leon remembered when he and Riley stopped at a rest area, end of August, somewhere in the lake district up north. They'd pulled off, smoked a fatty of strong bud, laced for sure, because they were high, too high, even for Riley, to drive. They'd sat on a small beach, tossed stones into the lake, sky colours, pinks and purples, rippling endlessly out. Then a flock of starlings flew overhead. Reflected black in the water as a cacophonous mass. They landed, hundreds of them, in trees near the outhouses. Riley tiptoed toward a picnic table, climbed on top and raised his arms.

The birds squawked and nattered, dropped to the ground and pecked it. Riley stomped his foot, lifted his arms higher, swung them wide. Eventually the birds rose into the sky, swarmed and circled, then flew away.

Riley had jumped off the table, grinning. "That was me, man," he'd said. "I keep doing that. Calling birds from the sky." He tapped his temple, nodded, agreeing with himself. "Don't be surprised," he'd said, "if I'm the next messiah."

Had he said that? The messiah? Leon tried to concentrate on remembering Riley's exact words. Before, he'd written the incident off and blamed it on that crazy-ass bud. But now that Riley was talking about voices, those birds replayed in his mind. Messiah? Really? Riley never mentioned God, or any Second Coming. But maybe he believed, truly believed, that his thoughts could bend and alter the world. That he could orchestrate flocks of birds from the sky, trust ridges and knolls to point him toward the future. Leon placed a single cashew in his mouth and sucked off the salt. For the first time he wondered how much longer he'd follow Riley and the open-road fantasy.

THE ROADS WERE DRY HEADING EAST AND A RACCOON appeared in front of the Sunbird, its humped back, its silver-blue eyes caught in the lights. Leon thought Riley would dodge it, swerve, but the passenger wheels thumped, first the front then the back.

"What the fuck?" the girlfriend said. "Did you hit something?"

Riley punched the radio back on and the car filled with static. The girlfriend reached forward, turned it off. "You hit something," she said.

"Not hard," Riley said.

"Not hard? It went under the tires."

"No," Riley said. "It got to the side."

"To the side? With its guts squished out?" she said. "God Riley. You killed it."

Riley slowed and clicked on the high beams. "Listen. I didn't." He swatted Leon. "Did I, man?"

But the animal had gone under, almost certainly dead or would be soon. Leon imagined innards stuck in the tire treads, fur clinging to the fender.

"You felt it," the girlfriend said to Leon. "You must have."

Leon said he had, pretty sure, and Riley shook his head, almost pityingly. "No, you guys," he said. "I didn't."

"Prove it then," the girlfriend said. "Turn the fucking car around and prove it."

The highway was now two lanes and Riley pulled a u-turn and drove back about twenty kilometres and turned again. He slowed and they all peered out the windshield, the girlfriend kneeling on the console, bracing herself against the dash. Nothing. No gory lump on the pavement. No dying animal on the shoulder. Leon half-wondered if later they'd find it under the wheel well, or if, as Riley believed, it had really survived and darted into the bush.

Headlights approached from the distance. Riley adjusted his beams to low, asked, "Everyone satisfied? I'd like to speed up again."

The girlfriend retreated off her perch. Leon heard a metal scrape. "You hit that thing, Riley. You did. You're just fucking lucky."

LEON HAD ONCE DISAPPEARED ALONG THIS SAME stretch of road. Not thin-air vanished like the raccoon. But a year ago, almost exactly, when for once Riley had relinquished the wheel, climbed into the back and actually slept, a green glow arched over the trees. Nothing at first, but then it brightened and Leon pulled over. Light undulated and spiralled across the sky like lasers at a stadium rock show. He left Riley sleeping. Slipped out of the car and stretched over the warm hood. The engine ticked and cooled, and after that, total silence. Not a single car passed and those lights danced and danced, time dissolving. Later, he decided he'd felt like Major Tom from that Bowie song. Major fucking Tom when his spaceship drifts away and he's left alone, floating like a tin can. For days after, he felt the charge. As if the strange aurora beauty had been injected into his veins, running green and alive through his body. He quit law school, just stopped going. He wanted to live, really live. Then, two weeks later, he showed up one Sunday ready to announce it to his parents, and instead his dad dropped dead at the dinner table.

Now he felt restless for that dazzling light show, wished he could show it to the girlfriend, conjure it for her. She'd love it, might render it with moss or seaweed on some future canvas. He screwed his eyes tight and tried to summon it. After all, maybe Riley was onto something, commanding nature, maybe Leon had it all wrong, investing too much in his own limitations, the limitations of the world. But when he opened his eyes, those grey clouds were still clamped across the dark sky.

RILEY TUNED IN TO A CONSPIRACY CALL-IN SHOW. Tonight: the Illuminati. A familiar, tiresome theme. Theorists posited that certain world leaders and movie stars carried bloodlines of an old French king. Somehow, sometimes, they were also reptiles, colluding to rule the world. Riley had extrapolated it for Leon many times. And Leon tried to reason him out of it, saying life was too random, too unpredictable for anyone to organize power over everything.

"God!" The girlfriend practically shouted, and Leon imagined her pulling her hair. "Can't we listen to some music?"

Riley fished out one of his three CDs from the console, stuck it in the player. It started mellow with "Helplessly Hoping" and ended mellow with Bob Dylan. Years ago, Leon had tried to incorporate reggae and blues into Riley's repertoire, but Riley allegedly lost those discs and now kept playing the same folksy, singsongy fare.

Mid-harmony the music stopped. "Not this shit." The girlfriend reached to remove the CD. "That decade is so over."

Riley grabbed her wrist. "Leave it okay," he said. "I like that decade."

She jerked her arm up, down, and then stilled it. "Let go of me, Riley."

He let go, pushed the CD back in.

"I wanted Bjork at least," she said. "Fuck Riley. First the raccoon . . . Why'd you promise me fun?"

"Never mind," he said. "We'll listen."

"What?"

"Put on yours." He ejected his CD, fumbled with the case.

"No," she whispered. "Fuck you."

THE RADIO STAYED OFF AND RILEY WHISTLED A SOFT, upbeat tune meant, Leon supposed, to transform the silence into something innocuous, curative even. More likely Riley had believed they'd come to an agreement. About the music. About the raccoon. Leon stayed close to the window, fogging it with his breath, and wondered how the girlfriend had ended up with Riley. Probably they'd gotten high, giggled, and Riley praised her art. Who knew? Riley had a mystical, infuriating way with women. A seduction artist, Leon had once regrettably called him. But true. He charmed them with their need to believe that matching Tragically Hip t-shirts signaled cosmic unity, or that shared dreams of rising water revealed messages from the psyche, or that praising some twisted metal at an art show exhibited sensitivity, wit, and genius.

He'd done that with Leon. Back in grade ten, when Leon was a geeky, solitary kid who'd read a lot of books, including Auden and Whitman, and Riley approached him on the bleachers during lunch hour. Pretty soon Leon spilled the story about his missing fingers, Riley whooping and laughing and dragging Leon into his large circle of friends. Their little routine began right then. For the first dozen times, maybe more, Leon felt that, because of Riley, he possessed a new and fluent currency.

Now he was a sidekick. Hitched to Riley in this odd parody of adventure. Driving from place to place, caching town names and land formations into the deep folds of his brain.

"What's it called?" The girlfriend's voice slid along the passenger door in a silky slur. Leon felt the boozy heat of her breath. He tried to look at her through the hole in the headrest, only saw a pale cheek reflected blue, hair looped behind her ear. She snaked her arm around the seat, groped for his hand which he gave her, circled his scar. "What's it called when you have too many fingers?"

He said the word, *polydactyly*, twice, hadn't said it in a while and now it sounded like a flying dinosaur.

"Ah," she said. "Hemingway cats." Leon hadn't read much Hemingway, except for the story with the fish. "We had one. A Hemingway cat. Mittens, we called him. A cat with too many claws."

Leon flattened himself against the seat to listen. Decided her name must be short, perfunctory: Mel, Jo, Sam. "Anyway, he shredded the couch and curtains, and my dear mother banished him," she said. "For days, I cried. Bawled! But my mom refused to reinstate him. So I went out."

"You went out?"

"On the front porch with my comforter and pillow."

Leon imagined her as a girl, two-toned hair and intense narrow eyes. "Did you sleep out there?"

"My mom scooped me inside after I'd fallen asleep. In the morning, she got Mittens declawed." She sighed, squeezed his hand. "But I cried over the stubs where they cut off his bone tips."

Leon's heart wouldn't stop beating. Then Riley hissed and guffawed. "Mittens!" he said. The girlfriend released her grip and reestablished herself in the centre space where she yawned and stretched.

"I need to pee," she said.

"You just went," Riley said.

"Fuck Riley," she said. "I need to pee all this Purple Jesus. Pull over."

"On the side of the road?"

"Yes on the side. Unless your magnetic fish brain tells you there's a toilet up ahead."

The wheels skidded onto the gravel shoulder, and the girlfriend disappeared behind the car.

WITH THE DOOR OPEN, THE INTERIOR LIGHT STAYED ON, breaking the darkness into grainy globs. The engine idled and they passed another joint back and forth. Riley spun the tuner up the bandwidth: call-in quiz show, a fire and brimstone preacher, interview with a novelist. Then back down until some country croon crackled over the speakers. Riley turned it off.

"I think we should build a shelter, man," Riley said. "In the morning we can cruise some logging roads, scout for a spot." He nodded and his face took on shadows, dark stubble, smudges beneath his eyes.

"What are you talking about?" Leon said.

"I think they might be tracking us."

"Who?"

Riley took the last haul off the joint, snubbed it in the ash-tray. He leaned toward Leon, whispered, "Reptile aliens."

Heat puffed from the dash and Leon cupped his hands over the vent. Messiah, reptile aliens, the fucking raccoon. Leon wanted Riley to snap out of it, like that night, when the paramedics jolted his dad with their paddles and he'd wanted his dad to sit up, just sit the fuck up. But Riley, not dead, not dying, could do it—stop his crazy-talk—couldn't he?

A breeze blew in through the open door and Leon turned towards the empty backseat. The black windshield reflected the interior light. After a moment he said, "Where's your girlfriend?"

They both studied the clock, but had no idea how long she'd been gone, three minutes or thirty.

Riley cranked the window and yelled out. "Jana! Hey!" He killed the engine, took out the keys. The light went off and with it the radio. "What the fuck," he said. "Where would she go?"

Leon thought bears, cougars, creepy murderers. "There a flashlight in the trunk?" He knew there would be. Along with jumper cables and blankets and emergency flares.

"You going out there?" Riley asked.

"You have a better idea?"

LEON FOUND THE FLASHLIGHT UNDER THE NYLON TENT bag, its beam meagre and dim, illuminating about a square foot of air in front of him. He switched it off, let his eyes adjust to the dark terrain, attuned his ears to sounds of wild animals or rustling, but he only heard rushing water. He headed, ten-tative and alert, in the direction they'd come from and called Jana's name. It buzzed in his mouth, his ears. He called it again and it felt familiar and solid on his tongue.

Something stirred in the brush and he turned the beam

back on, then off. Nothing. He quickened his pace, thinking maybe that damn raccoon had leaped from the wheel well, attacked her. Horror film stuff. Still, tonight could turn into that kind of story, raccoon and girlfriend vanishing in the dark. Christ, now *he* sounded all conspiracy. More likely she'd grown sick of the driving, of the stupid trip, of their elusive destination. She probably wanted to hitchhike home, get back to her art projects, her galaxy table, her bed. He called her name again, over and over, like a mantra.

Up ahead a diesel engine groaned. Light bowed around the bend, catching and backlighting a road sign. He spotted her, sitting with her back against the post, clutching the plaid shirt tight around her throat, legs lengthened out. The blaring truck noise swallowed Leon's calls, and fired up his need to save her, so he started running.

The truck lights flared fully, filling him completely: rumble, wind, spray, growl and grind. Then it passed and became a distant thing.

"Jana!"

She rose to her feet and slouched against the sign, pure silhouette. He believed she smiled, felt his own stupid grin as he jogged closer.

"Twelve-Fingered Man?" she said. "You here to rescue me?"

He turned away. The Sunbird's tail lights floated in the dark distance. He slowed down, heartbeat in his throat, under his ribs, his scars. "You didn't . . . come back."

"Very perceptive."

"We thought . . ."

"What did you think?"

"Bears . . . Aliens . . . Angry raccoon."

She laughed, but it sounded hard, granular. "And Riley?"

Leon glanced back again, tail lights still hovering. "Riley . . ." he said. "Riley isn't . . . can't . . ." The word never materialized because he didn't know it. Above them, an aperture of sky opened, a satellite at its centre. On, off. On, off. What the hell would happen to Riley?

BECAUSE THE FALL IS IN TWO WEEKS

WAKE UP. IT'S FIVE-FORTY-FIVE. YOU'VE HAD A whole summer of rising early, so despite darkness creeping closer and closer to seven, it shoudn't be hard. Plus, you're a light sleeper, and your boyfriend's right next to you, snoring away. Grab your flashlight and shine it on his face. Study his furrowed brow, the clover curve of his nostrils. He looks like someone you hardly know. Let the alarm beep until he moans and buries his head. Don't apologize. Turn it off and hustle into your long johns and two pairs of wool socks. Then crawl out of the tent and stuff your socked feet into Birkenstocks. Zip up the tent door and head to the converted school bus.

The sky is pure pitch; if you looked up, you'd see a silver peppering of stars. Since you insist on fastening your gaze to the flashlight beam, try to recollect the dream you've just surfaced from. The one with the baby boy who came out of you and started running along a riverbank. Your period should've come a week ago, and your breasts are so, so sore. Just because they've been sore before doesn't mean it's nothing. But go ahead—keep telling yourself it's nothing. Then pull the generator cord so the lights inside the bus flood on.

Climb aboard and fire up the stove. Even though you're a vegetarian, lay bacon strips affectionately across the pan. Tuck these into the oven and boil a dozen eggs. Fill the biggest pot with water and set it on the back burner. When it boils, toss in half a pack of Nabob and then, because you always doubt its strength, add the other half and let it simmer. The sky is paling outside, time to mix the pancake batter and start flipping. The first three pancakes will be raw and burnt. They'll always be raw and burnt. Just throw them away.

There's a pink streak in the sky, and the camp emerges from darkness—tents, trucks, trees. At six-thirty the crew boss steps onto the bus. He's wearing a toque and fogged-up glasses, and fiddles with hand-held radios. Pour cold water over the coffee to sink the grounds and exchange good mornings. Then set the coffee on the table with the long-handled ladle so he can pour some into his cup. He sips, raises his eyebrows, and adds a teaspoon of sugar. Load his plate with pancakes and bacon, point out the bottle of syrup—imitation maple—and the blueberry jam. Repeat this routine for the three French-Canadian guys, the woman with dreads, the crew boss girlfriend, and the couple with matching blond bowl cuts and wire-rimmed glasses. As the time approaches seven, brew yourself a cup of jasmine tea and let the stragglers fend for themselves.

Your boyfriend steps onto the bus ten minutes before the trucks leave. He squints against the morning. Grunts and slaps together three peanut-butter (no jam) sandwiches. The Stanfield he wears is pilly and grey and smells like cigarettes and a sour musk, not unlike the inside of your tent. A thick silence accompanies him, a dark underground anger. Nothing that'll clear with coffee, which he gulps and gulps. You've only known him three weeks and haven't yet heard about his teen-aged suicide attempt, or how long and hard he holds a grudge. Avoid eye contact and scrape some bacon grease into a tin, but don't recite his favourite scene from *Barfly* to make him smile, don't wait for him to peck your cheek, thinking it's all okay.

Last night, when you told him you were late, he said, *I'll marry you next day off.* You were both high so don't feel bad for shrieking *No way!* Instead, think about how he scoffed when you said you had two years left on your degree, how he asked what the hell that had to do with real life anyway. Remember how you backpedalled and apologized and told him he could move in with you in the fall. The fall is in two weeks.

At quarter past seven, people flurry through the camp, collecting boots and packs, grabbing last-minute apples and Rice Krispies squares. Doors slam and engines roar and all three trucks pull out, a wake of dust behind them.

You don't know where they're going. You don't even know where you are, except that it's sort of, kind of, near Williams Lake. To get here, you had no map, but followed a convoy of trucks east off the main highway along potholed pavement. But the car stalled out in a town called Likely and no one up ahead seemed to notice. Your heart freaked as though you'd been attacked by a bear, and you attempted to pop the clutch. Thankfully, your new boyfriend drove up in a company pickup and cable-jumped the battery. After that, you followed him, passing lake and forest, lake and forest, mountains, clearcuts, and logging roads. If you had to navigate out of here alone, you'd get totally lost.

The camp nestles into pines at the edge of what you think is a small lake but is actually the crooked arm of a larger lake. Ten times better than the gravel-pit camp near Mackenzie, and the clearcut south of Prince George. Also, the crew's small, the smallest you've cooked for this season—fifteen including you—which makes the work almost like camping.

Restock the lunch trays with sliced ham and salami, some of that marbled cheese. Peel what's left of the boiled eggs and mash them into mayo with some green onion. Cover with cellophane and stick in the fridge. Then dump pitted dates into a saucepan, simmer to a paste and bake into squares. While you're doing the dishes, feel a squeeze between your hip bones, a full-on cramp above your pubis. Leave the stainless bowl, the dish suds, and run behind the bus to pee. No blood on the toilet paper. None. Feel a little dizzy as you stand. You're officially ten days late.

Once you stack the dishes and cut the date squares, you really should eat. Rice Krispies squares do not count. The grilled cheeses you've eaten for weeks are not enough. You need sustenance, nourishment, a shit ton of iron. Those cigarettes someone left on the driver's seat will not satiate you. Besides, they're not yours; you're not a smoker, not even close. Sure, go ahead and light one up on the stove, but you're only punishing your body for its natural inclinations.

Step onto the pine-needled ground. Go behind the bus and glance at the place where you peed. Sigh. Sighing's good. Switch off the generator. The motor chugs to a standstill and the silence fills your ears. Crickets and cawing crows. Pine cones popping in the early heat. A gentle, barely-there rustle of end-of-summer leaves. Disregard the cigarette stink and catch something autumnal in the air. Feel the melancholic ache that summer's almost over, that soon you'll face textbooks and syllabuses and serious decisions.

Sit on a folding chair down by the campfire ring. Take a drag off the cigarette and let it induce nausea. You haven't felt remotely sick until this very second, evidence you've used to convince yourself you're not pregnant. Now you're not so sure. Count forwards and backwards from your last period, which started on July twenty-first, back when you and your new boyfriend were in Mackenzie and you only knew his first name. On the day-off after that, you had sex with him under a picnic table in a park, and then in that crappy motel. The first time you used a condom, the second time, not. But he did pull out. Then, back at camp, you were careful(ish) for a bit, and after, by some random calculation and a memory of a sex-ed chart, you figured you'd finished the ovulation part of your cycle. Did you really believe you weren't fertile? Did you really believe you were exempt from this whole mandate to propagate the species? The truth: he's the first boy to make you come. The truth: you've thrown out reason for orgasm. The truth: it will cost you.

Count again. Thirty-nine days.

You've never gone a day over thirty.

Drop the cigarette in among the charred logs. If it burns to the filter, you're pregnant; if it goes out, not. Smoke spirals up and up. Will it to stop. It won't; it doesn't. Make a list of what you love about kids: *r*'s rounded to *w*'s, endless whys about dinosaurs and infinity, apple juice breath, pants and skirts twisted at the waist. All those years babysitting and teaching swimming, counsellor at summer camp, you always had fun, though remember those kids went *home*. Remember how your baby brother cried for six months straight. Shake your head and replace that memory with the image of a plump and placid child nursing at your breast. Believe you're capable of loving such a being. Have a romantic vision of packing that child on your back as you wander the streets of India, mountains of Nepal.

Then think how your mother will react. How she'll suck in a bunch of air and hold it. When she finally releases it, her voice will pitch upward: *How will you manage? How will you finish your degree?* Listen to her. She knows how difficult raising children is; she's raised three. She will see, with crystal clarity, your wide-open future collapsing in on itself. Your father, on the other hand, will exclaim your name, the way he always does, with an inflection of enthusiasm. Then he'll say, *Isn't life amazing? We'll have so much fun!* Remember how many business trips he took during your upbringing, how many affairs.

Your ex has nothing to do with this but imagine him anyway. Do you think he'll feel scalded by the fact you're almost certainly carrying someone else's child? When you lived together, he watched *Cheers* and *Jeopardy* on TV and ate Chinese food from Safeway—these facts alone should overrule conversations the two of you had about raising children with cute hippie names: Dakota and Summer and Ocean Breeze. There's also the fact that he cashed in his inheritance and bought a VW van and drove to Baja without ever sending a postcard. If he reacts at all, it'll be with a loud guffaw.

Why not include your friends in this round-up of delivering news? Carly, your artsy roommate, will clap her hands and offer to plaster your belly and paint it. Maia will screech, *Oh my god! Oh my god!* and bring over a plush orca and sand-dollar mobile. For a while, Jane and Alice will treat you like a minor celebrity, calling for weekly updates about the *bump*, and asking to be aunties. Eventually, they'll all get back to their various pursuits: thesis for a marine biology master's, learning sculpture in Florence, apprenticing in interior design, picking up Spanish in Argentina. Things that, at your age, you should be doing too.

Check out the car parked by your tent. The 1980 Lada you and your boyfriend bought together in PG. You've never had a car before, and you've liked learning to drive its standard transmission. Don't get too attached. In a month your boyfriend will run it into a ditch and snap the axle. You really didn't want to fork out half the cost, but your boyfriend bounced with manic exuberance and said it'd be so fun to road trip together. When you asked how you'd share it once the planting season ended—you in one city, he in another—he said, *Don't overthink it.* And you were only discussing a *car*.

Forget it. Enjoy the blue blue sky. The temperature so perfect: not too hot or cold. And the sun fanning down through the canopy, anointing your feet in gold light. Remove your shoes and socks and admire the swooning dragonflies above the lake. A single cloud floats above, billowy, rotund—embryonic.

See? You can't go two minutes without thinking about it. Remember there's the possibility of not keeping the baby. *Terminating.* You're a Women's Studies major; you're absolutely pro-choice.

Just don't count on a miscarriage. Trust your intuition. What your boyfriend's calling love has you doubting, a healthy fear. Just because he's asked you to marry him, just because he calls you *babe* and introduced you to his parents doesn't mean he's in it for the long haul. Also, you're not defective because he's excited and you're not. Pay attention to the low-grade terror you feel. Here's the thing: he can leave if it doesn't work out. Spoiler: it won't work out.

And what will you do about money? Yes, the universe will provide, but *barely*. The cheques from this planting season will vanish into tuition and books and seven months' rent. Your student loans will only carry you for so long; eventually you'll graduate and be legally obliged to pay them back. If you default, if you claim poverty, the collection agencies will hound you without mercy. Assume that if you go through with it—life of the single mother—you'll depend on monthly subsistence cheques (aka welfare) for years.

Walk down the slope to the edge of the lake. Hike the long-johns up over your calves and wade in. Decide to buy a test from that dusty-looking drugstore you passed in Likely. For a minute, believe it'll present a clear and open window. Not a single blue line. Entertain the idea that you'd kiss your boyfriend goodbye and suggest he visit around Thanksgiving. By then you'd be close to midterms and, except for a letter and couple of phone calls, you'd mostly forget him. You'd tell Carly about your near-miss, and then go to a clinic for the pill or an IUD. Maybe you'd have a fling with that guy from your environmental philosophy class. Maybe with Maia's roommate too.

Bend over and scoop water into your hands, splash your face. When you stand upright again, feel a tug on the underside of your belly. Like a fish nibbling a line. Too early to feel the baby. It's more of a knowing, that you are, for sure—without a doubt—pregnant. And, for whatever reason, or lack of reason, you will keep it. You believe you'll love this baby, and you will. But you picture your infant sleeping in your arms as you sit in a seminar class and take notes. A docile child slung on your back as you flip pancakes for the masses. You even fantasize about nursing your babe under the silver light of a full and maternal moon. Right now, you're imagining this child as a cut-and-paste accessory you can simply add to your dreams, not as the son who'll be with you—and you alone—day after day after day after day after day.

Because where are the hourly night feedings? Teething? Milk soaked sheets. More teething. Your hands in the toilet—again. Anemia. Mastitis. Vomit over your friend's car. Spiked fevers. Sitting in the ER. Stitches (head and left shin). Endless snot streams. Grubby fingers in nostrils, in sockets, in every potted plant. *Teletubbies*. Failed time outs. Tantrums over dead ladybugs, over broccoli, over you leaving him with a sitter. Whining at the yellow playground. Whining at the grocery check-out. Whining on the city bus. "Baby Beluga" on repeat. Times you yell and he cries, heartbroken. Mother guilt. Freak outs over sharing a red fire engine. Bits of Lego underfoot. Marker and peanut butter smeared over your bedroom walls. Your thwarted creativity and the hundreds of hours you will not write. The molars. Those fucking molars. And *mama!mama!mama!* a thousand times a day.

Never mind. Feel the riffle of wind off the lake. Appreciate the silence. Let it soak into your cells, encode the primordial grooves of your brain. Months from now, and for years and years, you'll long for solitude like this. Alone on a lake in the middle of nowhere. Not a single voice crying—or calling for you.

BLISS AND A BOY I ONCE LOVED

BEFORE I MET JP, NOTHING REMARKABLE HAD happened in my life, but I felt an impatience that something should, and soon. I was twenty, worked at a health food store, and agonized over the phrases my boss had plastered above the bulk bins: "Live Your Potential!" and "Follow Your Bliss!" I asked him what they meant, how exactly one did those things, but he only cast me his one-with-the-universe look and said, "It's your journey, Claudia. You'll find your path."

So while I was elbows deep in red lentils or culling limp chard leaves from the produce bin, I wondered how I'd do it. Live my potential. Follow my bliss. I'd already given up on university. "Dropped out and quit," my academic mother told her friends, though I'd completed two whole years. But I'd skipped classes, daydreamed in the library or student union building about doing something mildly heroic instead: climbing Everest, say, or spooning pablum into the mouths of orphaned Third World babies. Lately, I fantasized that a film producer might walk through the door, on a hunt for carob chips, soy milk, and a woman with my exact colouring and bone structure.

A film producer never walked through the door, not on my shift anyway. Only JP with his spectacular bowed legs and what I mistook for an over-sized guitar case. "No money in the hat today," he said. He wore no hat, his dark hair in a low pony-tail, loose strands fallen around his face. "I need change for the bus." He set his instrument case down and though I stood right there, he tapped the service bell twice and positioned his ear to catch its resonant ping. Then he smiled, a lopsided smile I immediately fell for, but his eyes, and the eyelashes that sur-rounded them, were so intense, like two black stars, I had to look away. That's when I noticed his index finger, cocooned and swaddled in gauze.

"What happened?" I asked, and he rotated the finger to show all sides.

"This? Just a tousle with Daisy's dinner."

"Dinner?" I said. "What kind of dinner?"

He picked up one of my paper cranes. I'd been folding them all afternoon, a promotional idea for a protein powder sale, and now a whole origami flock roosted on the counter. He looked as if he might speak to the bird, blow on its wings and send it soaring. But he only said, "Cool." And put it on top of the leave-a-penny jar.

Then he pulled a crumpled five-dollar bill from his pocket, ironed it flat and handed it over. Against store policy, I broke it into quarters and dimes, which he dropped into a leather pouch that hung around his neck. He winked, thanked me, and grabbed his case to go.

I didn't want him to leave, so I offered him a handful of nuts. He scrunched his nose. "I hate the Brazils."

I agreed, no one but my mother ever ate the Brazils, and to show my allegiance, I picked out four total then filled his palm with almonds, hazelnuts and cashews. He closed a fist around them and dispensed one at a time into his mouth. Between

chewing and swallowing, I decided to say something, to intro-
duce myself, invite him for tea, coffee, whatever he liked, but
the bells above the door tinkled and a man, huffy and red-
faced, walked in and asked if we carried herbal laxatives.

THE NEXT WEEK, JULY NOW, I SAW HIM AGAIN. EVERY DAY
I lunched on a small swath of lawn outside the university
sports complex—hummus and crackers, overly-sprouted
sandwiches, concoctions involving TVP and ancient grains.
On that day, a Tuesday I think, it was muggy and hot, and
I was flipping through *Diet for a Small Planet*. My boss had
lent it to me and told me if I wanted to make a difference in
this troubled world (and I did, didn't I?) then I should start by
reading it.

After my sandwich and a chapter on rules for food-
combining, I cracked open a cup of soy-based pudding. It
came from a giveaway pyramid stacked in the staff room. The
first spoonful tasted more chalk than chocolate, the second
almost entirely calcite. I didn't venture for a third but got up to
toss the rest into a nearby garbage can.

It reeked, garbage soured by summer heat, and I stepped
quickly away, bumping into a runner drinking Powerade.
"Watch it!" he said. Too late, because I'd jolted his arm and an
alarming red stripe splashed across his shirt. "I'm sorry," I said,
and searched my purse for a napkin. "It's totally ruined," he
snapped. I apologized again and wanted to offer him laundry
tips, but he said *bitch* like a harsh sneeze, something I was and
wasn't supposed to hear.

If I hadn't felt chastised, I might've headed back up Spadina
toward the store. But flustered, I went west. For a whole block,
maybe two, I scurried as if that man were tracking me, his
bitch compounding with my every step. "You're hypersensi-
tive," my mother always said. "You need to let things roll off
your back." I passed a bistro, a bike repair, and dozens of summer students, trying to do just that.

Then, as I approached the yoga place, it did roll off. Not because I willed it to but because I heard a startling, hypnotic sound. First, I assumed it was a chant drifting from the yoga studio. I'd sat in during an open house the summer before, had joined four other strangers on a carpet as a woman dressed in white explained that *om* was the universal sound. The *seed* sound, whatever that meant. *This* sound, however, sounded more melodic, instrumental, and came from outside. A little farther along it grew louder and pretty soon I reached a young man cross-legged on the sidewalk, leaning against a locus tree. He cradled a sitar on his lap, strumming the opening of what I'd later learn was a classical Indian raga.

It took me a minute to recognize him, his head bowed. But a leather pouch swung gently across his sternum and a gauzy finger travelled the complicated fret. He plucked the strings slowly, a low twangy undertone to a sequence of higher notes, which sparkled and sounded like magic wands waving away city noise and unbearable heat.

I perched on a nearby step, hoping he'd notice me, but he closed his eyes and increased the tempo. I'd never heard such music, nor watched anyone so intensely concentrated, so utterly uninhibited and alone in their action. He curled his wiry arms around his instrument and shook his head in conversation with the music. His fingers slowed then sped up, and a couple times he strummed so fast I thought his hand might fly right off.

A small audience gathered. One woman planted herself in the shade of the tree. He took no notice of her, of any of us, though he was transporting us all. My own body loosened, swayed; my heart lifted and expanded across that map of sound.

My lunch hour was finished by the time he conjured a storm of notes that collided and crashed. Then he built them into a great spire and when he reached the very peak, he stopped. Held his strumming hand mid-air and let it all drop. I waited for more. Everyone did. Some finale. One or two notes to resolve the whole thing.

But it was over, and the city resumed its ordinary hustle. Traffic, grit, white glaring sky.

He caressed the gourd part of his instrument, his chest rising, falling, as if he'd run up twelve flights of stairs, and a single sweat bead rolled down his nose.

None of the bystanders clapped, though everyone quietly excavated their pockets for change. I had nothing in my purse, only a few pennies and a subway token, so I ripped an end page out of my book, folded it into a crane and placed it in his case amid a silver constellation.

FOR THE NEXT WEEKS, I CIRCLED THE NEIGHBOURHOOD over my lunch hours, and sometimes after work. In my mind, I called him Busker Boy, and rehearsed asking him out. But a whole month passed without a single sighting. School started and the sidewalks and streets became crowded with renewed seriousness. Days grew shorter, crisper; another month passed and still nothing. Eventually I stopped eating outside and the closer it got to October the more I dismissed my Busker Boy and his divine musical interlude as nothing more than an urban mirage.

Meanwhile, my mother asked me daily about my plans. She didn't want to hear about the bliss-factor, a metric I'd made up to help determine my next step. My heart had to soar, feel the way it used to on Christmas Eve or before summer camp. "That's completely irrational, Claudia," my mother said. "You need a concrete plan." And just so I could report back to her, tell her *something*, I visited travel agents and priced out plane tickets. "Maybe I'll go to Australia," I'd say one day. "Maybe Nepal." And she'd say, "To do what, exactly?"

At her urging, I sent letters to consulates inquiring about animal sanctuaries in Tasmania and Perth, about orphanages in Kathmandu and Delhi. She insisted I choose one thing and just do it. According to her I'd garner experience that way, a little something to put on a resume. But I had a persistent belief that the right thing, the *next* thing, would present itself. Someone might read the one poem I'd published in the university journal, track me down, and offer me a fellowship to write in Paris or Rome. Or a friend might call, telling me their aunt needed a house-sitter on a secluded island off the West Coast of British Columbia.

That's what I was thinking about when I passed by Futures Bakery on Bloor and heard a knock on the window.

There, on the opposite side of the glass, was my Busker Boy. He motioned for me to join him inside. I pointed to myself and looked around, mouthed, *Me?* Then he held up that folded crane and something inside my chest hummed and hummed.

AFTER THAT, JP AND I MET THERE EVERY DAY FOR A couple of weeks. He told me things like how his initials stood for nothing. How he'd spent a whole year in India—Benares—learning sitar from a guru. How before that, he'd played guitar and occasionally mandolin. He also told me his older brother had died four years before—a kid I remembered from the papers, who'd walked into Lake Ontario all fucked up on acid and drowned. "My parents split after that," he said, and he'd moved into his uncle's place, where he still lived. Toronto was a purgatory for him, he couldn't wait to return to India, hopefully in the new year. And after that? He planned on busking around the world, searching for and collecting the purest, sweetest sounds.

In my turn I told him my mother named me Claudette, but my father's Anglo tongue had twisted it, so they switched it to Claudia. I told him of my recent vegetarian conversion, my desire to avoid bovine hormones and land exploitation. Then I confessed my limited musical inclination; I'd played piano for three years and my teacher used to poke my spine, demanding I count! count! *count!* And because I had nothing to match his family tragedy, I admitted I'd accidentally wrenched my gerbil's neck in a door hinge. And that, at four-and-a-half, I'd swallowed an entire bottle of Gravol and had to have my stomach pumped.

One Friday, during our usual coffee date, I mentioned the sitar. That his music had opened something in me but left me hanging too. I couldn't describe it and kept widening my hands as if holding an unrestrainable cloud. "It's supposed to do that," he said, and tapped our spoons together so they chimed. "Induce a mood of ecstasy. Celebration." He hadn't been busking lately because he'd picked up a job sterilizing surgical instruments at one of the hospitals, but he practiced two or three hours nightly. He clattered his empty espresso cup into its saucer and invited me back to his uncle's house.

My heart rate tripled and, as I sipped the dregs of my latte, I felt the loose elastic of my underwear—an old, end of the laundry week pair. I excused myself to the ladies' room where I removed and stuffed them into a sanitary dispenser. A presumptuous move and I immediately regretted it. Maybe he didn't like me *that* way. I'd only had actual sex a handful of times, so I couldn't remember what the signs were or if there were any. Maybe all he really did want was to play me another raga. *Induce ecstasy.*

I splashed water onto my cheeks and gazed into the mirror. My face rarely impressed me. It wasn't bad, but I was always disappointed it hadn't evolved into something more dazzling since last I'd checked.

WE WALKED ALONG BLOOR, DUSK OVERTHROWING the afternoon and a sickle moon hanging in the sky. JP took long swaggered strides with those bowed legs and I got a stitch under my ribs throwing in the extra steps. He guided me into the Annex where tall brick houses squeezed together like heavy tomes and the trees, canopied and loosely leaved above us, swamped the street in shadow.

Before his brother died, JP had lived north of Eglinton like I did, though we'd gone to different high schools. Still I wondered why our paths had never crossed. "I didn't go out much," he said. "Always rushing home after school to play guitar or listen to The Smiths." Still I felt I must've seen him peripherally—on the subway or at a house party. Maybe a concert, nosebleeds at Exhibition Stadium, or someplace like *Lick's* where the line cooks sang out your order. He said, "Sure, I've hung out at all those places. So maybe." But we must've brushed by each other once or twice, sleeves touching, elbows rubbing, some ephemeral imprint to ensure we'd meet later. Because our meeting felt like chipping plaster away from a beautiful fresco, a mosaic that had stayed concealed for centuries.

A couple blocks on, he pointed to a corner house with a turret. A high brick fence, topped with wrought iron spikes, squared off the yard. He ushered me through a gate and jangled his many keys on the unlit porch. He hadn't told me much about his uncle, only that he was a benefactor of sorts, he'd bought JP the sitar, and had once won an Olympic bronze for equestrian dressage. "He's a bit eccentric," JP had said. "He collects things." So what had I expected? A lounge, I suppose, with burgundy hues and burning incense, floor to ceiling bookshelves, and exotic musical instruments around each room—djembes and didgeridoos.

We entered a foyer filled with dark bulky shapes. Creaks and pops and the slight asthmatic rattle in JP's breath. He closed the front door and the air smelled trapped, tinged with formaldehyde or ammonia, like the inside of a specimen jar.

He didn't remove his shoes, so neither did I, and he led me into a larger room where he flicked on a switch. A low-hanging chandelier produced a yellowish glow, revealing, in the centre of the room, a parlor couch and two chairs. These seemed to huddle around an area rug as if afraid of what surrounded them. The taxidermied dingo, for instance, that lunged from a wall-mount. The stuffed horned owl, strung to the ceiling, its wings spread and a wisp of fur dangling from the talons. Portraits could've been nailed to the dingy walls, with eyes that followed our every move; instead there were beetles and butterflies pinned behind glass. An entire shelving unit devoted to bones.

JP watched for a reaction and I shrugged my shoulders tentatively, wondering if he wasn't testing me somehow, making sure I wasn't squeamish or easily disgusted. When I stepped toward the laden shelves, he picked up a long, jagged jawbone. "Crocodile," he said, and encouraged me to touch the fierce teeth. Then he curated a lineup of vertebrae, stationed like Russian dolls along two shelves: rhino, giraffe, sea lion, gull, hummingbird. He let me hold a fossilized egg, duck-sized, and told me he imagined a stony embryo inside. I pictured something part-lizard, part-bird, folded and forever awaiting its birth.

JP took the egg back and nested it into the crocodile jaw and then he pulled a skull off a high shelf, handed it to me. There were dozens of animal skulls, but this one was human. "From the Ganges," JP said, and pointed to the nine other skeletal grins across the topmost shelf. "My uncle bought them off the black market."

I studied the yellowed bone, the threadlike sutures across the top. Then tried to imagine the bony plates covered with flesh and hair. "Why?" I asked. "What for?" And gave it back.

He placed the hollow neck base against his own ear and closed his eyes. His breath relaxed as he listened for some invisible and wondrous sound. After a whole minute, he returned the skull to its tribe and said, "Because he could."

"Who is he? Indiana Jones?"

"You'll meet him," JP said. "Don't worry. He's bound to appear. But first—Daisy." I should've known better than to suspect Daisy was an old aunt, but that's how I pictured her: doddery and drooling in a rocking chair.

I followed JP down a short hallway into a room infused with dim red light. It was hot in there, with a strong bestial stench. A humidifier whirred and released puffs of steam; I became instantly overheated and removed my sweater.

"Ready?" JP said, and several beds of fluorescent lights

flared up to reveal the corral-like pen that occupied over half the room. JP climbed onto the bottom slat and leaned over the top one. "Say hi to Daisy," he said. I followed his adoring gaze to a crosshatch of branches, scattered leaves and straw. Then, draped over the farthest and thickest branch: a series of heavy muscular loops. It could've been a diorama, a museum scene, because, except for the stink, she appeared decorative, another stuffed animal brought in from the wild.

"Isn't she amazing?"

"Yes," I said. And I did think that—this wild creature in a Toronto home—but I had a feeling that if he entered the pen, he'd kneel beside her, stroke her looped scaly back, and speak tender, loving words.

"When my uncle first brought her back," JP said slowly, picking at and retrieving those far-off days, "I was eight or nine, and my brother and I would beg our mom to drive us here. Eventually my brother got bored of her, but I never did. I'd catch the bus after school—three transfers—and my uncle and I would freshen Daisy's straw, watch her moult, feed and handle her."

I tried to imagine his fascinated boy self as he gathered Daisy up in his small arms. But none of that transmitted. Instead she seemed to me as elemental and unknowable as a mountain ridge or the bottom of a river.

A voice boomed behind me. "What do you think? My prize possession! All nine Amazon feet of her!"

BACK WHEN I WAS ELEVEN AND TWELVE, I PARTICIPATED in Saturday morning classes, kids sent from all over the city, every one supposedly gifted and in need of extracurricular learning. I never wanted to go, complained I'd miss my favourite cartoons, but my mother insisted, saying I might learn the exact thing I didn't know I wanted to know. Then she drove me to a downtown collegiate where every term I chose a different class. One session, I took *It's a Reptile's World!* where I learned a rhyme to distinguish coral snakes from scarlet kings (*red touches black, and you're safe, Jack!*), and where I'd signed out box turtles and leopard geckos like library books. One of the Saturdays a special guest showed up. He stood in front of the class, passing bones and rattles and snake skins around the room. The whole time he lectured us, a boa constrictor entwined around his arms and shoulders, and with great energetic bursts the man explained how boas strangled their prey, how their jaws unhinged. "Like this," he'd said, and forced the snake's mouth wide open. "To swallow her food whole." For weeks afterwards, I thought about that sort of engulfment, the claustrophobic fate of being encased inside a snake's body.

Now here, alongside JP, that special guest extended out his lean, almost rubbery arm, in my direction. "I'm Bernard," he said. "But call me Bernie." His hair bobbed above his shiny skull, a cloud of whitish-grey, and his eyes widened in permanent amazement.

"I've seen you . . . and Daisy . . . before," I said.

"Yes, yes," Bernie said, practically hissing his s's. "Daisy and I used to get around."

He didn't ask where, and neither did JP, but I felt a redemption, a giddy relief. This was the connection, the one that stitched my past to JP's. Because all those years ago, Bernie had draped Daisy over my outstretched arms and the memory of holding her, brief as it was, had visited me arbitrarily as I rode the subway, waited for the doctor or washed the dishes. The dry coolness of that snake's scales. Red and grey saddle markings across her back. Her diamond-shaped head lifting and twisting back. Now all those random images seemed bright again, polished with deeper meaning.

The humidifier exhaled a plume of steam and the fluorescent lights buzzed. JP stepped off the slat and whispered, "You want to hold her?" He unbolted the pen. But Bernie's arm whipped past me and clamped down on JP's hand. "She's very cranky today," he said. He retracted his arm and JP repositioned the lock. "Cranky, cranky." He paced behind us. "She's ready to shed, my dears. You know how she gets when she's ready to shed."

I tried to locate crankiness in Daisy's quiet unmoving body, but all I saw was a piece of clinging straw.

"Did you know?" Bernie wedged between us. "That boas have spurs on their pelvic bones? True fact. Evidence of their evolutionary defunct hind legs." This seemed the kind of thing he'd said often and indiscriminately and may have said on that Saturday long ago, though it sounded like new information to me. I studied Daisy as if legs might stretch right out and start her walking. Really, though, I had no idea where to find her pelvis.

Bernie let out a stagy little shriek and I stepped aside. "Did JP tell you the exciting news?"

JP had backed away and was propping himself against the far wall. "Tell her about what?" he said.

"The movie!" Bernie sidestepped toward me and I smelled traces of Speed Stick and something else rising through, garlic maybe, old sprouted onions. "Cronenberg! You must know his work?" he said. I nodded, though I'd only seen *The Fly*, and had spent most the movie covering my eyes. "They shot scenes for his next film right here," he said.

He'd spent last summer on the sweltering set (i.e. his living room) and had, just that day, received a personal invitation to the premiere. He couldn't wait because, unless they'd edited her out, Daisy would appear in the film. "She was so at ease in front of the camera," he said. "A natural. Everyone on the crew—except the usual herpetophobes—had their portraits taken with her. Come!"

THERE WAS A STEAM TRUNK BEHIND THE COUCH, AND JP and I knelt on either side of it; Bernie sat on a footstool, knees pointed out like scalene triangles. The first thing he pulled from the trunk was a tortoise shell. A fabulous olive-coloured dome he'd recovered from his first trip to the Galapagos. He'd visited three times since, hoping, one of these days, to bring back the live animal. "A cold-blooded fellow for Daisy," he said, and passed the shell to JP.

Next came a shoe box, full of newspaper clippings and photos, which revved Bernie into high storytelling gear. He embarked on a long narrative about an insect hunt that had taken him deep into the Amazon where he'd happened upon a band of poachers. They'd captured Daisy, planning to slaughter and skin her, but Bernie couldn't bear the idea. JP drummed on the tortoise shell, giving the action a steady soundtrack beat, and Bernie stood up on the stool to reenact the exchange with the poachers, the excruciating bargain he'd struck through a translator to keep Daisy alive. And then the headache, the nightmare, the absolute bureaucracy, to get her on a plane and bring her home.

The story ended and he hopped off the stool and dove back into the steam trunk. Out came a three-inch stack of papers, curled from their long stint in a box. "I've written an entire book about it," he said. Then released the manuscript onto my lap where it slipped and scattered. "I've yet to send it off." His protuberant eyes vibrated in their sockets. "You don't know anyone in publishing, do you?" I didn't know anyone in anything, so I politely reorganized his papers before handing them back. "Ah well," he said, and stuffed the pile into the trunk.

As he riffled through more stuff, JP leaned against the couch, pressing on his knuckles so they popped one by one. Then Bernie pulled back and JP twisted his fingers into an elaborate sign language. I couldn't get the gist of his message and puzzled my brow in response.

Before he could clarify, Bernie commandeered our exchange by waving a picture of a small crocodile in front of me. "Caiman," he said. "The one I almost wrestled in Columbia." He launched into a story that started in a jungle, then expanded, curved, dovetailed, and segued into a plane crash he'd walked away from. In my periphery, JP stood up, returning the tortoise shell to the trunk. He looked right at me, his face full of apology, and whispered, "I'll be back." He headed upstairs to the bathroom, I assumed, or to fetch his sitar.

Bernie just kept on, this time about a blundering expedition to the Arctic. Ten minutes passed, and another ten, and JP stayed away. Bernie presented me with an 8x10 black and white. In it, he stood a head taller than a dozen grass-skirted tribesmen, his hair dark, forehead gleaming like porcelain under a tropical sun. "The Hewa," he said. "In Papua New Guinea. I spent an entire year in their company. Have you heard of them?"

Pins and needles crept up my calves. Bernie didn't wait for my answer but shuffled into a dance that involved slapping his thighs and waving his hands. Too polite to interrupt, I shifted and stretched out my legs, firing JP a telepathic message to hurry back.

"A fascinating people," Bernie said when he stopped his dance. "The only indigenous people in that country to never practice cannibalism."

"I'm sorry?"

"Cannibalism." Bernie bared and clacked his teeth. Above and behind him was the row of human skulls, who, in that instant, he rather resembled.

"Are you an anthropologist?" I said.

"Why, dear," he replied. "I'm not any ologist at all." His face brightened and he fanned the photo in front of his bone collection. "I'm a humble lover of adventure and knowledge. An *explorer*."

Only then did JP's absence strike him. For my sake, or his own, he made a theatrical show of looking down the hall and scanning the stairs. "That boy," he said. "Sometimes I curse my decision to buy the sitar. He used to be such fun! Now he does nothing but hole up and practice."

He didn't suggest I go to JP's room. Nor did he holler upstairs to JP. He only said, "You must come back another time, dear. Perhaps on a dinner day." Then he disappeared behind a door and left me alone.

I stood up and felt the nakedness beneath my jeans. A dim, unwelcome shame. The lunging dingo mocked me. My tingling feet and all those shelved, dead bones. Was this all? A few coffee dates and a boa constrictor? Long audience with JP's uncle? My blood sugars dwindled. My bliss-metre took a downturn. I made one last effort to will JP downstairs before I put on my sweater and walked out the door.

THE FOLLOWING MONDAY, JP SHOWED UP AT THE STORE before lunch. He wore hospital scrubs under his jacket, and an army green knapsack studded with buttons. Siouxsie and the Banshees. The Cure. Psychedelic Furs. I tried to ignore him. Not ignore exactly but focus intently on the customer in front of me. An elderly woman with a slight tremor and an endless list of symptoms. My gaze, however, drifted toward him, catching the way he lifted bottles off the shelves and shook them next to his ear as if he expected to find an exquisite timbre in each one. There was a beauty to his gesture, and I almost forgot how I'd spent the past weekend sulking.

The old woman decided on magnesium to steady her nerves, and glucosomine for healthier joints. After a long wait for her to count bills and sort through change, JP escorted her to the door.

Then he rattled the leave-a-penny jar and I swiped a dry rag over the counter. He swept his finger around and around so the coins clinked and released a coppery smell. "I'm sorry I bailed," he said. "I get these migraines . . ." He placed the jar back down and vice-gripped his head. "And when Bernie goes on and on and on . . ." He composed himself, a few rogue hairs hanging in his eyes, and said, "Will you come again today?"

I smoothed the rag out, folded the corners toward the centre. Part of me wanted to snub him, tell him I was busy. But then he drummed the counter. "We'll bypass Bernie," he said. "Sneak in through the secret passage."

Secret passage? How could I say no?

THE ENTRANCE WAS CAMOUFLAGED ALONGSIDE THE house. Thorny brambles had grown unruly across the door and we had to pinch and lift them, stepping under and through. JP said it had been a while since he'd been in there, since anyone had, and he struggled with a rusty padlock before pushing the door.

Inside was like a crypt. Or how I imagined a crypt—a musty combination of wet cement smells and small entombed carcasses. We stepped into webs and brushed them apart, peeled them from our faces. JP procured a flashlight and thumped its base. The beam shot out strong, and glanced off cinder-block sidewalls and, about fifteen metres away, a ladder. I tried to imagine where the ladder led to, what part of the house, as the light shrunk, and JP cast its miserly glow against the base of the outer wall.

"I forgot about these," he whispered. I couldn't see what, so crept in close beside him. He squatted and I knelt. Cans. Dozens of them, some dented and unlabelled, stood in two haphazard rows against the wall. JP knuckled several lids, and then picked up baked beans and scoffed.

"Did you rob a food bank or something?" I asked.

I felt his head shake in the dark. A small nasally laugh. "My brother's idea of a fallout shelter."

Fallout. It took me a minute to get it. Bomb—as in nuclear. And I remembered my own small plans for survival, the garden shed where I'd stashed bags of jawbreakers and chewable vitamin Cs, a couple of second-rate teddy bears and a blanket.

JP asked me to hold the flashlight and point it downward. He shuffled cans around until he found a white plastic bag wrapped in twine. He unwound it and rustled the bag open, removing a mildewed copy of *Treasure Island*. On the title page was an inscription: *To JP, For the early days of the shipwreck, Adam.* I zoomed the light so it tightened and banded around the epigraph. JP scratched at the ink, delicately, like an archaeologist hoping to uncover another message beneath. But the paper only pilled, and JP sighed and said, "Have you read it? *Treasure Island*?" I'd never gotten past the first chapter, but I said, "Long John Silver, right?" And reached for the bag with something else still in it.

A spiral bound notebook. Pages swollen and warped and totally blank. Except for the third page in, that same script pronounced: *In the event of nuclear disaster, please write here. Day one: We're still alive . . .*

"He had this crazy idea to live down here," JP said. "He had a similar set up at my parents' house, more cushy than this, and wanted to spend a week in either bomb shelter, testing them out. He planned on eating nothing but canned goods, and writing his dystopia." He stuffed the books back into the bag and propped them on top of the cans as if his brother might return to find them.

A small anchor dragged across my heart at the thought of JP's brother suddenly and permanently deprived of the sun. I'd never lost a single person to death or anything else. Up until then it'd been pure abstraction. But I could picture JP's brother at the edge of Lake Ontario, believing in his immortality the way I believed in mine. And though I never knew him, I felt a sorrow for the book he'd never write, music he'd never hear, and that he'd never eat a fresh apple again or drink coffee with his brother or walk under a full moon.

Any one of us could be dead at any moment. Bomb. Car crash. Plane. Drowning. Whatever. And I didn't want to. Instead I wanted to be one of life's great champions, defeating tragedy and grief, age and mortality.

I kissed JP.

His lips were cool and unresponsive. I persisted for a moment, but my confidence waned and washed away and I pulled back. Maybe he didn't want anything to do with me. Maybe I was only an audience for his sitar. I felt the impulse to run, retreat down the passage and dissolve back into the night. I apologized and stepped back. "No," he said, and reached for my wrist. "I was distracted . . . thinking about my brother." He pulled me in and kissed me.

Soon we were groping, grabbing, skin on skin, and we made our urgent way toward the far wall. The flashlight flickered and extinguished. Total darkness. JP leaned me against the ladder, and soon enough my pants and newly-purchased underwear were all the way down and off one leg. My bum and spine ground into a splintery rung, but I didn't care. I wanted this. All of it. Life . . . love . . . everything at once.

But before I could calibrate all that, JP groaned and collapsed into me and my spine burned with a scraping pain. He nuzzled my neck, breath erratic, almost doleful, and mumbled sorry. I cooed, said it was fine, it was good.

It wasn't good. I'd only had sex with three other guys, and each time, only once or twice. The exciting build-up annulled by brief and empty intercourse; an "I'll call you later" followed by silence. Always I believed I hadn't measured up to their expectations, or even to my own, and that I never would. So, in the cool dark of that secret passage, as JP's breath settled into a soft wheeze, I felt a mounting anxiety that JP would simply escort me to the door. That he'd peck me on the cheek and send me on my way.

Something thundered overhead.

We both tensed. A clomp and rattle; a finicky click. The trapdoor hinged open and light dropped over our half-naked bodies. Above us loomed Bernie's manic face. "There you are!" he said, as though he'd found us in a game of Hide-n-Seek. "Did you forget it was dinner day? I was just about to give Daisy her rat."

I DIDN'T WONDER WHY BERNIE HADN'T FLINCHED WHEN he discovered us beneath the floor. Perhaps in his travels he'd come across numerous pairs of mating animals, and we were just one more. But I whispered to JP that I should go. He laughed. "Because of Bernie? No way. Not this time." Then he shooed Bernie away. "Give us a minute!" And Bernie gave a playful salute and disappeared.

JP helped refasten my bra. "He hasn't opened that door in years, I promise you. Not since he did tours."

After we dressed, we hoisted ourselves up through the living room floor, right below the sneering dingo. I felt chilled, a little dizzy, still wondering if I shouldn't leave. I fixed my hair, piling it into a bun, and at the same time, JP cinched his ponytail back into place. For some reason, our primping made us giggle. "How do I look?" JP said, and turned a full three-sixty. "The height of fashion," I said. "And me?" He gently tugged my collar to straighten it. Then pulled a long webby thread off my shirt. "Don't go," he said. "I forgot it was a feeding day. It's pretty cool. Daisy and her dinner."

My earlier hopefulness returned as we moved from the temperate living room zone into Daisy's tropical lair. I welcomed the heat, the humidifier working overtime, and the strong alive stench. JP fiddled with the gate latch and acknowledged that I still hadn't held Daisy. "Feeding days aren't the best," he said. "She's hungry after all. Maybe next time." My heart flip-flopped under my ribs, jubilant at the words *next time*, but I tried to keep steady and focus on Daisy.

She was on the water side of her pen, body shaped like a letter M, head altogether hidden in her folds. Beside her, a discarded skin lay in a crinkled heap, like a lacy garment she'd tossed away. JP cracked his knuckles and told me Daisy escaped all the time. "She loves wrapping around the banister," he said. "Coiling at the top of the fridge." And sometimes, in the summers, he brought her to his room, the hottest in the house, while he practiced. "It relaxes her," he said. "She always sleeps for hours after that."

"Doesn't she sleep for hours anyway?" I asked.

Bernie entered holding a small wire cage and winked at me. "It's a thrill every time," he said.

Inside the cage, a rat clawed the wire walls. Pawing every corner for a way out. Daisy must've heard or smelled its panic. She untucked her head and unwound her body and the room crackled with pure instinct. Everything pared down to the rat and its frenetic movements. To Daisy's flinty eyes; her alert, flickering tongue.

Bernie stretched his arms over the pen and opened the cage door. The rat clung to the wire and dangled, pedalling the air until its hind legs swung back onto the cage. It screeched and nipped Bernie's finger, and Bernie yanked its tail so it splatted onto the straw. It stood no chance. Daisy sprang, completely airborne, wrapping and coiling around it before it could right itself and run. It shrieked and she squeezed. It waved one free paw and she squeezed more. Soon enough the shrieks diminished into little pips and the one paw feebly twitched. Then everything went silent and still.

During that Saturday class years before, a gangly red-headed boy with freckles and army pants kept asking about what Daisy had strangled, what she'd killed. I'd dismissed him as bloodthirsty, typical boy, especially after Bernie replied; she ate rats, rabbits, and once a small pig, but the boy kept on, dissatisfied. Even with his arms stretched out beside me, holding Daisy's midsection, the kid wanted to know if Daisy had ever strangled any person. For some reason, as I watched Daisy now, squeezing every last drop out of the rat, the rat most certainly dead, I heard the boy's voice, his slight lisp. "Has she? Has she?"

Then Daisy slackened her coils and the boy's voice vanished, the dead rat thumped quietly to the floor. The high drama over, but Daisy wasn't finished. Almost lazily she flicked her tongue over the still-warm corpse. Then unhinged her jaw, exposing the bright pink cavity of her mouth. She scooped the rat into it, headfirst, and clamped down.

AFTER THAT, UPSTAIRS IN JP'S ATTIC ROOM, A LOCK ON the inside of the door, a bare bulb bright in the ceiling, JP said he owed me. I didn't know why, my mind still on Daisy and the rat lumped in her throat. He nudged me toward a low-lying futon, its blankets and sheets in a tangled heap. I thought he meant me to sit there while he played his sitar, that he owed me a show. But he didn't play, he removed, again, my clothes, slowly this time, and said, "Your turn." Then pressed his ear against my chest.

I was embarrassed by my heart's wild enthusiasm, the eager response of my nipples, but he was not. And his touch became so attentive, each finger seeking a particular note on my body, sustaining it, before sliding on to the next and the next and the next.

THAT NIGHT DOMINOED ONE INTO ANOTHER AND another until I'd all but moved in. I didn't go home for changes of underwear but bought a few pairs, plus a toothbrush and some provisions, down on Bloor. JP and I no longer met for coffee. There was no need. Invariably, since he finished work at four-thirty, he picked me up from the store and we hurried back to the Annex. The house smells became familiar, welcoming, even the dingo's expression transformed into something like home comfort.

Bernie, too. Who sprung into some of our quieter moments, but never again during a naked embrace. Instead he'd stop us on the stairs or leap from his office as we fixed or ate dinner. He monopolized small chunks of our time with his plans to return to the Galapagos next spring, or long lamentations about Cronenberg axing Daisy from the film, or simply rattling off facts about comet moths, giraffe weevils, Hercules beetles. Often I'd find myself leaning in, enjoying his infectious enthusiasm, his entertaining mania, while JP disappeared upstairs, where I'd later find him tuning his sitar.

He thought Bernie was lonely, which I didn't believe. "It's true," JP said. "He used to bring Daisy to the schools and give tours of the house, but since he was banned by the school board, it's like all his liberties have been seized." No one was ever hurt, not fatally, but some girl tried to peel off one of Daisy's scales and Daisy lashed and knocked her tail hard into another girl who screamed and writhed as she hit the floor. "Some drama queen," JP called her. She'd snapped her wrist and several parents complained, saying Daisy could've strangled them all. "So not true," JP said. "But people freak out. Anyway, it broke Bernie's heart because he's a showman, and without those kids he kind of withered."

"Maybe he could busk with Daisy," I said. "Like you. Take her to the streets."

"I doubt it," he said. "But you're here. Someone fresh and willing to listen." I felt strangely honoured and useful, though you couldn't call anything I had with Bernie a real conversation. More just him speaking while I interjected amazed and agreeable sounds.

I was a listener with JP too, different than with Bernie. Because every night JP practiced his sitar—between making love and sleeping, he'd roll off the futon and pull on a pair of pajama pants or wrap a blanket around his waist. We kept candles burning, three beeswax pillars I'd brought from the store. And every night he'd position himself on an area rug across from me, fold his legs and play scales before he embarked on a long, long raga. For hours I'd watch him: his skin amber and glowy. And, with that strange, beautiful instrument cradled in his bowed legs, he looked like a genie, newly bloomed from a jar, anointing me with his music, lulling me into a dreamy half-sleep I expected would last forever.

IN LATE NOVEMBER, SNOW STARTED FALLING. FIRST little wisps, sharp squalls churned up by the lake, and then fat-bottom clouds moved in and dropped layers of dense sticky snow to the ground. At the store, customers grumbled, their pockets stuffed with tissues and lozenges, on the hunt for echinacea, zinc, mega doses of vitamin C. I was immune to their misery, my brain so honeyed with hormones I could barely count change let alone recommend one flu remedy over another. All I wanted was to point out the sticker above the bulk bins, the one that said bliss, and preach the power of it. I had enough restraint not to, but barely.

I'm still amazed I didn't float out from under my own skin. Because in those weeks, I hardly touched the earth. I blew off my mother, left messages on the home answering machine when I knew she held office hours or attended committee meetings, and said, "Still alive and well and staying downtown. See you soon." I had no intention of seeing her soon. She was part of my past, a skin I'd cast off and shed, a thing I'd outgrown.

My mother, however, didn't think so, and one day dropped by the store. I hadn't seen her in month or more. She seemed shorter than I remembered, her hair more silver, face a little more pinched around the mouth, eyes filled with a robust and beady judgment. She asked me to go for lunch. I stammered that I didn't get my break for another hour. Maybe another day? One where she didn't have to wait. She shrugged in that Gallic way of hers and said her meeting with the dean got postponed, she had lots of time. So she browsed the aisles, scrutinizing labels, dusting bulk-bin scoops with scraps of paper towel, as I rang vitamins through at the till. Her presence made me prickle and sweat.

At the bistro she ordered spinach and bacon quiche with a glass of white wine. I had a roasted veggie sandwich with melted brie, a cup of black tea with lemon. She did most of the talking. First about the Berlin Wall, which so-called wall woodpeckers had started chipping away at three weeks before. I'd given the story only a fraction of my attention as I passed by newspaper boxes, feeling a fleeting reassurance we no longer had to worry about nuclear war. My mother waxed poetic about Gorbachev, about the end of an oppressive era, then slumped back and raised her glass as if she'd done the heavy lifting of global negotiations herself.

I polished off my sandwich while she catalogued the family gossip—her recent root canal, Nana's indigestion, Tante Helena's negative biopsy, and my cousin Marie in Montréal, involved in an international youth program, and who'd just left to spend three months in Tunisia. "You should apply," my mother said.

Over the last bite of my sandwich, I mumbled something about not knowing where Tunisia was.

"*Bon.* Tell me about this boy then," she said. "This JP."

I fiddled with the lemon slice, dribbling a bit of juice into my tea. "He's sweet," I said. "Cute." Language seemed altogether the wrong tool, like measuring a great distance with a stopwatch and a ball of string. I slapped together a few other words too, words I thought might, but probably didn't, please her. *Considerate, talented, a half-decent cook.*

Then, as a diversion, I explained the connection between the Saturday morning classes and Daisy.

"You were so scared back then," she said.

"What do you mean, scared?" I worked the lemon slice more intently, wrung it to nothing but pulp and rind. "I wasn't scared."

"You couldn't sleep, Claudia. You stayed for days in a sleeping bag at the foot of our bed." She dabbed at her mouth, placed the scrunched napkin on her empty plate.

"That was for something else," I said. "A movie."

She gestured for the bill and pulled out her wallet. "Really? Not the snake?"

"I've never been afraid of them."

"No?" She laughed, a note of bitterness in it. "I could've sworn." Then the bill came, and she counted out tens and a five, a couple of twos.

"It was a movie," I repeated, no longer sure.

She slipped the money into the little folder and pushed it to the edge of the table. One of the mints fell. Neither of us picked it up. "It doesn't matter, Claudia. That's the past. It's your future you need to worry about. Don't waylay your plans for some boy and his snake."

THE FUTURE. I'D FORGOTTEN ABOUT IT. I'D BEEN SO pleased with my bliss bubble that I wanted nothing more. But my mother's admonitions injected a low-grade anxiety into me, and I began testing JP. I dropped my cousin's youth program involvement into our conversation, told him I might apply. He only half-closed his eyes and popped his knuckles, and said, "Interesting." Another time, after we'd all fed Daisy and another rat bulged in her gullet, I brought up an animal sanctuary in Tasmania, how I'd considered volunteering there. Bernie clapped his hands. "A marvelous plan," he said. JP said nothing.

One night I interrupted his practice, something I rarely did, because it had been troubling me—was he still planning to go to India? The frets were movable, and he slid one up, another down. He strummed the playable strings, while the underneath strings, the *sympathetic* ones, sent out a dutiful resonance. "Yes," he said. "Of course."

Wax had softened around the candles and I pulled at it, feeding bits of it into the flame. I wanted him to invite me without prompting, but he only bowed his head and muttered several Sanskrit syllables. I knew he wouldn't ask me. That without a second thought he'd embark on his journey—alone. While I did what? Waited?

My invisible future materialized, then quickly greyed and became a lonely landscape. A neediness hijacked my nervous system, my voice. I stuttered. "Can I come too?"

He stopped toying with the sitar. "You want to come?" He didn't sound displeased but puzzled. "I practice six to eight hours a day," he said. "What would you do?"

The flame was totally exposed now, dancing higher, and wax spilled down the pillar into a pool. I pressed my finger into it, drew out a river. I hadn't thought of India as a place where I would do anything though I tried to rekindle earlier aspirations to help the poor orphans, but no. All I wanted was JP. I couldn't say it. It seemed so pathetic, a womanly role my mother had warned me against. So I pictured Bernie.

Imagined him among temples and crowded streets. "I'll dig up skulls," I said, my voice stronger, "on the banks of the Ganges."

WE WENT ALONG WITH THAT BELIEF, AT LEAST I DID, FOR a couple of weeks, though something had shifted. Bliss, as I'd known it, had become tarnished and I wanted it to shine again. Then, three days before Christmas, a blizzard swept in from the east. Fat flakes ticked against the window as JP and I made love. The snow fell harder, faster, and after, we lay facing its dizzy dance, backlit by a streetlamp glow. A drift built up on the windowpane and, silhouetted against it, was the origami bird I'd folded months ago. JP had placed it on the sill alongside a few river stones, the creases no longer sharp, the head stuck in condensation.

JP traced circles across my back, slid fingers between my ribs. "My brother and I used to build crazy snow forts," he said. "Multiple rooms and central chambers, pretending we ran an intergalactic superhero station."

"I was more of a snow angel kid," I said.

His hand slipped away, and I felt him roll to his back. "The winter before he died, it hardly snowed at all." His voice drifted like ash into the hole his brother had left behind.

I thought of the secret passage. His brother still down there in a weird way. The notebook. I flipped around to face JP, lightly shook his shoulder. "Hey! Why don't we finish his book?" I said. "Put snow forts in it. And whatever else. More homage than dystopia."

He shifted his gaze from the window to me, squinted as if battling the snow. "We?" he said.

My heart plunged; my cheeks flushed hot. "I thought I could help you," I said. "That's all. I thought I could."

"You didn't know him, Claudia," he said.

"Yes," I said. "But I know you."

He blew out the candles and I was glad for the dark. A

bereavement settled over me, for all the things that hadn't happened, for all that probably wouldn't.

I WISH I COULD SAY THAT WE WENT OFF TO INDIA. That we became buskers, the two of us, vagabonds who travelled from city to village to countryside, the entire globe over. I wish I could say that JP became a famous but humble musician, and that I continued to follow my bliss. But I can't. Because whatever fragile architecture was holding our plans together collapsed the next morning.

Neither of us had noticed the power out, it occurred in the night, lasting several hours, or so we gathered from JP's flashing clock when we woke up. Plough chains jostled outside, and when they passed, we heard morning shovellers, spinning tires and a handful of gleeful children. Outside the window, the trees and rooftops were saddled with snow. "How about we build a snow fort?" I said.

JP kissed my temple and I smelled his stale breath. "How about pancakes first?"

Downstairs was quiet. None of Bernie's frenetic scurryings, nothing except the furnace kicking on again and again, radiators gurgling, and the drone of Daisy's humidifier. "Weird Bernie's not up," JP said.

"Maybe he slept in," I offered.

"Bernie?"

He opened the front door to look for tracks in the snow, but the yard and the walkway were still pristine. Next he checked Daisy's room. No Bernie, and no Daisy either. He checked the fridge, the banister, and then took the stairs two at a time. Within a couple minutes he was shouting, and I was calling 911.

It took ages for the cops to arrive, and the ambulance, JP pacing around and around the parlor couch, saying Daisy would never do this. "I know her. She wouldn't. Never." He didn't let me into Bernie's room, and I didn't want to go in, but

I wish now I had. She hadn't swallowed Bernie whole, nothing so gruesome, but she'd wrapped herself around him, squeezed until there wasn't a single breath left. Probably he'd pulled her into his room, his bed, because of the power out, committed to keeping her warm.

The cops asked to see Daisy's pen. And an animal control guy arrived to administer Daisy with a lethal injection. JP tried to stay in the room, but the paramedics sat him on a chair in the hall and made him wait until she was fully dead. Then they carried Bernie's body out on a stretcher, Daisy's in a bag. I don't know how long we sat in the living room after they all left, but the light went blue, and then dark, and JP's sad, watery breath filled the room. I didn't have a clue how to touch his grief, and so when he finally said, "I need to be alone," I left.

I left, yes, in shoes and nothing more than a sweater. Snow had started falling again and ploughs were grinding along the streets. By the time I reached the subway I felt pitched back into the world, struck against all its sharp edges. There was something exquisite in it, that pain, something new and unequivocal and all my own.

I waited two days before I called JP. And when I did, he didn't pick up. On Christmas I drove down to the Annex with a slice of my mother's attempt at vegetarian tourtiére, but all Bernie's doors were locked, including the secret passage. I pressed my face to the front window and saw only the dingo and rows of bones. On Boxing Day, I found JP's mother's number in the phone book. "He flew to India yesterday," she told me. "He didn't want to wait for the funeral." She asked my name, and when I told her, she said, "Yes, Claudia. He left something here for you."

A shoe box. Bulky and held together with thick rubber-bands. Inside was a human skull—to remind me, I guess, of Bernie—and also his brother's near-empty notebook. Below his brother's words JP had written: *I'm sorry. I can't stay. But do it, okay? Write this story, this homage.* He also left me a Maxell tape. *Ecstasy* written on the A-side sticker; nothing at all on the B. It was JP. A poorly recorded version of him, sounding as if he'd set the tape recorder up on one side of the room, and strummed his sitar on the other. I listened to it twice and strained to hear the uplifting music I knew so well. But the notes only twanged and dissolved. And then they slipped away.

TRAIN IN THE DISTANCE

'M PERCHED ON THE TRAPEZE, NOT A REAL TRAPEZE, only a bar with chains on the new monkey bar set. There's a banana swing too, a couple of rings, and a bucket seat for the baby. I'm wearing cut-offs, my first pair, and though I wanted the frayed edge other girls have, my mother hemmed them, zigzag borders around both legs. I pick at the white thread and my younger sister, Laura, grips the rings, leaning forward as though diving midair off a cliff. She says, "What am I thinking of now?"

It's mid-July and I'm eleven, going on twelve. I practice my ESP powers regularly and am waiting for a premonition. For months, I've skipped ahead to the end of novels because I can no longer stand to *not* know what will happen. Also, I've marked all my *Choose Your Own Adventures*. Small red dots alongside choices that lead to safety or a triumphant end. And though I know we all die, I'm way more curious about *before* we're born, because despite the fact I've visited the King Tut exhibit at the museum and studied pioneers and Jacques Cartier, it's only recently dawned on me that millions of years have passed prior to my arrival. This shocks me, continues to shock me, in elaborate and intricate ways.

My mom traces everything back to sperm and egg: two cells joining up, evolving into eyes, nose, feet, etc. When I ask about the preceding nothingness, she shrugs, hoists the laundry basket or the baby onto her hip, and says, "Really, Heidi, I have seventeen other things to worry about today." My dad, on the other hand, espouses reincarnation, each human life a continuation of another, like volumes of encyclopedias. I ask if he remembers his other lives—as a sultan, a pyramid builder, a monk in Tibet—and he snorts a little, then says, no, most definitely not.

Today it's about a hundred and fifty degrees, the air heavy and still. We'd rather be back in the house, standing in front of the box fan, chopping up our voices and feeling the wind. But our mom kicked us out after lunch for laughing, even though it was the silent shaky kind. "Go practice for the circus," she said in her hissy voice. "Baby's sleeping."

When we're not training with numbers in the card deck, we stick to animals, rock stars, geography and food. So I say: "Animal?"

"Sort of," Laura says, somersaulting forwards and back, hands tight on the rings.

The ESP book suggests you relax when you run through the tests. They tell you to breathe three counts in and four out; that way you can focus on the face-down card or the other person's thoughts, information lifting out of your dark brain like a Polaroid. If you're really good, you dream the future or know it in a snap. Like the woman in the book who didn't have any money, and, while doing dishes, a series of numbers paraded past her mind's eye. The next day she bought a lottery ticket and won a hundred thousand dollars. My dad gets it whenever he goes to the horse races. "Like a train in the distance," he says. "A rumble through your feet before you hear the whistle." None of these things have so far happened to me, but the book says not to worry: ESP is a sense, like taste or smell, we all have it. Like a muscle you have to strengthen and exercise.

Laura releases the rings and smooths her boy haircut back

into place, saying, "I wish we were at the lake." I don't need ESP to know she'll say this. She says it every day. And it's true, we wish the baby hadn't been born *this* year, wish our mom still worked for the auction, wish our dad *had* won the Queen's Plate triactor. Then we could go to the usual summer camp, two hours away from this muggy city and its blank white sky. But the baby *was* born, our father didn't win, and our mother said, "We absolutely can't afford it," so she bought us the monkey bars instead.

Laura sprints across the yard, drags back the sprinkler. ESP doesn't work if either person breaks concentration, but she doesn't care. On average, she scores higher than me on the tests we take. When I ask how the answers come to her, she shrugs, tells me they just do. Not scientific or helpful at all. The book says younger children have an advantage over adults: *a natural propensity for clairvoyance.* Laura has a natural propensity for everything.

She turns on the water, which spurts, shoots higher than the back neighbour's chestnut, rains on my head. "Turn it down," I yell. And the arch settles to the top of the bars, plinking the metal, soaking my yellow halter with water still warm from the hose, and then oscillates away.

"Did you figure it out?" Laura says, galloping back.

"Is it a bug?"

Laura hooks her knees over the monkey bars and releases down into the spray. Her hair hangs and she squeezes her eyes as the water gets her. The Big Dipper, what my dad named the constellation of freckles on her cheek and nose, scrunches tight then spreads again once the spray passes. "That's better," she says. Her too-small Mickey Mouse t-shirt slides, showing her nipple and stretched-out belly button. She doesn't even try to tuck it in.

The water spritzes my face and I sputter. "A dragonfly?" I say, but I'm only guessing. There's no image twinkling behind my eyelids, no hum of its wings here in my brain.

"Not a bug at all," she says.

The water moves toward Laura, who releases her legs, clasps the bar and dangles. With toes pointed, her feet barely graze the grass. I slide my bum off the trapeze and, without touching the ground, shift my feet to the three-rung ladder. Every single day I see if I've grown. Laura already has an inch on me, will eventually have two, but this summer I still believe in a justice where the first born, if not the smartest, will at least be the taller.

LAURA ALMOST DIED ONCE, AND SOMETIMES I'M disappointed she never did. It happened at Marcy Whitman's Organ Grinder birthday party last June. All the kids were finishing up pepperoni and cheese pizzas, waiting for cake. The restaurant lights kept blinking like a pinball machine, the Wurlitzer playing requests. I wasn't there but imagine it playing *Music Box Dancer* because someone always, *always,* requests that song. Anyway, Kenny Whitman, Marcy's brother, started stabbing balloons with his sharp loot bag pencil. Laura had wanted to save hers and when she hid it by her knees Kenny crawled under the table and jabbed right through the balloon into her left thigh. Laura kicked the table, and Kenny's elbow, but she didn't even scream. Mrs. Whitman removed the lead best she could, but a tiny chunk remained. Back home, our mom called Poison Control while Laura and I got giddy on the front lawn. I've never known a dead person, unless you count my grandpa who died when I was two, so Laura crossed her heart, swearing that if she keeled over, she'd report back via dreams, mind-messages, and hauntings. Then we sprawled on the grass, holding hands, clouds amassing and dissipating overhead. "It's supposed to be peaceful," I said. "Like you're always floating."

That's when our mom came out, smiling with relief. "All in the clear," she said. "It's only graphite." The rest of that afternoon we played jacks on the front porch, which brought me no closer to knowing about life or death or anything.

I GRAB THE SECOND BAR IN, AND HANG IN FRONT OF Laura, but she lets go, thwumps to the ground, wipes her hands on her shirt. Her boy haircut plasters against her forehead and she shoves the bangs into a crest, straddles the sprinkler. I hand-walk my way across, swinging my legs, my body, around her, and over to the other side, the bars slippery and my hands cramping.

That's when I hear a loud *hem-hem* and turn toward Roz's yard. Sure enough, she's standing by the maple at the collapsed part of the fence, hugging the tree as though it's her boyfriend, which she doesn't have.

Roz lives in the semi-detached next door. Not the one attached to ours, but the one next to that. There aren't many kids on this street, especially compared to our last neighbourhood where we played Kick-the-Can and S.P.U.D. day after day after day. Now it's just Paddy Thompson—who only talks about farts and *Star Wars*—and Roz. Roz lives with her mom, and they rent the house from Rough Trio's band manager. I don't listen to their music, but Roz told us the whole band showed up in a limo last Christmas, took her for a ride in the snow and offered her champagne. Next time, if we want, she'll get us autographs.

"I have Pop Rocks," Roz says, shaking a small purple sack. "Want any?"

One thing about Roz: she always has candy. We're never allowed. Our mom uses carob instead of chocolate and cuts the sugar in half when she bakes cookies. Anything that isn't homemade, she deems *junk,* so when we're not getting it from Roz, Laura and I sneak quarters from our mom's change purse, tell her we're going to the park then zoom to the corner store for gobstoppers and bubble gum.

"Why don't you bring them over here?" I say. That way Laura can count Mississippis as I cross back over the monkey bars. I'm positive I can take two at a time. But then Laura's gone and the sprinkler jets into my face, the water cold and running down my halter and thighs. Then it's off, Laura dashing from the spigot, under the clothesline, through the next door people's hostas and over the fence.

"Come on, Heidi!" Laura sticks out her tongue and Roz stands tiptoe to pour a pile of candies onto it before dropping back onto her heels.

"Yeah, Heidi," Roz says, voice all sneery. "You coming?"

Even from across the neighbour's lawn, Roz's mouth glitters. Silver fillings on every single molar, and all along the bottom front row.

"Not much left," she says, tapping a little into her hand.

Lately I've been getting the glass feeling. Not the tempered window kind, but liquid; glass drawn from fire like electric red honey. Once our dad took us to watch those blowers at Harbourfront, spinning their pipes and blowing until the liquid transformed into an empty bubble, then hardened. From then on, it's happened. I get achy, trembly, as though the whole world will break. Like mid-minuet at the piano recital when I forgot the next note; or when I lie in bed, listening to my dad come in way too late; or when my mom tells friends over the phone that she's got four kids these days instead of three; and right this minute, something about Roz.

Still I land in a slosh of water and grass, water oozing into my flip-flops. My jean shorts completely soaked, threads loose and webbed along my leg. I don't run like Laura, never run like Laura, and saunter instead across the neighbour's lawn, humid air settling on my drenched skin making me feel dog-licked all over. I still haven't received Laura's transmission: the animal that's sort of an animal. I take in a three-second breath when plankton floats into my brain. Amoeba. I've recently learned about single-celled creatures, how their splotchy bodies creep around, not quite animal, beyond our sight.

I unhitch the wire gate and step into Roz's yard. Grass tickles my ankles and calves, lawn unmowed since one of Roz's mom's boyfriends hacked away at it a month or two ago. There's a cracked flying saucer, the one we used to slide down the snowbanks last winter, and a rusted push mower, weeds sprouting through the blades. I almost step on a board pronged with nails, but Roz says, "Watch out!" Then smiles, her lips a deep, candy red. "Put out your hand," she says. Her eyelashes are so blond you can hardly see them, and her scaly pink eyelids remind me of freshly hatched robins. I stretch out my hand for her to sprinkle in about seven Pop Rocks. When I bring my hand to my face it smells like iron and fake grape. I dump the candies into my mouth, and they hardly even fizz.

WE ENTER ROZ'S HOUSE THROUGH THE FRONT DOOR. Kick our flip-flops into a pile by the empty umbrella stand. My skin goes cold and shivery for the air conditioning and my vision fills with yellow blobs because, with every curtain closed, the light is dim.

Unlike our house, there are no partitions dividing hall from living room, living from dining, dining from kitchen. The walls are tiled in smoky mirror, even part of the ceiling. The tiles go all along, almost to the kitchen, making the house look like a jungle, three rubber plants turning to six, and the black leather couch stretching like a tunnel into the wall.

Laura leaps into the swivel chair, knees on the seat, hands on the floor, pushing herself in circles. My arms fill with goose-bumps and my teeth chatter. I wish I had a towel or a dry shirt, and I consider running home for one but whenever I interrupt my mom's reading or napping, her *quiet* time, she bursts like a dark cloud. So instead I walk toward my reflection, stick my tongue out, hating my nose, getting bumpy like my mom's, plus that cluster of tiny pimples on my forehead. Then I trace the edges of the tiles, the in-between cracks. I've read *Through the Looking-Glass,* and all the Narnias. I'm hoping one day it'll happen to me: an accidental stumble into another world. The tiles yield nothing though, so I slide my legs beneath the glass coffee table, lean into the couch, pick and twist the shag carpet.

"You hungry?" Roz says.

Laura stops, slips off the chair and crawls past the circular dining table to a stool. This she climbs and bangs her fist on the maroon counter. "Give me a meatball sandwich," she says in her best Bugs Bunny. It's the only voice she does; the one thing I do better.

Roz wags her finger, high blond ponytail wagging too. She reminds me of a gymnast, sway-backed and thin hair. The kind of girl whose leotard or bathing suit always gets stuck up her bum. "Something better," she says.

There's a crystal ashtray on the coffee table, reeking of Rothmans cigarette butts and ash. There's also a book, *Life Goes to the Movies,* velvet cover slipped into a gold case. I've flipped through it before. Mostly black and white photos of movie stars: Humphrey Bogart, Marilyn Monroe, all the people my mom likes. I'm more into *Grease*, having seen it six times at the half-price matinee. My favourite scene is the end, where the in-love John Travolta and Olivia Newton-John drive their souped-up car right into the sky. It'd be nice if middle school culminated in singalongs and carnivals next year, but I doubt it. I don't care about love or boys anyway. I'd settle for a couple of friends, more than just me and Ernestine Chow trading *Mork & Mindy* cards by the back fence.

I pick up a photo cube, picture of baby Roz in one square, Roz's mom, bouffant and Cleopatra eyeliner, in another. It's hard to recognize her because these days she wears thick round glasses and her hair's a frosted, fluffy blond. There's also a picture of her on a boat in a bikini. I've seen her walk around the house in her panties and bra, and once, last winter, when my mom went stomping through the February snow to dump the vacuum water, she glimpsed Roz's mom lounging on the deck, fur coat open, and breasts naked under the sun. My mom called her an exhibitionist. My dad, who's been to Europe, told us ladies there wear bottoms-only at the beach.

I roll the cube on the floor and it turns up a photo I've never noticed before. A black-and-white with smoothed out creases, as though it's spent years in someone's pocket or the bottom of a bag. It's of a man and woman standing on a cobbled street, dour stone buildings behind them, staring blank-faced into the lens. I try to imagine their world in colour and sound, but they look frozen, like props for the photograph.

"Who are they?" I ask, bringing the cube to the kitchen.

"My Nana," Roz says, slinging a bag of Wonder from a drawer and setting six slices side by side on the counter. I've seen Roz's Nana, a stout woman with enormous breasts, always calling Roz a *good girl*. "With my Papa. My *grand*father."

She spreads margarine across the bread, as though she's a painter painting a yellow sky. "He was knifed in the back," she says.

Laura stops spinning the stool, slaps the counter, eyes gobsmacked and wide. "Murdered?" she says.

Roz lifts the lid of a bright orange dish. "Shitdamn!" she says, slamming it down. She huffs across the kitchen, arms crossed, feet stomping to the cupboards next to the fridge. Using the bottom shelves as a stepladder, she hoists to the counter and reaches for the topmost shelf. "Hey, Heidi," she demands. "Stand there." She points right beneath her, so I stand, arms like a forklift, and Roz drops a sack of sugar, the size of a baby.

"Murdered?" Laura repeats. Then louder. "Murdered?"

Roz leaps, flutters her feet, and then lands steady, throwing hands into the air, pretending she's Nadia Comaneci or something. "Yes," she says. "Murdered! In Hungary. My Nana yammers on about it all the time. Crying about my poor Papa. Crying about the revolution."

The sugar goes from bag to bread, Roz dumping a measured tablespoon onto each slice, spreading it corner to corner like Christmas glitter onto glue. She closes the bread, leaving margarine and trails of sugar on the counter. Cuts the sandwiches into quadrants, places them on a plate and we each take a square.

"What happened?" I say.

She bites into the bread, chews mouth open and glittering.

Then she straightens her spine, says, "My Nana waited in her apartment listening to the gunshots and yelling from outside. My mom just a baby in her crib. Anyway, Nana didn't know Papa was dead, no one had come to tell her yet, when his ghost appeared in the steam of her stew and told her to leave the country."

"What did she do?" I say.

"She left the country, Dimwit."

I chew the sugar sandwich, sweet flooding my mouth, and imagine a body, fallen forward into the gutter, knife glinting between the shoulder blades like you see in TV murder mysteries. Then the ghost, writhing free, a genie from a jar, drifting along the streets through the wall to Roz's Nana. Every part of me tingles, and I'm suddenly envious of Roz. My grandfather only died in his sleep after a night playing bridge with my parents. Squeezed my grandmother's hand and off he went, like a sigh.

"What'd it look like?" I say. "His ghost?"

Laura scoots off the stool, takes three McDonald's collector glasses from the cupboard. "No such thing as ghosts." And I almost shout: *Since when?* Wanting to remind her how *she* was nearly a ghost. But Roz twirls her finger around her temple, rolling her eyes, says, "My Nana's a bit, you know, cuckoo."

Laura laughs and empties a whole ice tray into the glasses. Roz tops them with orange pop. For a moment I hate them both, think about running home. Instead, I leave the picture cube beside the toaster, baby Roz face up. I grab a glass and follow them up the narrow, dark stairs.

ROZ'S UPSTAIRS MAPS OUT SAME AS AT OUR HOUSE, her room exactly where Laura's used to be before the baby. Now we share the tiny middle one. Roz opens her door and light washes over us, the blinds wide open. The air feels like Florida.

There's a hopscotch woven into Roz's carpet. Three actually. None the size you'd draw on the sidewalk or playground but big enough if you hop on your toes. When Laura and I tried to convince our mom we needed to replace our thin brown rug with something like this, she handed us a roll of masking tape and told us to make our own.

One of the hopscotches goes under the bed, the other angles into the closet. The third is central, so we set down our snacks and clear away the *Charlie's Angels* dolls, the magic set, the tangled rainbow slinky, half a set of jacks, a stuffed unicorn and a dozen balled up socks. I'm still angry, wishing I could talk to Roz's Nana, knowing I never will, so I clamp my mouth shut and don't complain when Roz wants to go first or assigns me the Bionic Woman's arm as a throwing stone.

Roz starts hopping and Laura untangles the slinky. I slouch against the bed, sipping orange pop, and study the stack of games in the closet. Hungry Hungry Hippo, Life, and Operation. All the games they advertise during Saturday cartoons, none of which our mom will buy. She's all Scrabble Jr., Boggle, and jigsaws. My dad sometimes comes home with surprises, especially after he wins money at the track. Last week, he fanned five twenties onto the table, and then handed me and Laura keys to our very own roller skates.

Roz throws the Monopoly shoe to the number three square. She hops over number one, onto two, then the four-five, both feet down. But when she gets to six, she lands on a line, toes creeping into seven-eight.

"You're out," Laura says, tossing the slinky onto the bed. "My turn."

Roz drops her lifted foot, puts her hands on her hips and stoops toward Laura. "I get a do-over," she says.

"No you don't," Laura says. "You stepped on the line. You're out."

I say nothing, could care less who wins. But never Laura, Laura always stands up. Against the boy who used to kick me. Against the man whose raincoat was open at the bus stop, his thing hanging out. She even called Mrs. Whitman and demanded she punish Kenny for leaving a scar.

Roz kicks Laura's glass and ice cubes tumble like dice, orange pop puddles and fizzes.

"Look what you did," Roz yells.

I want to leave. Right now. Not home, but a *Bewitched* nose-wiggle disappear to the park up the street or my grandma's living room. The glass feeling overtakes my whole body, belly, arms, legs, everything.

"Did not, Roz." Laura crosses her arms and scowls. "*You* did."

Roz's face goes red and mean, red spreading up her forehead, right through her middle part. She hurls the Monopoly shoe at Laura, and it dings Laura's temple and bounces into the closet. "Let's leave, Heidi," Laura says. Roz lunges for the door, shuts it against Laura, who rubs her head and says, "You can't keep us prisoners."

Roz splays against the door, as though she's in the Graviton and pinned there. Laura reaches for the knob and Roz digs her fingernails into Laura's wrist. Laura yells, but Roz won't let go, her nails digging deeper as Laura thrashes her arms, hoofs Roz's shin. There's foam on Roz's lips and her eyes go funny. Not roll-up-spaz funny. Glassy funny. Laura gives her one more kick and I yell, "Stop! Stop it."

Roz's body suddenly empties. Not collapsing, but more like an insect, dried out from the inside. Or a cereal box you think is full, and when you pick it up, it isn't. My heart flips around like a coin, heads, tails, heads, tails, and I'm wondering if I should run for help, scream out the window, or what.

"Shit," Laura says, waving a hand in front of Roz's face. Not one flinch. "Is she dead, Heidi?" But Roz is still standing.

I step on an ice cube, cold shocking through my leg, and for some reason, I remember swimming lessons. Lying on the wet deck, playing the unconscious victim, peeking through eyelashes and chlorine fog at my teacher with his bulgy Speedo. "What do you check first?" To the class dripping in a circle around me. And I muttered, "The breath, the breath," in a Bugs Bunny whisper, even though I wasn't supposed to move or speak.

So I drop my ear beside Roz's mouth, feeling heat from her, a small sound, like a bubble pop. Then her eyelids stutter, her cheek twitches. "What the hell you looking at?" she says.

"What happened to you?" Laura says.

"What are you talking about?" Roz says. "We're playing hopscotch."

As Roz speaks, her baby robin eyelids flutter, her cheeks twitch, and I feel a rumble, like a train in the distance. It's not the future that comes clear, not Roz's doctor's appointments or brain scans, her epilepsy diagnosis or doses of strong medicine. Not my dad losing everything to the races, the quick sale of our house, or the move to my grandma's without him. Not the three middle schools I'll go to over the next two years, or the way Laura and I will play together less and less. No, these things I'll only know once I've lived them. It's the past that floods my brain. The past vibrant and full of colour: cobbled streets, rubble, gunfire. The haunted look in someone's eyes. The split second before the knife goes in.

ALMOST SISTERS

THEY STOOD ON THE GUNWALES. FIONA ON ONE end, Tiffany on the other, lifejackets pushed to their throats. They steadied themselves, widening arms like wings. Their mothers were sunbathing on the nearby dock. Occasionally one popped up, shielding her eyes and scouting the lake to make sure no one had drowned. Now it was Fiona's mother, cupping hands around her mouth, shouting so it echoed across the water. "Girls! Be careful!" The girls only glanced toward the dock, and both mothers, browned from the summer sun, flipped, one then the other, to work on their backs.

Fiona bent her knees and her thighs hardened. She straightened and bent again so the canoe lowered and lifted like a teeter-totter. She swung her arms, adding height and momentum. The canoe smacked the water, waves rippled from the boat, and Tiffany scrunched and shrunk on the other end. Another hard bounce and Tiffany flew into the air. Her skinny gymnast's body lost contact with the canoe, her limbs scrambled and her mouth formed a horrified "o" before she disappeared, briefly, under the gold-faced water.

Fiona began to bounce again, lightly at first, the emptiness of the canoe turning with her weight, spinning like a compass needle. Then she bounded down hard and launched herself into the air. A complete rainbow of a backbend.

She flubbed the landing. Too bulky with the floatation device and water surging up her nostrils. The canoe shot away, past Tiffany's head. "Don't!" Tiffany shrieked. "Don't!"

And the mothers chimed in. "What? What now?"

THEY WEREN'T SISTERS. PEOPLE ASKED BACK WHEN they'd lived together, back when they went around in matching colours and braided hair, when they shared a room with a blue carpet and star stickers that glowed on the ceiling. Before Tiffany's mother married Patrick, and Fiona and her mom moved into a townhouse.

Still, down in the village, when they rode their bikes from the cabin and bought their grape sodas and Sour Keys, people still asked. Mostly because of the freckles across their noses, though Tiffany's looked more like sprinkled cinnamon and Fiona's were more blotchy. Plus they each had brown hair with red threaded through it. Highlights, their mothers called them. But that's where the resemblance ended. Tiffany was fairer and flightier, always leaning forward like pushing against a heavy wind; Fiona a whole two inches taller, stronger too, able to lift her end of the canoe out of the water while Tiffany dragged hers and had to rest three times.

Fiona hadn't wanted to return to the cabin this year. At eleven, her mother let her go to the park by herself, where she climbed the big boulder and ate gummy bears without having to share or let her mother know. There were ponds covered in fluff from the trees, and she threw rocks to scare the ducks and geese, or drew pictures, funny jokes, that she stuffed under rocks. Once she found a trowel in one of the garden beds, and started packing it around to bury things. Pennies, mostly. Jokes she'd written on scrap paper. And once, her mother's cast-off earrings.

Her jokes turned serious and she wrote long poems and drew pictures that depicted life in the late twentieth century, crammed them into Mason jars and planted them all over the park, and in her tiny backyard. For people to find. When her house crumbled into ruins like the Romans' and the Greeks', they would come for her notes. Archaeologists would uncover her jars. They'd know of her, know her better than anyone, she thought.

During her first days back at the cabin, she invited Tiffany to try it. But Tiffany gnawed her nails and twisted her hair. She wanted to sketch out maps that would guide them back to the buried things. "It's not pirates," Fiona told her. "You have to leave the jars in the ground. You have to let them stay forever."

But Tiffany had wanted to stuff the jars full of cassette tapes or her set of jacks.

"Tiffany," Fiona said, "you want them to know *jacks* about you?"

FIONA FLOATED FACE DOWN, HER BODY LIKE A STARFISH, and exhaled long and slow, air leaving in a small bubbly track. She could hear the mothers' voices, shrieking or barking. Did they think she'd drowned? She hoped so. The air was gone and she needed to turn her head for more. But she stayed still, hair fanning overhead, body swaying with the water's movements. She wanted her mother to leap into the water, arms like a cartoon propeller, her voice ringing with panic, thinking she was dead. Because, after all, it was true. One day she would be dead. One day they'd all be dead.

Fiona's father was dead. He'd died quietly in a forest ranger cabin on the West Coast, asphyxiated by white gas fumes while he slept. Fiona had only seen him twice before that, if you counted the night after she was born. Where he went after that, she didn't know, only that two weeks after, he burnt their house down. No one had been inside, but her mother said, "Everything was lost." That's how she put it. *Everything.* Her mother also said, "He was crazy. Three trips to the mental hospital. And I called the cops on him twice."

"Did he steal something?" Fiona asked. "Did he try to steal me?"

But her mother shook her head. "He pulled a knife on me once. And twice on himself." She drew a line across her wrist. Though she swore the white gas wasn't suicide, that he'd gotten better, had turned things around. Even had that one visit with Fiona. "Remember that? I'm sure the gas was an accident."

Fiona didn't think it mattered if it was suicide. She understood what it meant to be curious about death. Not that she didn't want to live, it wasn't that. She just wondered what was on the other side, wondered what came *after*.

THE MOTHERS MET FOR THE FIRST TIME AT THE POOL. Sunday afternoon Tadpole swim lessons. Tiffany in waterwings, Fiona swimming wide frog-leg strokes underwater. Fiona doesn't remember this. She doesn't remember a lot; some things happen before you're ready to remember. She has that written in a poem, sealed in a jar and buried under the swings at the yellow playground.

"Remember when we were three?" Tiffany asked every time they visited. And at the lake, looking for the best skipping rocks, she asked again. "Remember how we called each other sisters?"

What Fiona remembered about being three was watery, like rain slashing across a window. The wavering chain of a park swing and her hands, cold, gripped around it.

It was Tiffany's mom, not her own, who stood behind her, gently pushing on her back as she sat on the swing. When Fiona asked about it, her mother said, "I had a restraining order against your dad. After the knife. That meant he couldn't come near me. But he wanted part-time custody and got a lawyer. The courts ordered supervised visits to start."

Fiona remembered a man crouched in front of the swing, holding his hands out to her as though wanting to catch her. In her mind, his face blurred like a finger painting. Only his voice was clear. "Fiona," he said, over and over, and sometimes in her dreams. "Remember me? I remember you. I have your picture. Remember me?"

To Tiffany she said, "No. What's there to remember? We were babies." She made the wailing sound of a baby. "Change my diaper, *whaa-whaa*. Give me milk. *Whaa*."

But the memory slammed like a door, over and over. Her father, a man like a smudge, pleaded with her to remember him more clearly. And no matter what, she could not.

TIFFANY TOWED THE CANOE BACK TO FIONA, sputtering. "Let's do it again," she said. Fiona lifted her head, her mother was laughing on the dock, not remotely worried. Fiona reclined back in the water, submerged her ears and heard her heartbeat fill the whole lake. "No," she said, her voice sounded echoy, like someone else's. Tiffany pouted and splashed Fiona's face.

"Let's make time capsules then."

Fiona ducked under the canoe and emerged at the stern ready to push it to shore. "Okay," she said. Her voice slipped around the belly of the boat. "But we're going to canoe out and drop them into the middle of the lake."

"But . . ."

They slid into the shallows, had to glide the canoe over the small patch of seaweed, which brushed and tickled their feet, and they both kicked faster to hurry through.

Tiffany said she'd once seen a man down at the other end of the lake, blood like blossoms over his skin. "Leeches covered his whole body. And he just plucked them all off."

"Put that in your capsule," Fiona said. "That's the kind of story you should put in your jar."

Tiffany hoisted the bow of the canoe onto the small beach, wedged it in the sand. "I wouldn't want to find a stupid story like that in the future," she said, and flung her lifejacket into the bottom of the boat.

"DO YOU THINK IT'LL BE ALL MOSSY WHEN WE FIND IT?" Tiffany was drawing, pencil crayon on card stock. A picture of the two of them, each on separate ends of the canoe. The lines precise, their features fine, and Fiona could tell who was who, though they had matching hair.

Fiona sighed. "We're not going to find it. I already told you. It'll be in the middle of the lake. No one will find it for a hundred thousand years."

Tiffany held the sharp tip of poppy red in the air. "I want us to find it," she said. "When we're older and have kids and live together again. I want us to find it so that we both remember."

"Remember what?"

"Remember that we were almost sisters."

THERE WAS ONE PHOTO OF HER FATHER. THE ONE HER mother had given her before her ninth birthday. She'd started thinking about him a lot back then, even though he'd died six years before. She asked her mother the exact colour of his eyes and what his favourite song was and did he like bananas as much as she did. That was around the time they'd moved out of Tiffany's house. Tiffany who had two fathers, one stepdad and one real. And Fiona had nothing. Dead equalled nothing.

So her mother gave her the photo. It had somehow survived the house fire. That and an old embroidered pillow that still smelled of smoke. The picture was of her parents. Her mother's arm wrapped around Fiona's father's neck, not knowing everything that would happen. And her father. The ordinary cut of his chin. The eyebrows that twisted up at the ends. And his eyes. Dark as the lake, a square of light in each one. Every night she pulled the photo off her dresser and studied those light squares. "What's it like?" she asked.

But his lips never moved. Never said a thing.

THE SUN HUNG LIKE A HEAVY MEDALLION WHERE THE bay opened to the wider part of the lake. The mothers chatted in the cottage now, drinking wine after dinner. "We're going," Fiona said. "Be careful!" they chimed. Fiona clutched a plastic bag to her chest. "We'll be back in a bit."

They flew down the steps and dropped the canoe into the lake. Tiffany climbed into the bow, Fiona, for her J-stroke, took the stern.

Air cooled around them; water lapped at the hull. They paddled and after a while, Tiffany took longer pauses between each stroke. "Can we change sides?" she asked. Fiona switched her paddle to the left, but her stroke was weaker on that side and the canoe drifted off course. She thought about what she'd sealed into the jar.

These are my parents. I live with my mother. But I only met my father from the seat of a swing. My father is dead. He's always been dead and will forever more be dead. My mother is not dead. And my sort-of-sister is not dead. Yet. But one day, when you find this, each one of us will be.

"Where's it going to be?" Tiffany leaned over the side as though she could see the bottom. "Not too deep, okay? In case."

"In case what?" Fiona knew Tiffany would back out, she always backed out. Fiona had gone over the time capsule rules and still Tiffany didn't get it. "You have to throw it in and never look back."

"I don't like when you say that." Tiffany had stopped and now her paddle dripped from its perch. "I don't like when we do it your way. I think we should bury it on the other shore and then dig it up next year. We can keep burying things and keep digging them up. Like always finding lost things." Her voice brimmed now. Fiona hated when Tiffany got sucky and cried.

Fiona tossed her paddle into the canoe. It bounced off the yoke and the blade caught Tiffany's bum. Tiffany didn't move. Fiona stood up and projected her voice into the bow of the boat, out to the whole of the bay. "You can't find them again! You can never find them again. Because it isn't the same. It isn't!"

The sun sank into the horizon and flaming cloud filled the sky. Orange into red, red into bright pink. Tiffany turned, listed to the starboard side. "You don't have to." Her voice trembled; her eyes puddled.

Fiona lifted the bag from the bottom of the canoe. She stood again and pinwheeled it over her head, around and around. Tiffany lunged for Fiona, but fumbled and fell forward, knocking her chin on the canoe's yoke as she did. "I want to remember. I want to keep the picture I drew. Of us!" She got up, her mouth bleeding a thin red streak. Fiona climbed onto the gunwales and lifted her arms higher, spinning the jars faster.

"Stop Fiona! Stop. You'll flip us."

But Fiona didn't stop. She bounced and spun the sack over her head. Faster and faster. Until she finally let it fly.

ACKNOWLEDGEMENTS

EARLIER VERSIONS OF THESE STORIES APPEARED IN the following publications: "To The Ravine," *december Magazine*; "Bliss and a Boy I Once Loved," "Promontory" and "Needs," *Prairie Fire;* "Almost Sisters" and "Kick," *Grain;* "At the Edge of Everything," *New Ohio Review* and *New Ohio Review Online;* "Elephant Shoe," *Little Fiction;* "Destination Scavengers," *The Antigonish Review;* "Intruder," *The New Quarterly;* "Train in the Distance," *Event;* and "Hunger Moon," *The Dalhousie Review.* Thank you to the editors of each.

Also, special appreciation to the Canada Council for the Arts and the British Columbia Arts Council for funding and support.

Big thanks to the crew at NeWest who believed in this manuscript, and a special shout out to Nicole Markotić, who came to know these characters intimately, and who encouraged fully realized versions of their worlds.

Heart-gushing gratitude for my Pacific University peeps. To all the tremendous MFA faculty, but especially to Claire Davis, David Long, Laura Hendrie, Valerie Laken, and Jack Driscoll, who influenced these stories directly or indirectly.

And, to my fellow students turned friends/first readers: Alex Regalado, Louis Whitford, Maureen Sullivan, Susan Urban, and Marti Mattia.

Much appreciation too for my on-again, off-again writing group in the Comox Valley. Particularly, Cornelia Hoogland, whose belief in my work and abilities has buoyed me up on many occasions.

Smooches to my writimin partners, Jenny Vester and Julie Paul, with whom I've been exchanging words and retreating for nearly two decades(!), and who have seen many iterations of these stories plus other bursts of creative rambling. Thanks beyond measure for all the support and encouragement.

To my boys, Seamus and Emile. Without whom, there'd be different stories. Without whom, I'd be someone else.

And my husband, Jim, who never stops reminding me how awesome he is, so I don't need to tell him here. But I will anyway.

And to the beautiful constellation of friends and family in my life, all beloved and inspiring.

And to you, dear reader. Thank you.

DISCUSSION QUESTIONS

1. In addition to being one of the story titles, how did the book's title work for the collection as a whole? What other titles might you choose?

2. The end of "Promontory" is left relatively open—judging from the characters' predicament, do you think they survive? Is there another possible ending?

3. Why does Tess remember wanting to go off with the kid thief at the end of "Elephant Shoe"? What does that desire tell her about herself?

4. "Hunger Moon" and "Because the Fall is in Two Weeks" are told in the second person. How does that shape your experience of the story? Do you think it's an effective use of point of view?

5. In what ways is "To The Ravine" a classic coming-of-age story? And in what ways does it differ?

6. Did you find your understanding of Heidi informed by "Kick" as you were reading "Train in the Distance"?

7. What was your attitude towards the aimless characters in "Destination Scavengers"?

8. Claudia, in "Bliss and a Boy I Once Loved", is motivated to find 'bliss' in her life. Do you think she—however briefly—actually achieved it? Why or why not?

Traci Skuce graduated from the Pacific University low-residency MFA program in 2015. Her short stories and non-fiction have appeared in several publications across North America including *Grain, New Ohio Review, The New Quarterly*, and *Prairie Fire*, and have been nominated for four Pushcart Prizes and two Journey prizes. For the past twenty years, Traci has lived in Cumberland, BC with her husband and two sons.